Haneen

Miriam Day

For Rosemary, Dorothy & Miriam

Prologue

It was with a word that this story began - one word said twice - a word I've often heard since, tossed about with casual ignorance. That night it was spoken with the longing the Arabs call *haneen* - a longing that haunts the imagination like the sound of water in the desert.

It was New Year's Eve 1989 - the year the Cold War ended. The papers were giddy with talk of a 'peace dividend' and everywhere you looked you saw pictures of the Brandenburg Gate, people scrambling up the Wall and soldiers with flowers in their guns. Every hack in the world was after an assignment in Prague, Bucharest or Berlin, but I was doing time as a stringer in Helsinki - 'The White City of the North', as it's fancifully known.

It was bitterly cold that night, as if the town had foundered in a sea of ice. I ended up in a bar in Katajannoka and hunkered down near the big, tiled stove. It was well past midnight and any jollity had

1

lapsed into dogged drinking as people steeled themselves to brave the polar wind that was pasting snow to the windows. A gaggle of students chattered by the dance floor, the girls in shiny frocks which looked out of place in the panelled bar. Behind them a few couples swayed to those baffling, melancholy tangos you only hear in Finland. An Estonian who sold candyfloss at Linnanmäki Park stood at the bar with two sailors, very drunk, and a bony-chested Russian girl in a fur coat. They had joined the landlord and his retinue and the whole party was wreathed in smoke. Dog-ends circled every stool like a fall of leaves but the barmaid, faced with the sobering thought that this year promised to be much like the last, didn't bother to sweep up. Instead she asked the landlord if she could go home. He had been at the aquavit all night and was peering at his watch, unsure if it was ten past twelve or two o'clock, when the door crashed open and two men burst into the bar.

The first swaggered in like a drunken dandy. His lips and hands were blue with cold and his coat was hemmed with snow. A squall of wind slammed the door shut behind him and the landlord lurched to his feet as the second man, a handsome, dark-eyed foreigner, stepped into the light.

'Happy New Year,' he said through chattering teeth. 'Do you serve coffee?'

'Coffee?' jeered the landlord, aping his accent. 'Sod off. We're closed.'

'Forget the coffee,' the first man cried. 'We want vodka - a bottle! This man just saved my life… ' He fished a handful of notes from his pocket and the landlord, grunting some reply, lumbered back to the bar with his booty clutched in his fist.

'Where do you think he's from?' asked the barmaid as he squeezed past her to the till.

'Who?'

'The dark one - the one with the lover-boy eyes.'

'How should I know?' he asked, squinting at her face. 'Why?'

'No reason.' She combed her hair with her fingers as she watched the men stamp snow from their boots. 'I recognise him, that's all.'

A little later the first man staggered off with one of the dancers. The foreigner sat by the stove for a while, staring into the flames. Slim and square shouldered with collar-length curls, his eyebrows arched like the silhouette of a bird in flight and his face had a look of beguiling candour. Turning away from the fire he wiped the table with his sleeve and took a pen and paper from his pocket. For a moment he sat in absolute stillness, his hand poised above the table. Then he started to write and a change came over him. His body seemed to soften and thaw and his expression flitted from mischief to longing, tenderness to remorse, shadowing the drama that was unfolding on his page like the face of a child listening to a story.

The barmaid - a Barbie blonde with a Miss Finland smile - leant over a chrome beer pump and retouched her lipstick. Then she sauntered over to the stove.

'So your friend got the girl,' she said, pretending to clear the table. 'And you got the vodka. Did you *really* save his life?'

The man looked up at her and gave a little shake of his head.

'I remember you, you know,' she said. 'Do you remember me?'

'Yes,' he answered with a shrug. 'You worked here last summer.'

'I used to wonder what your story was,' she said, flicking her hair behind her ears. 'I thought you might be a sailor, come north on a ship full of sugar and rum.'

'And you...' he paused, searching for a word. 'You're a -'

'I'm just a barmaid,' she said, sitting down. 'My name's Ritva. It means tree branch - in spring time.'

'Tree branch?'

'In spring time.' She filled his glass with vodka. 'What's your name?'

'Kamaran,' he replied.

'Does it mean anything?'

'It means... it means "lucky".'

'Oooh!' she shot him a saucy look. 'Well maybe tonight's your lucky night! *Kippis,*' she added, handing him his drink.

By two o'clock the bottle was half empty and the man sat slumped over the table, fast asleep. The Russian girl, meanwhile, had been sick on the floor and the Estonian was picking a fight with the sailors. It was time to close. The landlord flicked on the main light as the last of the drunks tottered out into the whirling snow. He nodded towards the foreigner who was still sleeping soundly, his head resting on his folded arms.

'No luck then, Ritva?'
She shrugged.

'He's drunk. I've called us a taxi. And don't *look* at me like that! I'm just seeing him home, that's all.'
A cab drew up outside. Pulling on her coat she hurried over to the sleeping stranger.

'Mister!' she cooed, shaking him gently by the shoulder. 'Wake up mister. It's time to go home.'
The man sat up with a groan, knocking his forgotten letter to the floor, and rubbed his face.

'The bar's closing, Kamram,' she said, stroking his hand. 'I've called a taxi. We can share it if you like. Just tell me where you want to go.'
He gazed at her, his dark eyes shining.

'Baghdad!' he said. 'Baghdad.'

Part I - Leyla

Iraq 1957

Chapter 1

Kamaran remembered little of his early life: an airless room blacked out against the heat, the yelping of jackals in the night, a sweaty old crone with a gold tooth who called him 'the unfortunate Jamila's boy'. The unfortunate Jamila was his mother. She lived in Wadi al Salaam - a sun-blasted city of tombs, treeless and desolate, the calamity of her death having turned the world to stone. Her son's heart too, apparently. For Kamaran never cried at his own mother's tomb but was found howling like a wolf pup with some orphan at a stranger's grave. 'Like his father,' the old woman muttered. 'A smile to the face and a knife to the heart.'

Kamaran knew his father's secrets. He had a casket where he locked vials of ointment and secret potions that were poisonous to drink. He had books with strange lettering and pictures of skeletons and people without skin. He had 'instruments' with red tubes like the bloody veins in the pictures, and an evil metal 'syringe' he kept hidden in a case. He had white cotton coats and *Al Mukhtar* magazines which arrived mysteriously each month and smelled of glue. These objects went with them, the one constant of their lives, as his father's quarrels sent them scurrying from one in-law to the next.

Kamaran didn't have many things. His prize possessions were a magnifying glass and a compass, Ramadan gifts from his father's father which arrived late as they had been sent to an old address. He had met his grandfather only once. His name was Sami. He had an owlish face with a long nose and staring eyes and he lived in the fabled city that Kamaran longed with all his heart to see - Baghdad.

By the time the compass arrived, he and his father were living by a canal and some wasteland where a broken plank dangled on a rope beneath a dusty tree. The warren of dark rooms in their new house reeked of the smoking palm fronds the villagers burned for fuel and the dried limes his dead mother's sister boiled to make tea. His dead mother's sister had two matching red-faced babies who mewled all night, and if ever Kamaran asked her a question she sighed like a camel and told him to go away. So he spent his days outside, making rafts, swinging on the broken plank, and playing knucklebones or football with boys who dodged barefoot across the stony ground.

One bright March morning, just before his sixth birthday, Kamaran's father announced he was sending him away. He would live with his grandfather, his uncle, aunt and cousin, and 'be made to learn some proper manners at a proper school.' Kamaran asked lots of questions which his father, who was late for work, didn't answer. Then he scrambled over the wall at the back of the yard and ran out across the wasteland.

It had been a dry winter and the earth was cracked with lines like a jigsaw puzzle. He hopped from piece to piece then raced along the path by the canal. Beneath a stand of trees a ruined house tumbled into the water, a place the village boys avoided because of the *si'luwa* - a hairy water-witch who kept finger bones in a Nidal milk tin and had bosoms which hung down to her knees. Kamaran found a sunny spot amongst the rushes and lay down to think.

He was going to Baghdad! The word alone set his mind awhirl with pictures. He shut his eyes, to see them more clearly, and opened them again as something rustled in the dried reeds by his head. Peeping at him through the rushes he saw a tabby kitten with silver fur and golden eyes. It was scabby and very thin. Some cruel boys had probably tried to drown it or scare it away with stones. After a moment it tottered out and gazed at Kamaran with such a trusting face that he picked it up, hid it under his shirt, and smuggled it back to the house.

He fed it milk from the end of his finger, laughing at the ticklish rasp of its tongue, and

11

stashed some lumps of stew in his pocket for its dinner. It capered about and ambushed his feet as he walked by, it chirruped when it wanted to be picked up and, when it tired of its games, it purred on his lap and talked to him with its golden eyes. By the next day Kamaran felt so confident of its charms he introduced it to his cross aunt. She sighed wearily and said he could keep 'the mangy flea-bitten wretch' if he must, since he was leaving so soon.

The kitten learned to ride on Kamaran's shoulder. To drink, it scooped up water with its paw. It liked dates and, if you pushed its chin forward, it looked like a grouchy old *Bedu* woman. At night it pounced on his feet under the blankets then curled up in the hollow of his neck and purred them both to sleep. Each day Kamaran loved it more and each night he asked his father the same question: 'Can I keep it, *baba*? Please?' And his father gave the same reply: 'You can keep it for now but you can't take it to Baghdad.'

The time soon came for him to leave. His grandfather was to collect him in the morning. Kamaran packed his things (which didn't take long) and was sent early to bed. As he lay in the dusk, unable to sleep, he listened to the scuttling lemon leaves and the whisper of the dead banana plant outside his window and he thought about Baghdad - its secret courtyards, its wide river, its orchards where rubies grew on trees. He thought about his kind grandfather, the home he had never had, the cousin he had never seen. Then he gazed at the kitten, so small and trusting, as it lay fast asleep in his arms.

Sami left the house long before dawn. His sister Rabia had risen with him and fussed about food and rugs for the journey. He gave her the slip at last and walked briskly through the alleyways to his car, relishing the sense of adventure as his solitary footsteps echoed in the dark.

The air felt damp. He tucked Rabia's rug over his legs as he settled into the driver's seat, making the springs creak, and sniffed the pleasant, musty smell of the leather. He loved his car, an old Alvis he had bought from a British pal ten years before, and he spoke to it fondly as it coughed and wheezed, coaxing it into life.

They were soon on their way. A lone truck rattled towards the *suq* leaving runaway oranges bouncing in the road. Sami swerved to avoid the fruit and hoped some urchin would find them. Ignoring the red lights on Rashid Street he crossed the Tigris, which looked silver in the moonlight, and headed out of the city.

He hummed happily to himself, his voice lurching at every bump, as he drove south through a forest of palms. They thinned, briefly, as he passed through a village, triggering a relay of noisy barking. A white dog lolloped alongside the car but gave up as they plunged back into the trees. A little later a gazelle bounced into the road and was gone. After that nothing stirred. The head lamps made a tunnel of light, leading deep into the murmuring forest, and Sami started singing to keep himself company.

'What need have you for apples, with those cheeks of yours?
What need you mint, smelling sweet as you do?
What need you pomegranates, with your lovely curves?
Yet I wish I was a farmer and could bring them to you!'

When dawn broke he found himself in flat, open country criss-crossed by waterways. Stands of date palms marked distant hamlets, marooned by the night's mist. A boy on a donkey waved cheerily as he trotted by. Here and there men made their way into the fields. By the time the fog had burned away, bands of rushes in silted canals were the only green in a dusty landscape. Salt glittered on bare earth in which nothing could now grow. He passed one abandoned farmhouse then another. The tenanted ones were little more than hovels and the people looked ragged and dirty. 'How typical of Nasir,' Sami thought, 'in a country full of wonders, to live in such a wretched place!' He stopped himself guiltily. His younger son always made him feel at fault. To distract himself he sang another half-forgotten folk tune and concentrated on recovering the words.

As he neared the village, he spotted a boy with a basket trudging along the road. He pulled over and wound down the window to call to him.

'I'm looking for the village doctor -' Sami broke off, studying the boy's impish face. 'Kamaran!' he exclaimed, opening the door. 'You're Kamaran, aren't you? It's me - your *Jiddu*!'

'Did baba send you to catch me?' the boy asked, watching him warily as he climbed out of the car.

'No... but I thought you were coming to Baghdad with me?'

'Basrah,' Kamaran mumbled. 'I'm running away to sea.' He put down his basket and flopped onto the dusty grass, suddenly limp.

'Have you had any breakfast?' Sami asked after a moment. 'You can't walk all the way to Basrah without breakfast - and besides, my sister has made us a wonderful picnic.' He rummaged in the hamper Rabia had given him and sat down beside his grandson. 'Try one of these,' he suggested, unwrapping a sticky package. 'They're called "the lady's belly button" and they taste marvellous!'
Kamaran took the sweetmeat and stuffed it into his mouth.

'Nice?'
The boy nodded. His thin shoulders drooped and his chin wobbled as he tried not to cry. Sami patted his

15

hand, wondering why everything to do with his younger son had to be so complicated.

'I *really* wanted to come to Baghdad!' his grandson wailed, as if in answer. 'But though baba's not even going to *be* there, he said I couldn't take my kitten! He said it would be a bother to everyone and I shouldn't make such a fuss because it was only a flea-bitten stray. But,' he wiped his nose with his cuff as indignant tears spilled onto his cheeks, 'he's *not* a flea-bitten stray. A stray means a cat with no home and he's found his home - with me.'

Sami nodded, considering his logic.

'How long have you had him?'

'Eight nights and seven days.' Kamaran glanced at his grandfather from under his long lashes. 'Baba said you liked birds and wouldn't want a cat in the house.'

'Did he?' Sami looked puzzled. 'Oh yes... yes I did go through an ornithology phase once. But I'm in a cat phase now. Is that what's in your basket? Can I see?' He undid the string that bound the lid and the kitten butted its head through the gap, staring at them with its yellow eyes. *'Ma sha'Allah!'* gasped Sami, stroking it under the chin. 'What a beautiful creature! Does he have a name?'

Kamaran shook his head.

'Well, if you're going to take him to sea, how about Sindbad?'

'Sindbad!' Kamaran grinned, delighted. He picked up the kitten, kissed it and gave it to his grandfather.

'He's got six toes, he eats dates and when he wants a drink he scoops up water with his paw.'

'Is that so?' Sami murmured, as if this was the information he had been waiting for. 'Well in *that* case I would consider it an honour - a very *great* honour - if Sindbad would put off his visit to Basrah and come to live with us in Baghdad.'

'But what about baba?' asked Kamaran. 'He'll be cross.'

'Every moustache has its scissors,' Sami murmured, patting Kamaran's hand again. 'Don't fret about baba - your old grandfather knows how to handle him!'

They quarrelled even so. Kamaran waited in the yard, pressed flat against the wall by the kitchen door. His heart thumped as he tried to listen. Through the clatter of dishes and the hiss of a kettle his grandfather's jolly voice grew suddenly louder. A moment later he strode out into the yard and Kamaran knew from his face that Sindbad had been saved.

His father winced as if he had toothache when they kissed him goodbye. Then they climbed into the car and bumped off along the pitted track, and his trim form grew smaller and fainter and was soon lost in a cloud of dust.

17

Chapter 2

By the time they got to the city Kamaran was fast asleep. His head banged against the window as they rattled over Shuhada Bridge, but still he didn't wake. Sami, smiling at the picture of oblivion he made, remembered drowsy homecomings in a pony and trap and fell to reminiscing about the Baghdad of his youth - a city as flat as a tablet of scored clay, quiet as a village at night and lit only by swaying lanterns and the stars. A city where a man's reputation was a jewel and to safeguard your house you made the local burglar swear 'on his moustache' not to rob it. A city where the expression 'colder than the water carrier's arse' still meant something, where black-clad women fluttered like leaves in the wind to wash clothes in the river, where wailing mothers kept candlelit vigil for their drowned sons and thunder struck fear into the heart.

For in the year of Sami's birth, seven times since, and seven times seven before, the Tigris had stirred itself. Swelling like a *djinni* it had left its bed to slip through the winding alleys into houses, bakeries, workshops and gardens, as though in search of something, turning everything upside down and leaving a trail of rejected pots and sodden corpses bobbing in its wake. Time and again the river sucked at the clay bricks of the houses and as soon as one dwelling crumbled another was built in its place. Above the slow rise and fall of this ochre sea the minarets stood stalwart, glimmering like beacons with the call to prayer, while the golden domes shone bright as jewels in a tomb where all else has turned to dust.

Like a shrivelled crone recalling young love, Baghdad invoked her past. For in her youth she was celebrated for her beauty, her brilliance and her roses, or in other quarters for her silks and jades, her perfumes and furs, and all the other enticements of her trade. She was legendary, too, for her showboat merchants, boastful sailors and lovesick fools, her bawdy porters, lying fishermen and crafty servants, her imaginative and quick-witted girls who could talk themselves out of the worst trouble and leave you wanting to hear more.

A city of poets, bookshops and libraries, when she fell to the Mongol hordes it was said the waters of the Tigris ran red with her blood and blue with her ink. Then she cast aside her jewels like a spent mother, while her children - Muslim, Jewish, Christian, Arab, Kurd - scrapped and squabbled and told mean jokes about each other. So they had all muddled along for centuries, keeping themselves to themselves, except for the merchants who traded tall stories in the old *caravanserai,* and the

19

poor, insane, and seditious of every sort who so crammed the humbler quarters of the city there was no room even for fleas.

Then, when Sami was twelve, along came the Brits with their promises of Liberty, new borders and new monarchy, fresh from the Raj with their progress and efficiency - and everything changed. Foreign china, bales of clothing and mountains of shoes appeared in the suqs and were found to be indistinguishable, each bowl or shirt identical to the one before, as if fashioned by a sorcerer's hand. People were so dazzled by this glut of cheap goods that the potters, tailors and cobblers closed down their workshops and disappeared into the crowd.

In the countryside the new rulers made private domains of common land. Proud tribesmen slaved like mules, were treated like dogs and ate like sparrows in fields that had once been theirs. Ruined families flocked to the city, they had been coming ever since, and their clustered hovels had sprawled into clamorous, stinking shanty towns. Tattered urchins and lean men scoured the streets, scavenging for food and work. Others became soldiers, policemen, government clerks - the fist, eyes and nose of the new state. They put up streetlamps which veiled the stars in a garish haze and the dusty roads were all tarred over, making them more convenient for cars but deadly for Baghdad's playful children.

Things became more and more orderly and less and less fun and for who and for what? Sami scorned the modern mania for 'saving time,' since the more time people saved the less they seemed to have and the worse they were at enjoying it. He lived in the family home in an old *Mahalla* - a quarter that had changed little in centuries. Here the houses, windowless at street level, joined in a labyrinth of passageways which were shaded by the shuttered balconies whispering overhead.

The entrance to the Old House, as it was known, he had renovated for his bride, Evin. Two carved lovebirds perched amidst a swirl of flowers above the door and a graceful 'hand of Fatima' knocker protected the family inside from the Evil Eye. His own parents had lived in the traditional way with little furniture so everything could be easily moved, for everyone in the old Mahallas decamped from sunny to shady rooms for the summer and escaped to the roof to eat and sleep under the stars. Evin had put a stop to this migration and rarely left her chamber now. Sami, ousted, had gone to sleep on a sofa in his study and was still there. His sister Rabia had a cot in Evin's room and his son Mazin lived with his wife and daughter on the north side of the gallery. Tables and wardrobes had begun to clutter the house. Mazin had bought a refrigerator. Rabia had danced like a madwoman when his daughter-in-law gave her a 'Lady of the House' with an electric whisk that spun like a dervish at the press of a button. Now they had installed a new bathroom and Sami was teaching his grand-daughter to say *'Astru ya sahib al-mahal* - with your permission, o spirit of this place!' before she flushed the toilet.

Sami adored children and there had never been enough in the house, for while most families could name at least a hundred cousins his one surviving sister was childless and he had only two sons himself. But he was not a person given to melancholy. When his business partner Yona had left Baghdad six years before - along with most of the city's Jews - Sami had sold their photography business, smuggled half the proceeds to his friend and now lived off the rest. He rose early and whiled away his mornings at the coffeehouse or drinking tea in a *chaikana*. In the evenings he listened to music or made calls to ailing friends and his dwindling flock of relations. Every other day he went to the barbers for a shave. On Fridays he went to mosque, and on Thursday afternoons he met with a circle of old friends who - having an exhaustive knowledge of each other's views on politics, religion and poetry - passed their time very amiably with gossip, banter, music and cards.

Sami had tired of politics long ago but for his sons it was different. Born into a British fiefdom, the battle for independence raged about them as they grew up. Drunk on dreams of freedom and the promise of a new republic, they turned away from their religion and cast themselves into the fray. Mazin was thrown into prison. Nasir was beaten. Both were nearly killed when they joined the students who marched across the bridge into a storm of bullets, fell into the river with their banners and leaflets, and dyed the Tigris red and blue once more with their blood and their ink.

That fateful day a girl called Reem helped Nasir as he staggered, bleeding, from the bridge. She had a delicate face and grave eyes, like him, and even the same smile which - when it came - put the rising sun to shame. Sami warned his son that the wind doesn't blow with the ship's desire. Nasir, just seventeen, was too young to listen. He never dreamt that an encounter that promised everlasting bliss would teach him, instead, the brutal vigour of unrequited love. Nor that Reem would prefer Mazin - his boisterous older brother whose curling eyelashes gave him a look of perpetual innocence even as he was marrying the only woman Nasir would ever want. He buried his pain like a shameful secret and with it his love. Then, despite Sami's wise counsel and Evin's maledictions, he made a foolish betrothal to a foolish girl. At the age of nineteen he was a married man and at the age of twenty the father of a son. At the age of twenty-one his bride was dead and gone, and he was left with this boy who was growing.

Kamaran had grown so much that Sami struggled to lift him from the car without waking him. Tucking the rug under his feet, he kissed his head. He felt full of tenderness and sudden hope that Kamaran's advent might change the fortunes of the family - that his sons would be reconciled, his house filled with merry, laughing children and that God, in his mercy, might yet bless a foolish old man with a happy ending.

Chapter 3

Kamaran was woken by the morning call to prayer. It spiralled into his dreams like a silky rope and, still half-asleep, he followed it. Padding past his snoring grandfather, he made his way along a gallery and up the stairs to the roof. A gust of wind slammed the door shut behind him and he had to fight his way through the white sheets that snapped on a clothes-line near the door.

A high parapet and a march of chimneys framed the flat roof. Standing on an orange box, he climbed up onto the wall and sniffed at the unfamiliar smell of the city. The house was marooned in a sea of rooftops, the colour of cinnamon in the dawn, breached here and there by billowing sprays of palm. To the right he saw a mosque with three honey-coloured domes and beyond it another, blue like the thin morning sky. As the *muezzins'* call faded away, a rhythmic squeak sounded from the alley below. Kamaran looked down gingerly. Two passages joined forces at the corner of the house and opened out into a small square with a tree in the middle. A boy about his age emerged from beneath its branches, pushing a barrow of hay and followed by a fat white duck. Kamaran waved and was about to shout when he heard footsteps behind him. A dumpy woman, her face swathed in a white *hijab*, was gathering the sheets from the line.

'God have mercy!' she shrieked when she saw him. 'What are you doing up there?'

'I was only looking,' Kamaran protested as she waddled towards him. 'I wanted to see what these chimney things are.'

'Did you indeed?' She grabbed his arm and hitched up her skirt to step onto the crate. 'Well they're wind-catchers. They suck the cold north winds into the cellar before they can make trouble - and if you're not careful they'll do the same to you!'

'And who's the boy with the white duck?' asked Kamaran, undaunted.

'That would be Yusuf, the dairyman's son, and the duck is his sister, turned into a birdie for asking questions and peeking over walls. Now come here you little Tartar,' she scolded, lifting him down and giving him a bristly kiss. 'It's bad manners to peek and besides, you might fall. I'm your great-aunt Rabia and you're going to make yourself useful rather than all this climbing on walls.' With that she took his hand firmly in her own and led him back downstairs.

It was lighter now and Kamaran looked about eagerly. The house looked splendid and shabby, like a ruined palace. The rooms faced inwards to a central courtyard, cloistered above and below, and the columns along the gallery were perfect for climbing up like a monkey. A starry dazzle of mosaic, speckled

26

with missing tiles, decorated the ceiling. The balcony sagged in one corner and creaked like a ship as he walked, and all along one side of the gallery ran a timberwork lattice, intricate as lace and studded with petals of coloured glass. These were the windows of a lofty drawing room where ripples of mirrored tiling shimmered across the ceiling to a chandelier that fell like crystal rain.

In the courtyard below the doors opened like secrets in walls of sandy brick. There was a persimmon tree for climbing, a swing-seat, a broken fountain which gurgled and splashed, and rooms with grilled windows for imprisoning his cousin or to use as dungeons in games they might play together. Everything played tricks with the sunlight, casting shady patterns which shifted with each step, and the homely smells of wood ash and rising dough filled the air.

'How old is my cousin Leyla?' Kamaran asked as he jumped down the stairs, two steps at a time. 'What time does she get up?'

'Little Kashkash? She's just five and she's not here at the moment. They're at a wedding with her mother's folks. They'll be home for Ramadan.'

'Jiddu said her name was Leyla.'

'Kashkash, Kashkash. Like poppy seeds in a pod. *Wis, wis, wis!* Always giggling and whispering, whispering and giggling!' Rabia giggled herself.

'Is there something wrong with her?' asked Kamaran.

27

'God smile on you, my child!' his aunt replied, laughing in earnest. 'She's a sniffer of air and a picker of roses, the little pigeon, but the sweetest thing you ever saw. Sweeter, even, than your little kitty-puss,' she added and, without drawing breath, she launched into a story about a tabby cat that lived with the Prophet Mohammed (peace be upon him).

Kamaran peeked at her as she nattered away. She had a hooked nose and eyes like the blinking eyes of the frogs he used to catch in the canal - eyes that were charming on frogs but which didn't suit his great-aunt Rabia at all.

'…and so he blessed the cat,' she concluded with a wistful smile. 'And that's why tabbies always have an "M" at the top of their noses.'

It was an interesting story but, Kamaran thought, unlikely to be true.

They had stopped at the back of the courtyard where a clay *tannur* squatted by the wall, a pile of twigs in its belly. Rabia got matches from her pocket, lit a twist of paper which she passed to Kamaran and jerked him back as he dropped it into the kindling. Flames erupted from the top of the oven, twisting six feet into the air. Kamaran laughed, delighted.

'Hmm,' said his aunt with a severe look. 'I thought you'd like that. Now go and find this kitten of yours, before it gets into mischief.'

Sindbad was not properly house-trained and nor was Kamaran. Sindbad galloped about the courtyard, getting under everyone's feet, and wriggled away when you tried to cuddle him - and so did Kamaran. Sindbad climbed up the tree and wouldn't come down, he yowled and bit if you tried to wash him, he vanished at meal times then raided the kitchen for things he wasn't supposed to eat, he escaped over the roof to prowl the alleyways then limped home with cuts on his face while the whole neighbourhood was in uproar looking for him - and so did Kamaran.

After three days of mayhem the kitten was confined for a week to the *kabishkan* - a small room that sat in the corner of the gallery and overlooked the whole house like a look-out deck. He mewed pitifully all night. Kamaran, who slept in his grandfather's room, pleaded to join him but Rabia put her foot down, intent on a new regime.

She woke Kamaran for prayers at dawn each morning, loaded him with baskets and marched him off to the markets before breakfast, taking fiendish detours to wear him out. For while the more decorous women of the neighbourhood sent maids, children or men folk to fetch the groceries, Rabia insisted on selecting everything the family ate herself. They crossed the river to the fish suq and she left Kamaran shivering in the mist or skidding about the pavement, slippery with scales, while she cross-examined the traders. She made him wait in the middle of the copper suq, blocking his ears against

29

the clatter of hammers. She sent him running to and fro for paper, needles and soap, and if she saw a horribly long queue she told him to join it, just to find out what was on offer at the other end.

Then she crossed Rashid Street and plunged into the labyrinthine market beyond. Wintry sunlight sliced through gaps in the awning, making sudden shadows of the passersby, and Kamaran trotted to keep up, frightened he would lose her, as each twist revealed a new scene. On and on they wound, dodging blasphemous porters and boys with trays of sweetmeats on their heads, until the smoky smell of coffee filled the air and they found themselves amongst mounds of sumac and paprika, bright as paint, which made him sneeze.

Rabia bought chickpeas, rice and lentils by the sack-full on a monthly raid and hoarded them in the cellar as if making ready for some new siege. Everything else she got on the day she wanted to cook it, choosing from amongst a thousand and one stalls - each one arranged with the artistry of a shrine. Kamaran was dragged from pillar to post while she inspected the merchandise, prodding, sniffing and querying its provenance like a madam in search of a whore with particular talents.

Her pilgrimage always ended at the same stall, where the *ziggurats* of fruit were so masterfully constructed even the naughtiest boy felt no urge to topple them. The dates had a sweetness to break the heart, the merchant promised as he offered one to taste. The apricots were blushing from the attentions of the sun, the sweet lemons were shameless and the oranges so juicy it was a sin to think of them. Rabia sniffed haughtily, oblivious to the honey in his voice and the spice in his eyes. Then she loaded Kamaran up with purple carrots and cabbages as big as his head, and made him trot back to the house like a pack-mule so she could bake fresh bread for her sister-in-law's breakfast.

This was another of Kamaran's chores. After hobbling back from the suq, he lit the tannur and helped shape the leavened dough into balls. These Rabia flipped from hand to hand, until they were thin discs, and threw onto the oven walls where they stuck like magic. Kamaran's job was to watch until the bread blistered, grab it with some tongs, and toss it into a basket to cool. Rabia shaped the last of the dough in little rounds which she sprinkled with *ghee* and sugar for his breakfast. While he was eating she prepared a tray with dainties - creamy buffalo *geymar* and date syrup, the hot bread, and tea in a little glass *istikan* with a silver filigree holder. Then she lit a cigarette and sat down to smoke it while Kamaran took the tray upstairs to his grandmother.

On the first day he had stopped in the doorway, scared to enter the gloomy room which stunk of old hyacinths. A brood of dolls stared at him from a chest at the foot of a four-poster bed, swathed in red drapes. In their midst sat a framed photograph. His grandmother claimed it was of her but Kamaran

31

didn't believe it. The girl in the picture looked plump and pretty with thick, curling hair, whereas his grandmother was a bony old woman with two thin plaits which coiled into her lap like wet rope.

'That's me you're gawking at,' she said.

He almost dropped the breakfast tray because he had been poking around, thinking she was asleep, and all the time she had been watching him.

'Come here,' she demanded, 'and let me have a look at you.'

He shuffled over to her, clasping the tray. A white arm reached out, pulling his face towards her own, and between the long green eyes Kamaran saw lines like the 'M' on the face of the Prophet Mohammed's cat.

At the end of the week Rabia told Kamaran that she wouldn't make him come to market any more, as long as he behaved. That night he was allowed to go and sleep with Sindbad in the kabishkan. She had furnished the little room with a carpet, a chest strewn with lemony leaves to scent his clothes, and a bed. Kamaran, who had never had a room of his own, moved the chest to the screened window that overlooked the drawing room. That way he could climb up in the evenings and spy on his grandfather's friends as they sat amidst the gorgeous rugs and cushions, telling jokes and smoking a *nargeela*. His bed was by the other window. This had a grilled balcony which overlooked the alley, like a crow's nest, and was just big enough for a watchful child.

As he curled up in bed with Sindbad that night, Kamaran vowed he would never get up to say dawn prayers again, nor would he make his children do it, nor his children's children. He was woken early, anyway, by a rustling outside his room. A shadow stirred in the doorway. A little girl was standing on the steps outside, leaning against the wall, one foot tucked behind her. She twisted shyly on the other, turned her face away and meowed like a cat. Kamaran meowed back to see what would happen. She answered with a husky purr and turned towards him, looking at him from behind a mop of curly hair, her head to one side. They stared at each other for a moment in silence.

'Can I see the kitten?' she whispered eventually, in a gruff little voice.

Kamaran nodded and his cousin Leyla (for it was she) sidled in and perched on the bed beside him. She sat very still and gazed at the sleepy kitten with her mouth open.

'Why have you called her Sindbad when she's a girl?' she asked.

'He's not a girl.'

'He *is.*'

Kamaran picked up Sindbad and held him briefly above their heads. Neither of them were the wiser for this examination but it made them giggle. Then they had a tickle fight and Leyla giggled some more. Then

33

Kamaran remembered what Aunt Rabia had said about the giggling and the whispering and he stopped suddenly, on the watch for signs of madness.

'Anyway,' said Leyla, 'I brought some special things to show you. If you like you can choose one to keep and we can be friends.' She put a folded square of silk on the bed. Wrapped inside he found a broken ivory comb, an assortment of buttons, a piece of mirror and a tiny silver box. This, she whispered, contained the greatest of her treasures - an ancient, fossilised pomegranate seed.

'It's not a fossil at all!' Kamaran protested when he prised open the lid. 'It's just an old bead.'

'*I* think it's very ancient,' replied Leyla, unmoved. She looked for an alternative offering and passed him a tiny glazed tile. 'I found this all by myself in the desert and Jiddu says it's thousands and thousands and *thousands* of years old.'

In the end Kamaran chose a charm, threaded on a twist of coloured cotton. It was made of tin and blue beads that protected the wearer against the Eye, and he told Leyla he wanted it for his cat.

Chapter 4

Ramadan fell that week. The days started in darkness with the rattle of a drum as the *musaharati* tottered across the square, calling the faithful to rise. The racket clattered about the narrow alleyways and Leyla came galloping into Kamaran's room and sent him diving for cover under the blankets. Scampering over his bed she flung open the shutters to watch the old man who drummed and shouted with such delinquent glee, and counted the windows lighting up in his wake.

When day had broken Rabia donned her long black *abaya* and set off for market like a ship in full sail, returning with provisions for an army. All day long she chopped, ground, sprinkled and stirred with the concentration of a witch, as if summoning the visitors who arrived to break their fast with the family each dusk. She cooked great cauldrons of stew for the imam and the poor, which Kamaran and Leyla helped carry to the mosque through teeming streets that stayed festive with light until dawn. The chicken soup she made for the joiner's sick wife, Blind Um Ghazi's lentils and the pastries she fried for the old couple on the corner, the children were allowed to deliver by themselves.

Before Kamaran's arrival the square of sky above the courtyard had been the horizon of Leyla's world. Now, as spring came and the mud dried, she was allowed to play with him in the passageway outside. They both started school and they walked there together and the two of them were sent on errands across the Mahalla, Leyla clutching Kamaran's hand the while. They ran for cigarettes to Jawad's General Store, where candles and strings of chilli dangled from the ceiling, they fetched Sami from the coffeehouse and they queued for rolls at the new *samun* bakery which belched heat and noise like a forge.

To start with every foray thrilled Leyla like a bold adventure in an alien land, but with time the web of alleys came to be as familiar as the house. Five lanes, linked by a tangle of passageways, branched out from the little square. The dwellings that surrounded it were still in the hands of the old families but the square itself was the province of Abu Adil - a gossiping newspaper vendor with hair like a sheep - and the vegetable barrow-boy who everyone called *Ibn* Potato.

To the north lived Poor Jasim the Cobbler, honoured for his soft kid leather slippers, his wooden leg and his broken heart. The passage beyond was the lair of ancient Um Salma, who sat in a sunless window hawking camphor and 'old man's hair' from a hoard of dusty jars. Her apothecary marked the limit of the children's expeditions, for the narrow

36

lane doubled back and joined a wider alley which led west towards the suqs and the river beyond.

When the wind blew from the south, the smell of cardamom and toasting flour drifted into the square from Hussein al Rusafi's *Kek-al-Sayid*. His shop had an illuminated sign - the only one in the neighbourhood - which said 'Pastries as Light as an Eastern Breeze' in letters of pink and blue. The layers of his *baklava* were, indeed, as thin as an onion skin and the tantalising dainties arrayed in his window were all made to family recipes, perfected over centuries and guarded as fiercely as a pretty girl's honour. Wealthy strangers, enticed by the famous sweetmeats, nudged their cars into the cramped alleys round his shop and got stuck fast, to be shepherded out again by hollering children under the vigilant gaze of the women - the moral guardians of the Mahalla.

Scandals great and small, tragedies, romance and farce were repeated down the generations like Chinese whispers, in a saga as intricate as any related by the sly Scheherazade. The lunatic who roamed the square like one possessed, wild-eyed and muttering, was on no account to be mocked out of respect for the heroic part his father played in the floods of 1914. The doctor, on the other hand, was shunned. Not because he bought pork chops from the Assyrian butcher when his wife was away, nor because he shouted at his children, but for some far worse transgression which, despite being unrepeatable, was universally known. Ranked

37

somewhere between these two was the smelly Magic Lantern Man who spent his days in the suq and shuffled back at nightfall, still croaking as he turned the handle of his box: 'Behold the Ziggurat of Ur - home to heathen kings of old! Behold the Turkish harlot - three coppers and all will be revealed!' His gaudy promises floated across the twilit square as he vanished down a narrow, stinking passage littered with vegetable scraps which seemed to have been left as a monument to the infamous flood. Here fetid water lingered in the gutters even during the conflagration of Baghdad's summer, and the walls of the houses had a tidemark, traced by tiers of crumbling brick.

These decaying dwellings backed onto the Old House and the children sometimes climbed over the wall between the rooftops to pay a visit to their neighbours. The mansion to the left now served as the dairy and hay and fodder spilled from the downstairs rooms. Two goats, a cow the colour of nutmeg and an operatic rooster, who competed with the morning call to prayer, sniffed and strutted about the once elegant courtyard. Upstairs lived Yusuf with his duck, his brothers and his pretty red-haired sister, who walked from door to door with silver pots stacked on her head in a fabulous crown and sold geymar which she sliced with a pin.

The house to the right belonged to the mechanic, Ibrahim, and bits of rusting metal littered the courtyard like desert bones. By day he hammered and cursed and smoked but as the sun went down each evening his tuneful whistle sang out across the alley and he stood, like Noah, with doves wheeling about him - for he kept a flock of pigeons on the roof. When the children climbed onto the wall to watch him he gave them handfuls of corn and told them stories while the birds fluttered about and pecked the seed from their palms. In the time of the Caliphs, he said, there were dovecotes from the sea to the mountains, and if the Sultan's daughter wanted sweet plums from Lebanon for breakfast, a flock of doves arrived in Baghdad the next day, each with a plum tied to its leg. Sometimes a stray bird came to the roof to eat and Ibrahim trapped it and sold it the next day, knowing it would fly straight home. This kidnap game was a sport amongst the pigeon fanciers, he said, although he kept his own prize pigeons locked up in a coop. He took them to Samarra and Mosul to race them. When Leyla asked how they remembered their way home, he pinched her cheek and said it was because the old Mahalla was such a special place to live.

The children's shortest way home from school cut through a warren of ramshackle alleys behind Ibrahim's repair shop. Here the walls of the houses sagged and bulged as if exhausted by the effort of being respectable. The balconied windows were nodding off into the street. Cracks ran amok across the carved lintels. Cables and washing-lines looped promiscuously over buildings let piecemeal and so crammed with children that one was always crying in every house. Toddlers played in the dirt, spilling out into the alleyways along with greetings, curses and slang from the rural south. Whole villages seemed to have decamped together, bringing their donkeys and okra plants with them, to mingle with the turbaned Afghans who ran the cockfights and knife-grinders from Uzbekistan. Old men crouched in the doorways making paper windmills and birdcages of palm to sell in the market, or hawked vegetables, swatting the flies from sorry piles of blighted onions. Thorn sellers, pot riveters, charcoal vendors, shoe-shine boys, fortune-tellers - all set off each morning in the wake of the labourers who left before dawn and trudged home at nightfall caked with oil and grime, blistered and limping, reeking of the slaughterhouse and plagued with flies. Then they shared some stale bread, downed a bottle of arak as remedy for the day's humiliations, and crawled into infested beds to vanish again before first light the following day. Some were rumoured to be pickpockets, hired thugs, government informers and worse. Their wives looked like their own mothers by the time they were thirty and they dragged their children to mosque on Fridays, waiting for alms with a practised air of pious dejection.

These, evidently, were 'the poor' who Rabia liked to cook for at Ramadan. But, try as they might, Kamaran and Leyla could not persuade her to extend her goodwill into the wretched slums where they

40

spent the rest of the year. The children should on no account go there, she warned. Fleas, lice, cockroaches and vermin of every kind infested the streets. The air itself was alive with pestilence and murder because the fathers were feckless, the mother's spent, the children unruly and diseased, and nobody knew their neighbours anymore or cared much what they did.

It was true they sometimes saw weeping men carry little coffins through the alleys, but Kamaran loved it there. He exaggerated the southern twang which got him mocked as a clod-hopping yokel at school, he played barefoot football in the dirt like he used to do, organised games of chase across the rooftops and flew paper kites with the boys. Leyla, meanwhile, bossed their little sisters, carried about the babies left in their charge and delivered spelling lessons, drawing letters in the dirt. Then one afternoon a group of Kamaran's playmates minced after her, laughing at her white socks and her new kilt which - until that moment - she had thought the smartest outfit in all Baghdad. She reached for her cousin's hand but Kamaran stepped away and laughed at her too. Leyla ran all the way home without looking at him. He sauntered behind her, pretending he didn't care, but when he got home she hid in the cellar and howled with such fury he could not bear to hear it. Her tears triumphed where Rabia's exhortations had failed, and she made him swear on his compass, on Sindbad's life, on his own dead mother's grave that he would never, ever go home that way again.

41

After that the children were inseparable. They lolled on the swing-seat for hours at a time, whispering and laughing and waving their arms. They capered around the gallery with tea-towels on their heads, brandishing wooden spoons, and set up camp between the colonnades in a secret epic which stopped only for meal times. They pretended Sami's antique Damascus desk, inlaid with mother-of-pearl flowers, was a sultan's palace and they raided its secret little drawers and were discovered amidst a sea of crumpled paper, their hands covered with blobs of sealing wax and India ink. They sneaked into his study and stowed away in the old Kuwaiti chest, and when Leyla's parents woke to find her gone they knew she would be asleep with Kamaran and Sindbad, having crept to the kabishkan after bedtime. From here the children spied on Sami's guests in the room below, or hummed along to the old songs he played when he was alone, or eavesdropped on his evening chats with Mazin until the merry voices, the scent of rose tobacco and the rhythmic hubble-bubble of the nargeela lulled them both to sleep.

In May, encouraged by Sami and inspired by the storks in an old nest on Um Gahzi's roof, the children started an Ornithological Society. They spent their Ramadan money on crayons and a book for their survey: *The Birds of Baghdad*. Kamaran did the writing.

Date: Friday

Place: Roof

Sort of bird: Laughing doves on roof. Two of them.

Comments: They are called laughing doves because they go o-kuk kuk-oo-oo-o-kuk

Then Leyla drew the pictures.

Kamaran built a hide with orange boxes and dried palm leaves in a corner of the roof. They smuggled cushions and a rug from the house, to make it more comfortable, and stocked it with stolen biscuits which they forgot about until the crumbs inspired a pilgrimage of ants. This hide doubled as a tent in various games, provided shelter from the sunshine and was to be home to a number of initiations. It was here, having heard that sailors chew tobacco, that they ate one of Mazin's cigarettes. It was here they sniggered over the mystifying *Porter's Tale* in Sami's *Thousand and One Nights*. It was here they first tasted alcohol - the sun-warmed dregs of a Diana beer left on the roof the previous night. It was here, on a windy February day in 1963 when Rabia had to stop their fathers punching each other, that they swore to remain forever true - an oath they sealed with a kiss on wetted lips, something else which neither of them had done before.

That first year the only squabbles the children knew about were their own - when Kamaran found Sindbad dressed in a doll's bonnet, or Leyla looked in the mirror after he cut her fringe. Leyla's parents made a fuss of Kamaran, although they were always busy. They both worked as teachers and arrived home laden with books and smelling of pencil sharpenings and chalk. Mazin, forever whistling, bounded about in a flurry of dropped paper and cigarettes. He told jokes, juggled, made coins disappear and, pouncing on the children, scooped them both up to run round the courtyard roaring like a lion.

Reem clipped about the house in her pleated skirts and chignon, quiet and dainty as a wading bird. But at night she changed into a traditional *jellabiya* and slippers and - Kamaran to her left and Leyla to her right - they took it in turns to brush and plait her silky black hair. Then she encircled them in her arms and told them stories about clever orphans, courageous heroes and the sparrow who gathered seven grains of corn to throw a party for his friends. The tyrant's rage, the mother's passion and the slave-girl's cunning possessed all who listened, until she ended her tale with a rhyme: 'so mulberry, there ends my story!' Or: 'if you lived close and it wasn't late, I'd bring you almonds on a glass plate.' Then she smiled and her face was the moon in the night of her hair and Kamaran beamed at Leyla who thumped him, even though he hadn't done anything.

One weekend in July Sami introduced Kamaran and Leyla to his old friend Yona's grandson, Solomon. He took the three children to an island in the Tigris. They crossed the river in a boat with a striped canopy and had a picnic in the shade of some trees. Parakeets rustled about in the branches and screeching swifts wheeled above the water. Solomon sat next to Leyla, sharpening her pencils while she drew the birds, until Kamaran got bored and made him play football instead.

The next weekend Kamaran and Solomon went to the open-air pictures together and Leyla stayed at home. The weekend after that Kamaran went to Solomon's house to make kites. It was the Jewish Festival of *Tesh a Bab* and Sami told Kamaran that the skyline used to dance with kites on this day but 'the children have all gone because of Nuri and that monkey-business with the Brits.' Solomon was still there, however, and as his neighbours had gone to the synagogue the boys climbed over the scorching rooftops to Suq Al Shorja and had fun tipping water through a gap in the awning onto the crowd below. In the afternoon they made the kites. Kamaran's was blue, Solomon's red and they spent a long time making a beautiful white kite for Leyla.

When Kamaran went home that night Leyla refused to even look at it. Neither would she speak to him and she pretended not to hear when he asked what was wrong. Instead she wrote a note which explained that she didn't like kites anymore and she didn't like Solomon either. The next day Kamaran loitered on the swing-seat, got tea-towels and wooden spoons, waited in the Kuwaiti chest, mended the hide - all to no avail. Leyla sat alone in the courtyard drawing secret pictures and muttering to a doll with real hair, the colour of saffron, who had escaped Evin's room and blinked her china eyes as if unaccustomed to the light.

Stubborn as an ox, Leyla did not speak to him for more than a week. It was the start of *Muharram* - a time of pageantry and drama - and the Battle of Kerbala, where Hussein the Prophet's grandson died, was to be fought once again in the square. Abu Adil, preparing for the fray, squatted outside his newspaper kiosk in the shade of the tree and made severed arms and legs out of papier maché. Rabia fasted from dawn to dusk and vanished for hours at a time in puffs of steam as she cooked rice and mince to take to the mosque. Then, her clothes reeking of cumin and fried onions, she retired to the cool of the cellar and spent the afternoon stitching paper flowers for the wedding march to be held in honour of Hussein's daughter. As darkness fell she broke her fast with a cigarette, ate a light supper with the children, changed into her best silk abaya and hurried off to prayer meetings, taking blind Um Ghazi with her.

As the evening of the first parade drew near, the sultry air thrilled with chanting and lamentations. Sami shut himself away in the drawing room, playing his favourite records, and grumbled about 'the Brits' again.

'Why?' he growled when Kamaran asked him to explain. 'Because they encouraged these theatrics - that's why! To make problems between *Sunni* and *Shi'a*. Before that people only did it to spite the Ottomans, who were Sunni, you see. It's all very heartfelt and pious I'm sure,' he added. 'But I just can't abide all that weeping and wailing!'

'Were the Brits Sunni, too?' Kamaran asked.

'No my boy,' Sami chuckled. 'They were not. Shi'a or Sunni - what does it mean, anyway? It means nothing at all, except that my wife and sister bicker about which day to collect the lamb for *Eid* and drive the poor butcher to distraction!'

'What are you, Jiddu?' Kamaran asked. 'Shi'a or Sunni?'

'I'm a Muslim,' his grandfather replied, 'and an old sinner.'

Rabia told a different story. She said that Hussein was a hero who died fighting for justice and his people, and she took Kamaran to the wedding pageant where he joined the other children carrying candles and paper garlands through the streets.

On the eve of *Ashura*, the day of grief, the neighbourhood men lit fires in the alleys and cooked great vats of soup. The smell of cinnamon and smouldering dung filled the lanes and, from the rooftop, Kamaran could see plumes of smoke rising like incense to the stars. The next night Rabia took him to a friend's house to see the mourning pageant. Reem and Leyla decided to come at the last minute and ran after them across the square, but still Leyla refused to speak to Kamaran.

A febrile quiet seemed to have fallen with the dark. Shadowy figures stood behind the shutters, waiting for the procession to pass below. Rabia led the way into a courtyard. They hurried up the stairs to join the crowd of women on the gallery and jostled to the front so the children could see. As they peered through the railings of the balcony, the women behind them began a low chant which spread like a breeze over a lake.

'Hussein was slain at Kerbala,
A water-skin fell where he lay,
And the birds which fly in the heavens
Weep to remember that day.'

In the pauses they could hear the rhythmic rattle of chains and a sombre drumming which crept ever nearer. The women on the gallery began to ululate - a wild, keening cry which eddied around them and made the hot air quiver. At last the procession swayed into the courtyard. The air filled with stinging smoke and the smell of rosewater. A horse, nervous amidst the flaming torches, skittered across the cobbles. Black and green banners rippled with firelight - and then came the black-clad men. They moved as one, beating heavy chains across their bleeding shoulders with each step. *Shuffle-jangle-taq!* Kamaran winced at each blow. *Shuffle-jangle-taq!* The women took up the rhythm and started to beat their breasts and sob.

'*Ya Hussein!*' Rabia wailed, dabbing her cheeks with her sleeve. 'Ya Hussein!'

Kamaran turned to Reem. She stood still amidst the swaying throng, her face stricken, and he watched aghast as tears, red in the firelight, gathered on her lashes and made their own procession down her face. Even the men were crying. Some terrible force had been unleashed and was growing stronger and wilder and would sweep them all away in a new flood of tears. He tried to wriggle his way out through the crowd. At that moment Leyla grabbed his arm, her eyes full of mischief.

'Ghoulish, ghastly and grim!' she shouted. 'Extremely ghoulish, terribly ghastly and horribly, horribly grim!'

By day the sun drove everyone inside. The air felt hot as smoke and smelled of molten tar. The women used the rooftops as ovens and left trays of tomato pulp, quince and peach to cook to a sweet

49

jam in the sunshine. Sindbad panted in the shade and Kamaran and Leyla, their quarrel forgotten, fled the incandescent sky for the cellar. They sat in the draft of the wind-catchers, with stout needles and string, and made long necklaces of okra which festooned the gallery as they dried.

At sunset, when Ibrahim's pigeons came flitting home for supper, the children climbed up to the roof and splashed water over each other and the hot tiles. As the breeze from the river stirred the air, people dragged themselves up to the rooftops to eat. Contented murmurs, the chink of china and the scent of lemons and mint drifted across the alleys and away into the resting sky. Reem told stories and pointed out the stars of Leyla and her mad lover, Majnun, whose paths crossed once each summer and granted the beholder a wish. The children lay side by side, watching for the moment of re-union in the lonely heavens, and whispered until their own drowsy voices and the cooing of the pigeons lulled them both to sleep.

At last peddlers arrived from the country with the first baskets of soft green figs, harbingers of autumn. A *titipampa* man went from house to house with a wooden tool, to fluff the cotton stuffing in the mattresses. The storks and swallows left and the family abandoned the roof, too, and prepared for winter. Pelicans sailed in from the north on currents of still-warm air and one evening, as the sun set, they heard the clamour of a flock of cranes, the young birds whistling for their parents above the din.

Kamaran searched out the *Birds of Baghdad* survey, forgotten since their island picnic. Leyla had done nice pictures of the parakeets and swifts but on the next page she had drawn some other birds he didn't recall. Someone - Evin - had helped her with the writing and the pages were blotched with crossed out words and smears of ink.

Date:

Place:

Sort of Bird: Greater Spitting Dove in courtyard. One of them.

Comment: They are fierce with red eyes and sharp beaks. They peck boys.

They are called spitting doves because when they are angry they spit.

After the Spitting Doves Leyla had drawn a Pomegranate Bird who laid fruit instead of eggs. It was then Kamaran realised she had made the birds up. There was a Mesopotamian Cake Eater who nested on pastry shops, a Moon-faced Owl, and a Promises Crane who foretold the future and sang songs that made other birds dance. Kamaran told Leyla her pictures were a load of old nonsense. Leyla replied that they were real birds he didn't know about yet. Kamaran told her she was silly and couldn't be in the Ornithological Society anymore. Leyla said it wasn't up to him, but they soon forgot about it anyway as it was getting too cold to linger outside.

Damp fog crept out of the river at dusk and the night rang with ghostly cries as the last of the cranes returned from Russia, bringing their song of ice even to Baghdad. Mud clogged the alleys. The smell of turnips simmering in syrup hung in the damp air, and the night's silence was broken by the patter of ripe fruit dropping from the persimmon tree in the courtyard. In the evenings the family cuddled up together under woollen blankets and sat on a low bench set around a brazier. They passed round dishes of nuts and seeds, or roasted chestnuts in the embers, and the children drank glasses of 'silver and gold' - warm, sugary water topped with a magically floating spoonful of tea. On good nights Reem told them stories and Leyla sat still, with her mouth open, from the first word to the closing rhyme. Then Reem released them from her spell with a smile, and Kamaran beamed at Leyla, and Leyla thumped him - even though he hadn't done anything.

By February the days felt warm enough to venture onto the roof once more. The first of the swallows returned and the alleyways were soon noisy with the annual drama. In a month's time Kamaran's father was going to come and live with them but Kamaran, having found a home at last, welcomed each day with little thought of the night to come. His new family, the Old House, the Mahalla, Baghdad itself - all seemed part of some inviolable order, as constant as the stars, as natural as rain.

Chapter 5

The grove was layered with birdsong. Chirps and chattering, seductive whistles and watery trills dropped from the canopy of palms. Bees hummed in the white-starred lemon trees and a slight breeze rustled the branches, making hot patches of sunlight, and wafted the scent of blossom from the orchard. A samovar, cushions, rugs, baskets of crockery and food and a football lay scattered in the dry grass while Sami collected Leyla and her parents from the station. Then, laden with provisions, they wound their way through the trees in single file like a caravan of dromedaries.

The farmer, who rented the date grove from Sami, had planted citrus trees amongst the palms in the traditional way and grew vegetables in the shade beneath. Little brown birds hopped about the freshly dug beds and the soft soil clogged Kamaran's shoes as he skipped off the path. He was trying to catch up with his father who had arrived the previous night. He was wearing a new, tweed suit and he looked handsome but hot and out of place as he picked his way through the long grass, talking about the hospital where he was going to work.

Just imagine!' Mazin chuckled, turning to his wife. 'My baby brother - training to be a surgeon!'
Reem looked at him with a frown which made Kamaran feel sorry for his uncle.

'I don't suppose it seems strange to Nasir,' she murmured. 'He must have worked very hard to get so far.'
There was a silence and Kamaran dodged in front of Mazin to walk next to his father.

'If you're going to be a surgeon, baba,' he asked, trying to take his hand, 'does that mean you'll do operations on people?'

'Yes Kamaran. That's what a surgeon does.'

'Will you cut them open?'

'Yes.'

'Will you be the one who says "scalpel"?'
Everyone laughed, except Nasir, and then they arrived.

The women sat in the shade of a mulberry tree while the men squabbled over how to build the fire. Rabia sent the children off with a bottle of sherbet, telling them to put it into the stream to cool. They unbuckled their shoes and dabbled their feet in the water and Kamaran asked Leyla if she would like to go fishing for tadpoles. They drank all the sherbet so they could put the tadpoles in the bottle. Then they forgot all about them as they splashed their way up the creek, seeing who could

55

do the loudest belch and admiring the green bee-eaters that flashed amongst the leaves. Leyla suggested they race to the 'ancient ruin' at the end of the orchard.

They cantered like horses, whinnying as they wove their way between the palms, but as they caught sight of the mud walls Leyla skidded to a halt.

'There's *people* there!' she hissed, snatching at Kamaran's jumper.

They ducked to the ground and lay on their bellies, peeping through the long grass. The house really was half-ruined but some vagrants had found it and decided to make it their home. A man was sitting on the roof with a heap of palm fronds, and mildew puffed into the warm air as he pulled at the rotten thatch. A woman was sorting through a pile of dusty belongings below - an old stove, bedrolls, a tin chest. Both looked careworn and their clothes were patched and shabby. Even their donkey, tethered to one side and still half-loaded, looked weary and thin.

'Do you think Jiddu knows?' whispered Kamaran.

'No!' Leyla muttered with an indignant frown. 'I bet they don't belong here at all.'

A sudden splash made them both jump. A little girl was climbing out of the stream behind them. She stopped to poke two dry palm fronds into the sleeves of her grubby jellabiya and skipped off towards the house, pretending to fly.

Ten minutes later, squawking and waving palm wings of their own, Kamaran and Leyla flapped back into the clearing by the mulberry tree. Everyone had disappeared. Skewers of lamb hissed and sizzled over the embers of the abandoned fire and filled the air with a delicious smell.

'Look!' cried Leyla, pointing to the mulberry tree. 'A magic feast!'

A dozen dishes, covered with plates and cloths, lay spread out on a rug in the dappled shade. The children peeked at them one by one, oblivious to the anxious voices calling for them from the orchard. They found pickles, salads, sweetmeats and other good things to eat - each one as fragrant and tempting as the last.

'Shall we try a little something?' Leyla whispered.

'Aunt Rabia will be cross if we do,' warned Kamaran. 'She'll make us do chores for a week!'

Leyla looked at him so wistfully that he filched one little baklava for her and arranged the others so no-one would see. Soon they had eaten so many he couldn't fill in the gaps. They had just decided to finish them off and hide the plate when they heard Mazin's voice, and they scampered off into the trees.

When the whole family had returned they galloped into the grove once more, hooting and

57

screeching and beating their wings. Everyone laughed, no-one mentioned the sherbet, and Mazin joked about magic baklava that vanished in thin air.

'Or maybe a little bird got them,' Sami said to Leyla as they sat down to eat. 'I did see a little bird with sticky fingers and crumbs on its beak.'

'A *little* bird?' grumbled Rabia. 'No, no. To gobble up an *entire* box of Hussein al Rusafi's best baklava it must have been a big bird - a pair of birds. Two great fat greedy geese!'

It was then that Kamaran noticed the children standing at the edge of the clearing. One of them was the flying girl and the other was a boy about his age. They looked wild, with their matted hair and bare feet, and the little girl's wings still sprouted from her sleeves. He nudged Leyla and she looked up, a yoghurty smile on her cheeks.

'Are they the farmer's children?' Rabia asked, following his gaze.

'No,' replied Sami. 'They're probably from the village.'

Everyone stopped eating and stared at the ragged children. The little girl took her brother's hand and stared back, shifting from foot to foot.

'Perhaps *they* ate the baklava!' suggested Leyla in an excited whisper. 'I 'spect it *was* them, don't you, Jiddu? Not geese at all!'

'I wouldn't be at all surprised if it was,' Nasir agreed, brushing crumbs from his jacket. 'They run wild, these country children.'

58

'Well if it really *was* them,' said Mazin, 'they must have been very, very hungry or they never would have helped themselves to someone else's food.' He stood up with a friendly wave and walked towards them.

Reem had been staring at Leyla. She turned to Kamaran with the same steady gaze as the wild children followed Mazin out of the trees. They hung back by the fire while he heaped meat and bread onto a dish. Covering it with a cloth, he handed it carefully to the boy and gave the little girl some money. The two of them thanked him shyly and hurried back into the orchard.

'Very generous of you, Mazin,' Nasir said as his brother sat down again. 'Every child in the village will be here in a minute.'

'Oh well,' replied Mazin with a shrug, 'we've got plenty to go round.' He glanced at Reem then picked up his plate and they continued eating in silence.

Reem stared at Kamaran again and Kamaran nudged Leyla but she ignored him. He looked down, unable to meet his aunt's gaze.

'Charity is all well and good,' Nasir remarked. 'Except when people abuse it...'

'Those kids were dressed in rags,' said Mazin. 'I'm sure they and their parents are genuinely destitute and as poor as you could want them to be.'

'Poor?' Nasir asked. 'Or lazy?'

'Lazy?' Mazin echoed with an attempt at a laugh. 'You know the hours these people slave - and for nothing.'

'I'm not as naive as I used to be,' said Nasir, wiping his fingers in turn on his handkerchief. 'The country's full of people like this and we shouldn't encourage them.'

'People like what? Encourage who? All I did was give some hungry kids a scrap of food and a handful of coins!'

Kamaran glanced at his father. His cheek was starting to twitch as it always did when he was upset.

'If you both choose to forget your religion that's your own affair,' Sami put in. 'But compassion -'

'Your compassion is misplaced, father,' Nasir interrupted. 'These beggars -'

'But baba!' Kamaran blurted out, dodging Leyla's pinch. 'It wasn't *them* what ate the baklava. 'It was *me!*' He looked from his father to Sami, and then to Mazin, and waited for them to tell him off, or laugh at their mistake, and get on with eating all the nice food. But everyone looked just as miserable as before.

'Your compassion is misplaced,' Nasir repeated. 'These beggars pick your pocket given half a chance. Just because they *look* innocent it doesn't mean you can trust them. The father will get the money, anyway, and for all you know he'll spend it all on horses or drink.'

'But these people have *nothing*, Nasir!' protested Mazin. 'And you're right - the country *is* full of them, working for a pittance on land which -'

'Better to work for a pittance,' Nasir cut in, 'than to take what's not theirs.'

'This!' Mazin gestured to the trees around them. 'This plantation we're sitting in, *all* this land *was* once theirs.'

'And it really *wasn't* them baba!' Kamaran cried. 'It was *me* what ate the baklava! Just me!'

'And now father rents our land for some tomatoes and a sack of dates,' Nasir went on, ignoring his son, 'and makes us the laughing stock of the whole village.'

'Laughing stock?' snapped Sami. 'What rubbish! But let's not talk about it anymore.'

'I just don't want to be taken for a fool,' muttered Nasir. 'That's all.'

Nobody said anything for a moment. Then Rabia stood up to get tea from the samovar and the children handed round a plate of biscuits, topped with nuts.

The train clacked slowly north, tooting its whistle to warn animals off the tracks. Smells of raw onion and mutton fat from someone else's dinner hung in the empty carriage. The metal window frame was too hot to touch and Kamaran's shirt stuck to the back of the seat. He had begged to travel home with his aunt and uncle, leaving his father to go with Rabia and Sami in the car. Leyla sprawled beside him, open-mouthed and limp as a wilting flower. She and Mazin were both asleep. Reem had shaken out her hair and was twisting it up again, the hairpins in her mouth, as she looked out of the window. She seemed distracted and long tresses kept slipping from her fingers. She turned suddenly and caught Kamaran staring at her.

'What were you thinking about?' she asked with a solemn smile.

'I was looking at your hair,' he answered, blushing. 'It's all different colours in the light, like a black feather. Shall I help you put it up again?'
She smiled her assent and he sprang up to sit beside her. He could smell the perfume on her neck as he lifted her hair, which felt hot from the sun

'What were *you* thinking about, *ammati*?' he asked.

'I was looking at those women washing clothes in the canal,' she answered, pointing with a hairpin towards the squatting figures. 'Do you know, Kamaran, I'm the only woman in my family who can read - and that's only because my brother, God rest his soul, taught me. Without Mohammed I'd have stayed in the village, washed clothes in the canal and cleaned rice like my sisters have to do. Have you ever considered what life would be like if you couldn't read?'

'I can remember,' Kamaran mumbled, 'almost.'

'When the train stopped at a station how would you know where you were? If you couldn't read numbers how would you know which coin was which? And all those books - all those lovely stories...' Reem fixed the last pin behind her ear and twisted round to face him. 'It would be like standing outside a cave of treasures without the magic word to crack open its doors. And yet here in Iraq, where writing was first invented, most people still can't read!'

'Can't they?' Kamaran asked. 'Why not?'

'Because there aren't enough schools. Because families are poor and their children must work.' Reem glanced around the carriage and leant towards him, taking his hand. 'Because teachers spy on their students,' she whispered, 'and students on their teachers, and anyone who fights for justice is thrown into prison or killed. Because here in Iraq, *so* rich with its oil, Nuri and the Brits live like kings amongst roses while our children beg barefoot in the streets!'

Kamaran looked at her ardent face and tried to think of something suitable to say.

'What about the Ottomans?' he asked eventually.

Reem let go of his hand and covered her mouth. For a terrible moment he thought she was going to cry.

'Forgive me!' She flopped back in her seat. 'I got carried away. Forget what I just said.'

'I won't tell anyone,' Kamaran assured her, eager to redeem himself. 'And I *promise* I won't tell father,' he added.

She looked away, a red flush spreading over her neck.

'Is that how your brother died?' he asked, longing for her to talk to him again. 'Fighting for justice and the people?'

'No,' Reem said. 'Mohammed was ill and we couldn't afford medicine.' She leant her head against the window and shut her eyes.

Kamaran could see she didn't want to talk any more, and he felt as if he was standing outside a cave of treasures and had forgotten the magic word that would crack open its doors.

'He had tuberculosis,' Reem murmured after a moment. 'I held his hand while he drowned in his own blood.'

Dusk fell as they approached Baghdad. The track cut through a shanty town of palm-thatched huts at the city's edge. Leyla woke and gazed drowsily at the ramshackle dwellings.

'What are they?' she asked with a yawn.

'They're the homes of people who've come to Baghdad in search of work,' her mother replied. 'And cover your mouth when you yawn,' she added. 'Kamaran doesn't want to examine your tonsils!'

'Is that really where they live?'

'Some of them. Others sleep in the streets to save money and leave at the end of the summer.'
Leyla thought about this for a moment.

'Like the storks,' she said.

The name 'Nuri as-Said' was as familiar to Kamaran as Haroun al Rashid or Ala'ad Din or even Sindbad. In some stories Nuri was a hero who fought for freedom against the Turks. In others he was a stooge and a villain. Then there was Sami's tale about how he banished the Jewish children from the rooftops and now there was this new one from Reem.

Kamaran knew about the barefoot children, of course, but he had not realised they were Nuri's fault, or that Nuri lived with the Brits like kings amongst roses. Even so, he still didn't understand why people were always going on about him. He looked so very ordinary, with his suits and his paunch, and he never had any real adventures of his own. Not, that is, until the fourteenth of July that year. On that morning, according to Abu Adil and his newspapers, the army marched into Baghdad and told everyone that they were going to run things now. They shelled the Royal Palace and set it on fire. The palace guard, all two thousand of them, gave themselves up to a handful of rebels. Then the king and everyone came running out and they were all shot! Abu Adil looked doubtful about this bit of the story. But he got excited again when he talked about the happy crowds who had torn down statues of General Maude (a Brit) and King Faisal and their great jubilation. As for Nuri, he said, while his bodyguards fought the rebels 'the old dog' had dressed up as a woman and climbed out of a bathroom window with his face covered by a veil. Later he was discovered and shot, buried and dug up again, and his corpse was dragged through the streets by the mob. Kamaran listened to the bit about the veil with a strange sense of satisfaction. He couldn't help feeling that Nuri had finally had a proper adventure, worthy of his fame, even though the ending was ghastly, ghoulish and grim.

Chapter 6

The swallows were leaving again. Leyla watched as they twittered above the rooftops and performed daredevil swoops to skim water from the gutter below. Sindbad, now five years old and grown plump and stately, was too lazy even to snap his jaws at them. Stretching sleepily, he wandered over to the door and scratched to be let out. It felt stuffy in the kabishkan and the children had both grown so much that only one of them could sit in the little window. Tonight it was Leyla. She had homework to do but her books lay abandoned on the floor, mixed up with her socks and sandals, while she dangled her bare legs through the metal grille of the balcony. Kamaran, dressed in the long trousers and white shirt of his new school, was kneeling on the chest with Solomon. They were peeking through the shutters into the drawing room where Reem and Mazin were holding a meeting with some other teachers. Leyla couldn't be bothered to spy because these meetings were always the same - boring to start with and quarrelsome at the end. She preferred Sami's guests. His friends didn't talk as much. They listened to music and told jokes and sometimes her father joined them and lay on the chaise-longue with his shoes off, smoking the nargeela - something he never did with the teachers.

'Your mum's talking about Cuba,' Solomon said, jumping off the chest and coming over to the window.

'What's Cuba?' asked Leyla without bothering to turn round.

'An island. Christopher Columbus discovered it but he thought it was India.'

'Donkey!' Leyla giggled.

Solomon sat down on the bed and picked up an abandoned exercise book.

'Would you like me to help you with your homework?'

'Yes please!' She disentangled her legs from the grille and slid across the floor to face him.

'"Mayada has got three rose bushes",' he read aloud. '"The first bush has four times as many roses as the second, the second has two thirds as many roses as the third, and the third has twenty seven. How many roses has the first bush got?"' He glanced up at her. 'Do you understand the question?'

'No,' Leyla answered with a yawn.

'It's just an ordinary sum really.'

'Well it's not very *rational!*' she grumbled, stressing her favourite new word. '*Bibi* Evin has got that rose tree in the courtyard but she doesn't go round counting the flowers! And I don't like my teacher. She's got too many teeth.'

'That's not very rational either, is it?' Kamaran remarked, glancing at her over his shoulder. '*You're* not rational at all or you wouldn't hide sugared almonds in your pocket and pretend to fast at Ramadan.'

'I was *trying*,' Leyla answered pettishly. 'I'm just not old enough yet. Anyway, Jiddu says Ramadan is a festival of food.'

'He means you fast so you remember what it's like to really want food. Then you really, really enjoy it.'

'Well I really, really wanted the almonds. That's why I ate them, to save time. So you see I *was* being rational, *muhabal!*'

'You were being sneaky *m'habla* and anyway -'

'My brother says religion is "the opium of the masses",' Solomon interrupted, hoping to divert them. 'Because it makes poor people feel better about being poor.'

'Then it's a good thing, isn't it?' retorted Leyla.

'Not if it stops people from trying to make things fairer,' said Kamaran.

'Well until then, until things are fairer, it's a good thing.'

'But then nothing will ever change!'

'Maybe nothing will ever change anyway,' Leyla pointed out. 'At least this way people *feel* better.'

Kamaran told her to be quiet because Reem was talking. Then Rabia called up from the gallery and asked him to go and get her some cigarettes.

'Ammati!' Kamaran pleaded as she appeared at the top of the steps. 'Can't I go a bit later? I want to listen…'

'Go sweep up the desert,' replied his aunt - which meant he shouldn't be lazy.

'*I'll* go - with Leyla,' Solomon suggested, 'and you can stay here.'

But Kamaran jumped from the chest and loped down the steps after his great-aunt. He called for Solomon to follow him and the two of them set off on their bikes.

Sami had bought Kamaran a bicycle at Ramadan that year, urging him to explore Baghdad 'before they knock it all down.' Solomon already had a bike and every weekend the two boys went on expeditions with Leyla. She was learning how to pedal in the courtyard but she perched on the handlebars when they went out, letting Kamaran do the work.

If they were feeling lazy they headed up river where the coffee-milk water slid quietly past the mansions of Askari Street. Here everything was still ochre and green, and they sat on the bank and watched the round *quffa* boats careen downstream with their cargo of pumpkins or frightened sheep. In livelier moods they crossed the bridge and rode to the race track at Al Mansur to see the stable boys and prancing horses, or sauntered past the old coffeehouses on 'Sharia Nylon.' Most of all they liked to follow the river south and count off the bridges - Ahrar, Sinak, Jumariyah - to leafy Abu Nawas Street, where wood smoke and the smell of sizzling fish wafted through the trees. Then they bought samun *amba* - egg rolls oozing mango pickle - which they shared by the water before they peddled on to the last and newest bridge, named 'Fourteenth of July' in honour of the revolution.

'A master plan for Baghdad' was reshaping their city. A new Ministry of Planning towered like a fortress over the west bank and a firm from America was building a huge university downstream. Bulldozers growled around the old town, butting their way through the serpentine alleys and leaving pitiless vistas of sun-baked rubble behind them. The palm-thatched shanty towns had gone and beyond the Army Canal a vast grid of boxed housing had been built for the poor of the slums. The district was named *Medina al Thawra* - Revolution Town - and Nasir complained it was impossible to give directions, now, without sounding like a Communist.

As the suburbs spread many old families left the Mahalla, eager to replace their flooded cellars and flaking plaster for a villa with new plumbing and a patch of lawn. Some of the courtyard houses around the square had been let. Strange faces made their appearance in the shops and streets. The entire row opposite the bakery was up for rent and a new family moved in next to Um Salma's apothecary, bringing a flock of pigeons with them.

71

'Abu Adil says the new family with the pigeons are a "bad lot",' Kamaran announced at dinner one night. It was a Friday and the whole family had sat down to eat together.

'Who?' asked Sami.

'Abu Adil,' Kamaran replied. 'You know - the newspaper man!'

'The new people next to Um Salma,' Rabia explained. 'The father's name is Khalid Sha'ban but the pigeons belong to his son - a handsome, swaggering boy called Osman.'

'And what's wrong with them?' asked Sami.

'They're pigeon fanciers, that's what!' She looked meaningfully at Reem. 'We all know it's just an excuse to peek onto other people's roofs and... you know...'

'Does that make them a bad lot?' Kamaran asked.

'Yes!' declared Rabia, breaking up the chewy crust from the bottom of the rice-pot and handing him a piece.

'It's nothing to do with pigeons,' said Mazin. 'They're Ba'athists, father and son.'

'And that's censure enough, is it,' asked Nasir, 'according to that old rascal Abu Adil?'

'Osman Sha'ban is a notorious thug. He was a ring-leader in the riots in Mosul.'

'Well I don't think we should give credence to gossip,' Nasir said as he helped himself to some chicken. 'We should take them some kind of a gift or at least pay them a visit. It's discourteous not to.'

72

'Please don't have anything to do with them, Nasir,' Mazin urged his brother. 'I know for a *fact* there's blood on their hands.'

'They're practically our neighbours and we should make them welcome. Besides, despite what the esteemed Abu Adil thinks, the Ba'athists are a useful bulwark against the Communists. The more extreme elements can be dealt with in time.'

'It's the Communists who are a "bulwark" against the Ba'ath!' declared Mazin.

'Who's a bullock?' asked Leyla hopefully. 'And what's the Ba'ath?'

'The Ba'athists,' Reem explained, 'tried to kill President Qasim.'

'And Qasim is good,' said Kamaran with a glance at his aunt, 'isn't he?'

'Yes,' said Mazin. 'He's a lot better than the Ba'athists, anyway.'

'No,' said Nasir at the same time. 'He's weak. He survives by pitting one half of the rabble against the other.'

'For all his faults,' countered Mazin, 'you must at least admit that he's honest and has the interests of the people at heart.'

'Ah yes!' Nasir flicked some crumbs from his sleeve. 'The People! Has it ever occurred to you, Mazin, that not everyone shares your touching faith in "The People"? Or that "The People", when you condescend to save them, might not respond with the gratitude you seem to expect? I met "The People" every day when I worked in the south and some of them couldn't even remember to boil their water before they drank it. You tell them to do so, they forget, another child ends up dead. I'm not convinced it would be wise to put the country in their hands.'

'They shouldn't have to boil the water before they drink it,' said Reem.

'I agree. So let's give them clean water and modern hospitals - but not power which they're too ignorant to wield.'

'If you taught the people to read,' Kamaran ventured, 'like in Cuba, they wouldn't *be* ignorant.'

'I do wish,' Nasir said, ignoring Kamaran and turning to Mazin, 'that you would stop filling my son's head with your lofty ideals. He's quite foolish enough already.'

'He's smart enough to make up his own mind,' Mazin replied with a wink at Kamaran, 'despite what his teachers think.'

Nasir flushed.

'I don't complain when you hold your interminable meetings here, but I must ask you not to indoctrinate *my* son. '

'And I'm asking *you* not to befriend those Ba'athist thugs…'

'Nationalist poppycock from Europe!' declared Sami. 'That's what I call it.' Everyone turned to him in surprise as he rarely joined in these arguments. 'First that Khairallah Tulfah, now his nephew, this

Saddam Hussein! Jumped up lawyers, peevish students, officers with a grudge... weak men, hungry for power, who want to strut about and tell everyone what to think. Mazin's right. They're thugs and they're dangerous. As for the Communists, they missed their chance - thankfully. The dogs may bark but the caravan moves on.'

There was silence.

'Whatever you say, father,' murmured Nasir, pushing his plate away.

Leyla yawned and sneaked a bit of chicken to Sindbad. Family meals were no fun any more. They were like the meetings - dull to start with and quarrelsome at the end.

It was Leyla who saw them first. Sami and her parents had gone out. By the time she got up to the kabishkan Nasir had already ushered them into the drawing room. One of their pigeons had gone missing, she told Kamaran breathlessly, and they suspected Sindbad. Kamaran jumped up and they both climbed onto the chest to peer through the shutters into the room.

'.... my lad's very keen on his birds,' Khalid Sha'ban was saying in a friendly voice. 'And the one that's missing is his best racer.'

Kamaran waited for his father to say 'my lad's very keen on his cat' but he just nodded sympathetically.

'I'll stop the cat from going on the roof, if it puts your mind at rest.'

'But that's not fair!' Kamaran exclaimed, turning to Leyla. 'Sindbad's never caught a bird in his life!' He jumped off the chest.

Leyla heard him clattering down the steps to the gallery and a moment later he burst into the drawing room. The three men looked round in surprise.

'Ibrahim keeps pigeons!' Kamaran cried from the doorway. 'And *he's* never moaned about Sindbad!'

'Who's Ibrahim?' asked Osman Sha'ban, getting to his feet. 'And where does he live?'

At that moment Leyla heard her father calling for her. By the time she got back up to the kabishkan she had missed everything. Kamaran lay spread-eagled on his bed.

'Abu Adil's right!' he groaned. 'Khalid Sha'ban *is* a bad lot and his son Osman is even *badder*.'

'But baba's going to talk to them now,' Leyla reassured him cheerfully. 'I told him all about it. Yep! Here he is. Come on!' She climbed back onto the chest. 'Baba's talking now. He says he knows all about Mosul... now the nasty old son's getting cross... Kamaran? Kamaran? Come *here* Kamaran-you're missing it!' She glanced round but Kamaran shook his head. 'You tell them baba!' she whispered gleefully. 'Tell those wicked Sindbad-haters! They're leaving... they've gone. You'll be able to see them in the alley in a minute.'

Kamaran rolled to the end of the bed and looked out of the window.

'Your dad and my dad are quarrelling now,' Leyla continued. '*Your* dad's in a right old temper! He's gone all red. He's saying they were his guests… he's saying baba's got no manners… he's saying he's been made to look a fool and… have they come out yet, the enemies of Sindbad? They *must* be round the corner by now!'

Kamaran held up his hand to hush her as the two men passed below him.

'Do they look cross?' Leyla whispered eagerly. 'That'll teach 'em, won't it?' She jumped down and went to sit beside Kamaran on his bed. 'Won't it Kamaran?'

'Why don't you take things seriously for once!' Kamaran snapped. 'It makes no difference now. Baba said he'd *drown* Sindbad if I let him on the roof again!'

'He doesn't really mean it,' Leyla said earnestly. 'He just wanted to look tough in front of those horrible men.'

Kamaran didn't answer. He was watching his father hurry down the alley after Khalid and Osman Sha'ban.

Chapter 7

'You like birds, don't you my boy?' Abu Adil called out as Kamaran crossed the square the next day. 'Well that new lot don't - pigeons or no pigeons.' He beckoned Kamaran to come closer. 'They saw one of their birds with Ibrahim's flock yesterday,' he whispered, scratching at his woolly hair. 'He gave it back, no hard feelings and all. But what do you think he found when he went up there this morning? *Somebody* crept over the rooftops in the night and there they were - his six best racers, covered in blood and their heads pulled off, all dead in their coop!'

Despite this evidence that they were a bad lot, Nasir took to visiting their new neighbours and he made Kamaran come with him. Khalid Sha'ban had a mottled scar on his leg which he liked to show off and tell stories about.

'Ten thousand of us died,' he finished each time, 'getting rid of the Brits, and now they want to give the country to the Russians!'

Every evening as the lamps came on he passed under the kabishkan window, whistling through his teeth as he headed towards the square. Kamaran always hid behind the shutters until he was out of sight. He was afraid that his father and uncle would quarrel again if Mazin knew about their visits, and he told no-one about them - not even Leyla. When the two of them went out together he took care they didn't pass Khalid Sha'ban in the street, because he had a habit of stopping and joking with him. Sometimes he asked about the meetings at the house but Kamaran, remembering Ibrahim's pigeons, said nothing.

One windy Thursday in Ramadan, which fell in February that year, Mazin announced that he and Reem were going to have another baby. That evening he and Nasir had their most ferocious fight and the courtyard rang with angry voices and slamming doors. Leyla and Kamaran escaped to the roof and sat cuddled together in the hide. Eager to escape the ill-tempered atmosphere, they decided to go out with Solomon at daybreak next day and watch the birds at Um Khanazir Island.

They were woken by the suhoor drum and went downstairs while the sky was still dark to join their great-aunt for breakfast. Then they wrapped scarves around their heads to keep out the wind and set off to meet Solomon. Leyla sat on Kamaran's handlebars, waving her arms to make shadows in the low sun as the three of them sped along deserted Abu Nawas Street. When they reached the island they settled on the riverbank and waited for the shreds of mist to clear. They spotted some black francolins and a pied kingfisher, but they didn't see as many birds as they had hoped and it was cold.

'I heard some explosions earlier,' Solomon remarked. 'From the building works at the university or something. Maybe it's frightened them off. Shall we go to the races instead?'

It was still early so they decided to stay by the river for a while. They kept warm by practicing tricks on their bikes. After that they sat in the shelter of a wall and shared out the biscuits and oranges that Rabia had given them. Conversation stopped as they ate.

'It's awfully quiet, isn't it?' Leyla remarked. 'What time is it?'

The two boys stopped chewing and listened. They could hear no sound from the streets nearby, no stop-start of distant traffic, no car horns, no costermongers' cries. Baghdad's morning chorus was stilled.

'It *is* quiet!' Kamaran agreed. 'I wonder why?'

They washed their sticky hands in the river and set off, expecting to leave the eerie calm behind as they cycled north. The river bank was still deserted, the cafés on Abu Nawas Street all closed. They turned into Karada and here, too, the normally lively streets were silent and empty. Then, as they rounded a corner, they saw a gaggle of people spilling from a coffeehouse. An elderly man broke away from the crowd with a wail and began trotting towards them.

80

'What's happened *Haji*?' Solomon asked.

'They've killed him! Killed him - the dogs!' He looked at the children as if he hoped they would contradict him.

'Killed who?' asked Kamaran.

'Karim!' he wailed as he trotted on.

'Who's Karim?' asked Leyla.

They stopped at the edge of the throng. A short fellow in a crumpled suit was trying to push his way into the shop.

'Let me in,' he pleaded. 'I can't see!'

There was a laugh.

'It's the radio you fool!'

'What's happening?' Kamaran asked him.

'There's been a coup...' he explained, but the crowd shushed him as a new announcement crackled from within the shop:

The National Council of the Revolutionary Command...'

'National Council of your arse more like!' muttered a round-bellied man as he pushed his way out. Leyla giggled but Solomon looked uneasy.

'Karim Qasim,' he said. 'They've killed the President. I think we should go home.'

They cycled hard for a while then stopped to catch their breath under the apricot trees near Kahramana Square. From here they made their way through the backstreets. As they twisted and turned a loud bang made them all jump. It was only the noise of shutters being flung open overhead. An old woman leant out and shouted down the street.

'He's alive! Karim is alive!'

They heard the drub of footsteps and another woman ran out of a doorway, her abaya flapping behind her like a banner.

'He's alive! He's alive!' she shouted, tears of joy streaming down her face. 'We saw him on the telly!'

The old woman in the window above threw back her head and started to ululate. The call was picked up and answered from house to house, passage to passage. Soon the whole quarter rang with the strange, whooping cry.

As the children headed north the alleyways began to fill with people. Some scurried along keeping their heads down. Others clustered together, talking low, glum faced. A crowd had gathered outside a bakery to listen to a young woman who stood on the bonnet of a car, waving a flyer above her head.

'To the streets! To the streets!' she cried, her voice already hoarse. 'We must defend ourselves against the fascists! Defend our beloved Iraq!'

Kamaran wanted to listen but Solomon urged him on. Soon they found themselves caught up in a noisy crush of people and they were shoved along with the herd until they emerged, stumbling, into Rashid Street. A dense crowd already blocked the road. With every minute more people flocked in from the side streets to the east, adding to the commotion. Two men with buckets hurried along the arcade, stopping to stick posters on the columns. Kamaran took a flyer from the pile at their feet.

'"The gains of the Revolution are in peril,"' he read aloud.

'Read the poster!' one of the men said, holding his hand out for the flyer. 'I haven't got enough of these. And take your sister home!' he added with a worried look, before hurrying on his way.

'Where's Solomon?' Sami cried as Kamaran pushed his bike into the courtyard.

'He's gone home.'

'Alone? Which way did he go?'

'We split up by the church.'

'Which church?'

'The Chaldean church,' Kamaran replied, his face flushing because Sami was cross with him. 'I'll go back and find him - but what's happening?'

'I'll go,' said Mazin, grabbing Kamaran's bike.

'What's happening?' Kamaran asked again. 'Is it good or bad?'

But Mazin had already gone.

'It's bad,' said Reem. 'It's terrible!' and she started to cry.

Chapter 8

By the time the children were allowed out again Baghdad had changed. Broken glass scrunched underfoot near buildings pock-marked by gunfire. Burnt-out cars, checkpoints and barbed wire choked the narrow roads. Tanks lumbered about the streets and kept watch at every junction. The Ba'athist Militia, identified by their green armbands, stalked the alleyways and there was a three o'clock curfew.

Kamaran and his friends at school played 'Battle for the Ministry,' drawing lots to see which side they were on. They clustered together to pass round the spent bullets they found in the gutter, and traded whispered rumours of arrests and gunfights. The older boys arrived breathless with news each morning, and they tried to scare the younger ones with ghoulish stories. The Militia was on the move, they said. Street by street, house by house, they were rounding up their enemies. Cinemas and sports arenas were being turned into prison camps. Whole families had vanished in the dead of night. Their captives were condemned to days of beating and torture too awful to be named, and they worked from lists, the Ba'ath, lists of names drawn up by the Brits and the *Amrikiyeen*.

By the end of the week some of the older boys had disappeared themselves and their ghoulish stories all turned out to be true. Kamaran and his friends stopped playing their games and they looked away as they walked past the proclamation that had been pasted to the gates of the school.

'In view of the desperate attempt of Communist agents to sow confusion in the ranks of the people, the Nationalist Guard are authorised to annihilate anyone who disturbs the peace. The loyal sons of Iraq are called upon to cooperate with the authorities by informing against these criminals and exterminating them.'

In the Mahalla, too, whispers and rumours gathered like bats in the darkness. They flittered through the alleyways, twittering at doors and windows, to alight for a moment before veering off on some new course. Then a hush spread over the city, the river, the house. Gunfire peppered the night's silence and all Baghdad seemed to lie awake, listening out for the tramp of jackboots, the blows on the door. They waited for the terror to end - but it didn't. The storks returned, indifferent, to Um

Ghazi's roof and the cranes flew over the city with their mournful cry, as if lamenting the folly they saw beneath them.

Leyla and Kamaran took sanctuary in re-discovered games. They lay under the Damascus desk and drew pictures as they used to do. They teased Sinbad with pieces of string, fenced with wooden spoons, and talked in a squeaky parody of their younger selves as they plotted together on the swing-seat.

'Let's 'tend the swing is a ship...'

''tend the fountain's an island...'

''tend the island's a whale!'

They used an old sheet for a sail and floated away.

'Can I play?' Reem asked one afternoon.

She never left the house now and they had got used to her presence. The chignon, the pleated skirts and clipping heels had gone. Instead she wore slippers and walked with the steady, duck-footed gait peculiar to pregnant women. She dressed in a blue and gold jellabiya which stretched over her round belly, and wore her hair in a thick plait that hung below her waist like a tail.

'Can I?' she asked again, cradling the curve of her stomach as she waddled towards them.

'No!' said Leyla.

'Why not?' Kamaran asked. 'We're only *pretending* to play.'

'Because she'll spoil it!'

'I could be a stow-away,' Reem suggested. Leyla sighed as Kamaran moved to let his aunt on board. She sat down and gave a little shriek as the seat swung backwards.

'Lord it's rough today!' she exclaimed. 'Have we got far to go?' They swung back and forth for a moment and she put her feet down to steady them. 'Do I have to "tend" to be little to join in?'

'*Shush!*' groaned Leyla.

'Come here my Kashkash,' Reem laughed. 'Are you growing up too fast?' She pulled her close and tickled her. 'I'll get you a nice long abaya and *then* you'll have to behave! No more scampering up the rigging for you!'

Leyla, who had been giggling, sat bolt upright and glared at her.

'Oh yes!' Reem continued, wagging her finger. 'You can scowl all you like but I'm going to cover you up! We don't want any nasty strangers staring at you... and then we'll marry you off to one of your cousins in the old-fashioned way.'

Leyla slapped her hand.

'Yes, marry a cousin who knows just how silly you are and none of this running off with strangers.'

'Is baba *your* cousin?' asked Leyla pointedly. 'No. So you're not being very rational, are you, *youma*?'

'Rational or not,' her mother replied with another tickle, 'it's an abaya and a cousin for you! You'll marry her, won't you Kamaran?' She touched his hand and looked at him with her sober smile. 'Or take care of her at least?'

'See!' protested Leyla, getting off the seat in disgust. 'I *told* you she'd spoil the game!'

'Promise me?' Reem said, stroking Kamaran's cheek. Then, leaning on his arm, she heaved herself up and went to pacify her sulking daughter.

Later that day Kamaran sat reading in the kabishkan window with Sindbad curled in his lap. Engrossed in his book he barely noticed the distinctive, sibilant whistle as Khalid Sha'ban passed below, nor the greeting. He only stopped reading when he heard the second voice.

'So are they beginning to see sense at last?' asked Khalid Sha'ban.

'You would have thought so but they're very... very obdurate.'

Kamaran peeped down into the alley and felt a blaze of shame. He was right. The second man was his father. Who were they talking about? He felt an uneasy ripple in his belly and wished he had not heard them.

'They're still carping, then?' Khalid Sha'ban asked. 'Still finding fault?'

'Yes, but you know how it is,' his father replied. 'The dogs may bark but the caravan moves on.'

Intent on eavesdropping, Kamaran hadn't heard the door open. He turned round with a start to see Reem standing by his bed.

'Is that your father?' she asked.

'Yes,' said Kamaran, closing the shutter.

'Who's he talking to?'

'To Ibrahim,' Kamaran lied.

The rain fell hard that evening - a late spring storm which made a gurgling stream in the alley outside. Drifts of bedraggled rose petals stuck to the tiles in the courtyard, pale splodges between puddles of murky sky. They all went to bed early. Kamaran fell asleep to the water bubbling in the gutter outside. The sound rippled like a song through his dreams until - *taq-taq-taq!* - something rattled against the window. He wriggled to the end of his bed, still half asleep, pulled open the shutter and yelped as a hail of chickpeas hit his face. Someone was standing in the darkened window across the alley.

'Mazin... Mazin!'

'It's me - Kamaran!' he protested, rubbing his cheek.

A pale face floated into the lamplight and then a woman's voice, hissing with the rain.

'Go and wake Mazin! Tell him they're coming! Tell him and his wife - *hah!*' she broke off suddenly. 'Go, go! They're already here!'

Her fear jumped like lightning across the alley and made Kamaran's heart thump and buck so he could barely breathe. As she snapped the shutters together a sombre booming rumbled up from inside the house, followed by a long, splintering crash. By the time Kamaran had stumbled down to the gallery Rabia was there, blocking his way. She tried to shoo him back up the steps then gave up and hugged him close to her so he couldn't see. Kamaran heard shouting and gritty footsteps. He wriggled and ducked as torchlight flashed across the wet courtyard. Beneath Rabia's arm he saw the men in green armbands and there, swaggering in their midst, was Osman Sha'ban. A light came on as Reem and Mazin, barefoot in their nightgowns, stepped out onto the gallery. Then the rushing in Kamaran's ears overwhelmed him and he hid his face in Rabia's lap.

Only when the soldiers had left the courtyard, taking his aunt and uncle with them, did Kamaran think to go back to his room to see. He scrambled up the stairs and ran to the open window. The lamplight glinted on a chain of puddles in the narrow alleyway. Mazin had already vanished. Reem was passing below. One man walked beside her and a second, impatient with her pregnant waddle, was dragging her forward by her arm.

90

Again and again she tried to pull away from him, while with her free hand she snatched and clawed like one possessed at her own head. As she was dragged into a pool of light Kamaran saw why. On the wet ground behind her, like a trail for him to follow, lay handfuls of her long black hair.

Chapter 9

The next day Leyla and Kamaran were sent to stay with Reem's family in the country. It was the start of Muharram. In the evening the chanting from the prayer meetings thrummed with the pulse of cicadas. Reem's mother and sisters went to the gatherings every night and returned with faces reddened by tears.

One evening the children heard the familiar *shuffle-jangle-taq!* of a mourning procession. As it drew near the house they slipped away into an orchard. They lay down in the dappled moonlight and Kamaran began to see the pictures that stopped him sleeping at night. He thought about Reem's hair and how she had stroked his cheek and told him to look after Leyla. He thought how different things would have been if he had told Sami sooner about the meetings with Khalid Sha'ban, or the conversation he had overheard in the alley. Then he looked at Leyla under his lashes, longing to talk to her about what had happened, and tried to work out if she was thinking about it too.

'Kashkash?' he began.

'Shush!' she replied. 'I'm looking for Leyla and Majnun.'

The Muharram passion plays were held in a field near the village. For the Battle of Kerbala horses draped in red and green cantered in a storm of dust. The next day the children were taken to watch the burial ceremony for the martyr Hussein. They were jostled to the front of the crowd but there wasn't much to see and they could hardly breathe in the choking heat. Eventually a solitary horseman plodded into the circle of spectators. The horse was swathed in green. The pale rider drooped upon its back, his face averted, and trailed a long white handkerchief in the dirt behind him. The crowd fell silent as they saw his dreadful face, wrapped in bandages with two dark holes for eyes. In silence horse and rider shambled round again. Then Leyla began to make a noise like a laughing dove.

'O-kuk kuk-oo-oo o-kuk!' She turned to Kamaran, struggling to speak, a look of terror on her face. 'O-kk k... I want to go home!'

'Alright!' he cried. 'I'll walk back with you.' He took her hand and started to push into the crowd.

'No - I mean *home!*' she shrieked, pulling her hand away. 'I want to go *home!* I want to go *home!*' And then she stopped and looked at Kamaran with a dreadful face, white as bandages, two dark holes for eyes. 'They're dead!' she whispered - and collapsed in the dust.

Reem's father took the children back to Baghdad the next day. Rabia gathered Leyla in her arms and carried her off to Evin's room. Kamaran went straight up to the kabishkan. Sindbad was lying curled up by the window, as usual, but the rest of his room had changed. Someone had taken away his books and his football and his clothes had gone from the chest. He banged the lid shut and sat down. There was a knock on the door and he clamped his hands over his ears as his grandfather walked into the room.

Part II
The White City of the North

Helsinki 1989

Chapter 10

The north wind moaned and rattled at the windows like a lonesome ghost, the only sound besides the tap and scrape of his pen. Withering blasts of air swirled around the flat, spiriting bits of paper from the table and leaving them to hop and flutter across the floor like a chorus of dancing swans. Kamaran's back, wedged against the radiator, felt deliciously warm. Lost in his own world, he barely noticed the icy drafts which had turned his nose red, though every now and then he dropped his pen and rubbed his hands together to thaw his deadened fingers. Eventually he stood up, collected the stray pages from the floor, and went to the window.

A matrix of lights pricked the darkness outside, where a clutch of tower-blocks sprouted from the ice like an outpost on an alien planet. He folded his letter with a sigh and put it in his pocket. The whole world was celebrating. There must be somewhere he could find a drink and someone to talk to. He pulled on another jumper and tugged at the cuffs as he worked his arms into the sleeves of his new overcoat. His fingers fumbled at the straining buttons and when he was done he felt like an overstuffed toy.

Even in the hallway the air was icy and the cold started its incursion through the soles of his boots. The building was as drafty as a fortress. In summer sly breezes puffed the stench of garbage up the stairwell, and autumn gales pounded the doors like a battering ram and catapulted rain and hail at the windows. Kamaran thrust his hands into his pockets as he clattered down the steps, letting the door slam shut in the wind. As the echo died away he heard footsteps and voices, chirruping below him like canaries in a mine shaft. He rarely saw the other inmates and by the time he reached the vestibule they had gone.

It was snowing hard. Big flakes dropped from the sky in a stealthy airborne invasion and swarmed round the street-lamps like moths around a flame. The grubby road, the parked cars, the overflowing bins and bags of holiday rubbish, all lay under a thick thatch and the whole scene was irradiated in an eerie orange monochrome. Everything was closed and there was nowhere to go. A car swished past leaving tracks in the soft snow then all fell quiet again, save the nautical creaking of his footsteps. Damp flakes caught on his eyelashes and started to settle on the shoulders of his coat. He pulled his scarf tight around his neck and turned up his collar. He would never get used to this cold.

He had left Jordan on a sultry, star-spangled autumn night, flown into a city shrouded in fog, and shivered through the first winter in a jacket because he refused to believe he was staying. For three months he had barely seen daylight. A niggardly sun crawled out of bed an hour after he arrived at the office, dragged itself along the horizon and gave up the ghost at three. By the time he finished work darkness had fallen again. Twice he was nearly run down by the trams - painted the same beetle green and yellow as the trains at home - which trundled patiently around Helsinki, looking for a way out. Everything was a riddle to him. Crossing the road, remembering which shop sold paper or matches, deciphering the packages of food in the supermarket - each act had to be learned afresh, as if the city itself had been lost in translation. 'Home' was a flat in a stark parade of glassy-eyed tenements. The nearby 'market' - a word which conjured voluptuous sun-drenched fruit, spicy aromas and tall tales - was a sturdy municipal building of red brick, redolent of fish, where hefty matrons sold reindeer sausages and tins of bear meat.

Even the old town, decked out in the Empire fashions and grand white marble of Saint Petersburg, had the respectable, thrifty air of a well-to-do provincial port. Stolid women swaddled in fox fur and mink braved the snow for coffee and cake. The taxi drivers who ferried them about had weather-beaten, peasant faces and wore trapper hats of rabbit skin.

On Thursdays, *every* Thursday, eager workers flocked to the city's restaurants for their weekly dose of pea soup and pancake - and never had Kamaran heard such silence in a crowd. He soon learned not to talk to strangers. On buses, in trams and at cafés, people endeavoured to sit alone and shrank from conversation as if they were wary of catching some horrible disease. In the streets they plodded about quietly, like shy lumbering beasts forced into the open by a forest fire. His colleagues at work were thoughtful, modest, patient - but Kamaran soon abandoned any hope of making friends. He worked hard, saved his salary, and continued to buy the smallest packets of rice, soap and toothpaste because he was always on the brink of leaving.

In February his work permit had expired. He lost his job with the company and learned the Finnish for 'applicant', 'ethnic', and 'restricted period' as he was dispatched on a bewildering paper chase which sent him scurrying down a series of dead ends, and then deposited him right back where he started. They required documents - his draft papers - to prove he was at risk if he returned to Iraq. To write home for them was impossible as it might endanger his family. His life had been reduced to a devilish practical joke.

He took the first casual job he could find and added 'bucket', 'mop', 'disinfectant' and 'broom' to his Finnish lexicon. Dark days gave way suddenly to white nights. The shops filled with Easter eggs and winsome marzipan pigs. Cruise ships and migrant birds alighted, briefly, in the harbour. Café tables jammed the boulevards, lovers danced the tango in the strange twilight of the long summer evenings, and it became impossible to sleep. Then the icebreakers, tethered for the summer, were set free to roam the bay again and the vagrant birds fled south. In November he watched the last of the geese trawl across the wintry sky and the thump of their wings seemed to cry *Baghdad! Baghdad!* Rusty leaves hopped along the pavements like sparks from a dying fire and the city, marooned by the sea, braced itself as darkness fell again like a shroud. Snow followed fog, brushing colour from the town, and frosted the trees so they spiked the dark sky like a negative. In December, when the sea itself had frozen and the wind creaked at his window like a sheet of ice, Kamaran had finally bought a coat, but there were tears in his eyes as he left the shop.

He stepped into the road as another car hissed by. Up the hill to the right he could see the tower of the church, a granite space-rocket, his landmark amidst the tenements. An anaemic light spilled from the cluster of shops opposite. The Café of the Exiles,

101

whose real name he could not pronounce, was sandwiched between a pizza bar and a hot-dog shop. Only the café was open. He could see the owner through the steam on the window and, despite what he knew of the place, it looked almost inviting in the snowy street.

A brew of smoke, coffee and sour milk belched over him as he opened the door. The patron, whose sullen face had the translucent pallour of raw fish, showed no sign of recognising him. A few regulars were huddled at the bar watching the television. Kamaran felt too shy to join them and he took his coffee to a table near the front of the shop. Someone had been unable to resist the temptation of the misty window and had written 'Hapy New Year' in a childish, looping hand. Cold tears ran from the letters and chased each other down the glass. From the snowy pavement outside the effigy of an oversized hot-dog watched him with demonic eyes as it squeezed ketchup onto its own head. He sat down with his back to the window and took the pen and paper from his pocket.

Standing nearest the door was a professor who had fled Saigon in a leaky junk, been robbed by pirates in the South China Seas, and now ran a convenience store on *Hämeentie*. Next to him sat the Vietnamese chef who worked as a kitchen porter in Hotel Kamp and a Cambodian with the saddest eyes Kamaran had ever seen. Mateo, a tall, blonde swashbuckling Chilean, sat sprawled on a stool at the end of the bar. He had escaped Pinochet's thugs by crawling along a riverbed and breathing through a reed - an epic tale which became more heroic with each telling - and he still described himself as a 'medical student' though he had been driving a taxi for fifteen years. They had traded their stories like shipwrecked sailors, each dreaming of a different shore. Men from the South, like him, whose lives, started in one language, had been re-invented in another and whose brown skin had faded to the colour of nicotine for want of sunlight. Here they sat, in this depressing, strip-lit dive, hunched over drinks that would last the whole night and smoking cigarettes down to the filter as they watched the New Year festivities on television. Only Mateo looked happy. Pinochet had been kicked out three weeks earlier and he was planning to go home.

Someone turned up the volume. The picture cut to Berlin and a beaming reporter in a fur hat. A vast, cheering throng had gathered round the Brandenburg gate, their faces lit by the fireworks exploding in the sky above them. The Cold War was over. The spectre of nuclear genocide had been consigned to history and the celebrating crowds were wild with hope and joy. The soldiers on the wall had flowers in their guns and people were scrambling up to join them, waving flags and bottles. Kamaran put his letter back in his pocket and went to stand with the others at the bar.

'*Hei Compañero,*' Mateo said, moving his stool to make room for him. 'I'm going to a pub in a minute if you want to come.'

The picture cut again to a montage of the year's events. A solitary man stood before a convoy of tanks near Tiananmen Square. Jubilant demonstrators marched in Prague, or maybe Budapest. Gorbachev and Bush shook hands in Malta. American soldiers stalked the streets of Panama.

'No-one to stop those Yankees now,' Mateo muttered. 'Let's see how long the party lasts.'

Chapter 11

Kamaran was woken by a fitful clatter from the street below - a loose shutter or a bin that had been knocked over and was trundling about in the wind like a drunk. His eyes throbbed and the queasy smell of last night's alcohol engulfed him as he pulled the quilt over his head.

An hour or so later he made himself get up. Wrapping his bedclothes round his shoulders, he went to make some coffee. He warmed his hands on the kettle as the water came to the boil and, cup in hand, went to sit down by the radiator. It was then that he discovered his letter was missing.

'*Majnun,* majnun - you *fool*!' he groaned, as he crashed about the room pulling on his clothes.

By the time he got outside a pale yellow smear was all that remained of the day. Too anxious to wait for a tram he took a short-cut towards the Pitkäsilta bridge, following the trail they had taken the previous night. What if some diligent Finn found his letter and it made its way, step by dutiful step, to the Iraqi embassy? He knew it was far-fetched but the idea made his skin crawl. The letter was a soliloquy he had never hoped to send and it was, to say the least, indiscreet. It would be easy enough to trace him - and then it was a short step to identifying *her*. His heart turned over at the thought.

Darkness had fallen by the time he reached the bridge. A glacial wind howled across the ice and nipped at his ears as he left the shelter of the buildings. He trudged on doggedly, trying to recall the night's events. He had definitely had the letter when they left the café - he could remember putting it in his pocket. From there they had walked to Senate Square, stopping to buy mulled wine from a stall on the way. After the fireworks had finished they stumbled from one pub to another like a bad joke - a Latino and an Arab walked into a bar - and Kamaran began to feel as if he was tailing a rampaging bear that had escaped from the zoo. As they walked along the water-front an impish squall whisked Mateo's hat from his head and sent it sailing over the frozen harbour. He declared he was going onto the ice to find it, Kamaran's words of caution inflamed his bravado and they had a tussle at the quayside. Eventually Kamaran diverted him with a snowball fight. The running skirmish had allowed his companion to conserve his dignity - and possibly his life - even as he was led uphill to the safety of Katajannoka. There they shambled about in search of a café Kamaran knew, Mateo lured on by the promise of tango. Kamaran omitted to say it was Finnish Tango - forlorn tunes from a bygone world which reminded him of his grandfather, the melody stamped out by a plodding trombone. 'Tango as played by an elephant!' Mateo griped as he sashayed onto the dance floor. There he had pranced around one of the girls like a matador and, after two songs, the two of them had left the bar together. That was it! That was when he had gone back to the letter. And then the barmaid. 'Majnun - you fool!' Kamaran groaned again.

The café was open. He stood in the doorway for a moment, stamping the snow from his boots, and blinked idiotically as he looked around him. A log fire crackled in the stove and cast a rosy blush on the checked tablecloths. A handful of diners were tucking into hearty piles of bread and stew which filled the room with the smell of gravy. It was blissfully snug. The warm colours and homely smells, the old-time music and the inquisitive looks which followed him to the bar, all gave Kamaran the feeling he had blundered into some private world. Slumped on a stool at the end of the counter, engrossed in a magazine, her face veiled by her long blonde hair, was the barmaid Ritva.

'Well, well,' she said as he came towards her. 'I hope you slept soundly in the *privacy* of your own bed?'

'Yes thank you,' Kamaran answered, 'I did. And you?'

She gave him an evil look and went back to her magazine.

107

'Thank you for helping me home.'

Ritva didn't respond. Kamaran stepped a little closer and leant over the counter.

'I'm sorry if I offended you,' he murmured, putting his hand to his heart. 'I didn't mean to be ungrateful but -'

'Yes,' she interrupted. 'You said.'

He asked if anyone had found a letter. Ritva gave a theatrical sigh, dropped the magazine, slid off her stool and sauntered over to the kitchen.

'Some Irish woman's got it,' she said when she came back. 'She left a number.' Ritva slapped a card onto the bar and then, yawning like a cat, she wriggled onto the stool and turned back to her magazine.

The instant Erin walked into the restaurant Kamaran remembered her. Huddled away on the other side of the stove, she too had been writing something in a small, hard book. Every now and then she had looked up and gazed in his direction, lost in thought. He had just been able to make out her face, a pale will-o-the wisp in the firelight, and he had wondered if she, too, used writing as a remedy for loneliness. Their eyes had met once and they had exchanged a smile of recognition. She smiled again as she dodged through the tables towards him. In the daylight she looked like a street urchin - young and rather tough.

'Here you go!' she said, presenting the letter to him with a flourish. 'I only took it because that landlord's a pig and I knew it would wind up in the bin. I do speak a bit of Arabic as it happens,' she added as she sat down. 'But I can't read a thing. Your secrets, regrettably, were quite safe with me.' She wriggled out of her coat, whipped off her hat and leant towards him, her dark hair crackling about her face in a storm of static. 'Just tell me one thing,' she said, dropping her voice to a stage whisper. 'How in *god's* name did you wash up in Helsinki?'

Chapter 12

Erin was a journalist and she had worked in Beirut during the Lebanese civil war - 'and I *mean* Beirut, not swanning round Cyprus getting news from the wires like the rest of the pack!' She said she wanted to improve her Arabic and they met every other weekend, ostensibly for lessons though they generally ended up in a pub. She always arrived exactly fifteen minutes late and swept into the room in a breathless state, as if she had urgent business to attend to. Apologies, confessions, excuses, cracks about the weather and asides on the bar and its clientele were dispatched along with her outdoor clothes. Then she settled before him a spent force. Elbows on the table, her chin in her clasped hands, she gazed at him with her storm-cloud eyes and asked him about his week.

Her own opinions she dispensed with freely and unasked, as if she was chewing sunflower seeds and spitting out the husks. On an Irish pub near the station: '*Oirish* bloody pub more like - they're everywhere! Same green paint, same pictures, same songs. Nostalgia - it's a desperate business!' She was bored and lonely and she regarded herself as an exile, too, as she had found herself 'banished' to Finland on account of a professional indiscretion.

'It happened while I was in Beirut,' she confessed eventually. 'I used to work as a stringer for a radio station in the US. One day I phoned in with news of a car bomb. The editor gave me five seconds. Then: "Any *American* casualties?" she asks. No - but twenty people killed. 'Any Brits? Europeans? Guys from the UN?" No, I tell her. All of the dead were Arabs. "Erin," she says. Dramatic pause. "You're wasting my time." Dramatic pause. "And *I*," dramatic pause, "don't have time to waste."'

'So what did you say?' asked Kamaran.

'Nothing,' she replied. 'That's the way it goes. They're all the same. So I shut my gob and didn't make the same mistake again. But one day, six months later, that same editor had some minor quibble with my report. I objected. She overruled. I told her to fuck off.'

In April Erin went to London for three weeks and returned laden with booty from the Edgeware Road. Kamaran arrived at her flat to find an oriental bivouac in the corner of her sitting room. She had pressed an Indian bedspread into service as an awning and used another to disguise a sofa in sultry swirls of indigo and red. The low table between them was covered in exotic offerings - bottles of Arak, Ceylon tea, Turkish baklava, glass istikans and

111

saucers, packs of apple and rose tobacco. Coiled in their midst, like a contortionist waiting to start her act, stood an arabesque nargeela of sky blue glass.

'It's all a bit naff, I know,' Erin said. 'But I thought it would be fun.'

So they set up camp. Kamaran sought out the ingredients to cook his favourite dishes from home, and they lounged amongst the silky cushions, nibbling exotic delicacies and drinking tea out of little glasses like children playing at *Arabian Nights*.

As spring gales gave way to summer showers they found themselves talking late into the night. Or rather Erin listened, her chin in her hands, as Kamaran answered her questions about his life. She quizzed him about his student days in Basrah and he entertained her with spicy stories of the city's past. He told her about the merchant ships from the Malabar Coast which had swept into port on the Monsoon, the camel caravans crossing oceans of sand with their cargo of cochineal and Venetian glass, pack mules laden with Persian saffron and rhubarb, and cutters full of indigo and Yemeni coffee. He told her about the English schooner that sunk in calm waters in 1739 and left no trace, save a family of mice who floated ashore in a powdered periwig. He told her about the East India Company coins found in the belly of a bull shark, along with a spurred boot, after a British officer dived into the river to rescue a ball during a game of polo. He conjured the colonial port with its dirt streets, flyblown fish suqs and gardens of okra and roses, the chandlers, coopers and rope-makers which lined the wharves, the prancing Arab stallions traded for chests of Indian silver, the turbaned stevedores, eyes red from tobacco dust, their hands skinned from lugging sacks of sugar to shore, and the little boys who dived from the packet ships into the dock for a copper penny.

He sung her epic sea shanties and folk songs, tapping the slinky rhythm of the *khashabah* on the table, until both of them wiggled their hips like gypsies to the *dum-taq-taq* of his hands. He described how the streets still yielded salty secrets of the city's past: African curls from rebel slaves who had run their own republic, flashes of corn-coloured hair and strange eyes, river green, the smells of India - chopped chilli, ginger and coriander - the steam from the kitchens, redolent of dried limes and an alleyway in a heat-stricken harbour.

He painted the river, glimmering blue and silver as a fish in the dawn, and recalled lingering to watch the last boat come in like a straggling duckling at sunset, when the trees on the far shore grew out of a lake of gold. He told her about the forests of date palms billowing like seaweed in a current and the canals which ebbed and flowed with the tides; the disembarked sailors who lurched along the waterfront, their sea legs stumbling on solid ground; the proud families who gathered in ice-cream parlours on Thursday nights, the little girls dizzy

113

with ribbons and flounces; the playboys from the Gulf, their wallets stuffed with cash, who trawled the streets for pleasures forbidden them at home - nightclubs and gambling, liquor and girls.

She asked him about his work and he told her about weekends with his friends in Baghdad. How they played football on the riverside and watched the pretty girls sashaying along the Corniche; or wandered past the fish restaurants at sunset when the air smelled fragrant with wood-smoke; or followed the crowds to Suq al-Ghazal to admire the songbirds, falcons and snakes; or ambled round the flea-market, examining the bric-a-brac like detectives, and jostled amongst the hustlers in Tayaran Square to buy kebabs and tea from barrows which sizzled and steamed in the wintry air.

He described the gaily painted hand-carts of the sandwich vendors, decked with giddy ziggurats of beetroot, pickles, and hard boiled eggs, the weekly soup of beans and marsh mint, the chickpea broth whose aroma filled the streets and which, to him, would always be the smell of Baghdad in winter. He showed her how to shell pumpkin seeds with her teeth, and recalled trips to the cinema where the whole audience chomped *karazaat* in a seesawing rhythm which kept tempo with the drama. He described taking his grandfather to the barber to be shaved, plucked and massaged until they were both smooth and fragrant as brides; and how they went on to the old coffeehouses on Rashid Street, where

114

kettles and wooden tables worn smooth with use gleamed in the smoky twilight, to play chess and listen to the chatter and the clack of dominoes, the tinkle of teaspoons, the sleepy bubbling of nargeelas.

She asked him about his family and he told her about his reclusive Kurdish grandmother, her flowered shawls and sad nursery of dolls, and the great-aunt who had tended her like a maid, carrying her clogs and ointments to the baths, massaging her hands with almond oil and getting up in the night to make her lime tea. He recalled the scent of the cardamom coffee Rabia brewed for her friends - black clad women who ate sticky pastries, smoked, read fortunes in the coffee grounds and squawked like crows as they told each other saucy jokes. He remembered the folk stories Reem had loved - the tale of Tantal, dark and shaggy as a wolf, who stalked forsaken places at night; the black beetle's lament for her beloved mouse who drowned in a vat of honey; superstitions about shrieking jujube trees and storks who became pilgrims for lost souls, and the fable of the shooting stars, each one said to be a flaming djinni pushed from heaven for eavesdropping on the angels. Finally, inevitably, Kamaran told Erin about Leyla, their games in the Old House, their escapades in the Mahalla, and the Baghdad of his childhood which barely existed now, outside his imagination.

After Reem and Mazin's murder his father had taken him to the north. There he had started to drink and Kamaran had often been woken by the sound of his footsteps as he paced about the flat in the dead of night. In his darkest moments - mumbling, tearful, drunk - Nasir had sought to justify himself to his son. Mazin had been reckless, Sami blind, and it was he who was the real victim. It wasn't until Kamaran was thirty and his father finally drank himself to death that he discovered the truth. Amongst his papers he found a sheaf of letters his grandfather had sent to him - letters which he had never seen. Some had little postscripts from Leyla embellished by drawings and jokes, others were addressed to Nasir himself, entreating him to visit. Sami had not banished them from the family as his father had led him to believe. Rather Nasir had chosen to go and he had dragged his son into exile with him.

By the time Kamaran returned to the old Mahalla, the billowing sea of tawny rooftops and feathery palms was encircled by the concrete blocks beloved of Western architects. Lowering high-rises, monstrous tenements and a network of roads, bridges and flyovers had transformed the city's scale like the crude marks of a giant's pen. Broad, straight lines sliced through the shady haven of the alleyways, and the old neighbourhoods that survived were left to wither in quiet obscurity like backward country cousins. Around the Al Galaini Mosque and

116

south of Kifah Street, acres of rubble were all that remained of the beautiful courtyard houses, bulldozed in the name of development. The labyrinth of passageways around the square had, as yet, been spared and the Old House stood like a citadel in their midst. Rabia and Evin had long since died but Sami welcomed him home with open arms. Leyla, who he had feared could never forgive him, re-conquered his heart with her first smile - but by then it was already too late.

Sometimes Erin steered him back to the present and asked why he had left. Kamaran evaded the question, nursing his secrets like an oyster making a pearl around a painful chip of grit. The more he dodged it, the more curious she became. She wanted to help him, she said. She could use her contacts to get a message to Baghdad. She even offered to drum up some work and travel there herself. Kamaran was too unhappy to question her motives, though she listened to his stories with the attention of a lover.

In June, Erin invited him to spend midsummer's eve at a cottage that belonged to some friends. They left Helsinki in the afternoon. The shops had all closed at midday and - despite the rain that had fallen all morning - it seemed that everyone had already decamped to the countryside for the

Juhannus holiday. Erin chatted gaily as they sped through the suburbs, telling Kamaran about the traditions of the festival. She had dressed up for the occasion - earrings, a silk shirt, her black hair twisted about her head - and her blithe mood was infectious. As he watched her pretty, animated face Kamaran felt grateful that she had included him in her party and found himself looking forward to the evening's revelries.

They kept to the motorway for more than an hour, cutting through rolling farmland which grew wilder and craggier as they drove north. Then they turned along a narrow road that led deep into a forest, and finally they bumped their way along a straight dirt track, a diminishing arrow of earth between the trees.

The summerhouse, a wooden cabin with a pitched roof, was on the shore of a small lake. They parked in a clearing fifty yards from the cottage and carried their bags through the woods. The leaves were still wet and the slightest breeze sent raindrops pattering into the undergrowth, but the sky had cleared. Shafts of misty sunlight sliced through the branches and lit up tangles of bracken and a sea of white flowers which grew in the dappled shade beneath the birches. The air was sweet with their perfume and the spicy scent of the pine needles that lay thick upon the path. Somewhere in the distance Kamaran could hear the tinkle of a stream. Other than that all was still.

118

Their scrunching footsteps marked the silence and, as they climbed the wooden steps to the cottage, it was clear there was no-one home.

'Your friends must have gone out,' he said.

'My friends?' Erin took a key from her pocket and turned to him with a smile. 'My friends are in Estonia. We've got the whole place to our selves.'

Chapter 13

A ramshackle jetty snaked over the water, ending in two wooden benches which framed a view of an island in the middle of the lake. Erin took Kamaran's hand as she clopped gingerly over the weathered planks, making little waves that slapped against the wood. It was a magical spot, poised between earth, water and sky. The island, the dark spikes of pine on the far shore, the arching branches of the silver birch - everything was mirrored in the glassy lake. Bullrushes and plumes of meadowsweet edged the bank and a drift of white lilies floated in water that became sky, crossed by silent, gliding clouds. Erin had brought a bottle of champagne - two bottles as it turned out - and they sat on the jetty looking out over the water as the sun began its slow descent towards the trees.

'I like these white summer nights,' she said as she poured them both a second glass. 'They remind me of home. Ireland's beautiful,' she added, handing Kamaran his drink. 'You should come to Kerry with me.'

A brown mallard darted from the rushes and got entangled in the water-lilies. Kamaran watched as it splashed about, plunging the leaves beneath the surface with its broad feet, and swam off with a vigorous quack.

'You're very *mysterious*, aren't you?' Erin had leant back against the bench and she was staring at him with a quizzical smile. 'You never really talk about yourself, for all your pretty tales of Basrah and Baghdad.'

'Don't I?' Kamaran looked away. 'Perhaps it's a question of culture. We are more... discreet with one another.'

'Discreet, eh?' She looked at him steadily. 'I'm beginning to think you're harbouring some guilty secret.'

'Are you?' Kamaran said with an attempt at a smile. 'Well it's true there are some things I prefer not to talk about. What is it in particular you want to know?'

'Everything!' She took a swig of champagne. 'Everything about you! What did you get up to when you left college, for example? Have you ever been married? Are you *still* -'

'After I left college,' Kamaran said, cutting her short, 'in Basrah, I studied architecture in London.'

'Really?' She looked at him in surprise. 'When was that?'

'I went to England in nineteen seventy-five and stayed for three years.'

'That must have cost a pretty penny.'

'No. We get scholarships to study abroad. School, university, hospital - they're all free.'

'And what happened then?'

'What happened then?' He shrugged. 'I went back home.'

'And?'

'And things looked good - good for the country I mean.' He held out his glass as she poured more champagne. 'The oil industry had been nationalised a few years before, everyone had work to do and money to spend and Iraq was booming. We took mains water, electricity and phone lines into every village. We built railways, roads, schools, hospitals...' A note of pride had crept into his voice and he stopped, silenced by an unexpected pang of nostalgia. There were more cranes than palm trees in Baghdad - that was what they used to say. 'Well anyway,' he went on, 'I worked with a Finnish firm, I became friends with one of the managers and he always said... he told me he could arrange a job here with the company. And that, as you put it when we first met, is why I "washed up" in Helsinki.'

There was a moment's silence as he looked out over the lake. A fish flopped from the reeds with a loud plunk and sent ripples shimmying across the water.

'And so,' Erin prompted him, 'you went back home in seventy-eight and ten years later you wind up here. What happened?'

'Saddam Hussein happened,' Kamaran said, standing up. 'And Ayatollah Khomeini happened, and our countries went to war.'

It was dark under the trees and the damp air smelled of bracken and moss. Twigs snapped under Kamaran's feet as he hobbled about, gathering pine cones. Erin's friends had built a Juhannus fire for them - a tall wigwam of branches on a spit of pebbles that poked into the lake. The boughs were green with pine needles and Kamaran had gone to fetch kindling while Erin went for a swim. She had tried to persuade him to come with her but the water was icy and he was glad of the opportunity to be alone. He felt rattled and on edge. It had never occurred to him that Erin saw the weekend as a romantic assignment. He wanted to recover the light-hearted mood they had shared earlier and spare her the awkwardness of any intimate disclosures. But her questions had stirred up painful memories and now he could think of nothing else.

He had forgotten the optimism he had once felt, despite his loathing for the regime, and he had forgotten the bitterness that had gripped him as it faded. Weary of turmoil, eager to work for the development of his country, he had allowed himself to hope. But little by little, law by law, things had changed. As the rhetoric against Iran had sharpened, each new trespass was justified in the name of 'National Security' and even friends who hated the Ba'ath had accepted what was happening, as if there was some inexorable force pushing them to war.

It started with the bomb attacks in Baghdad - the work of an Iranian group. After that all things 'Persian' were damned. The government issued edicts about foreigners, fifth columnists, the Islamists in their midst - and then they started rounding up and deporting people of Iranian descent. Whole households vanished overnight, the doors on their forsaken homes sealed with a disc of red wax. When the fighting began they said it would be over in weeks. It lasted eight years. Many of his friends were injured, others killed. The black mourning banners draped from their houses were emblazoned with government slogans which praised the heroism of the soldiers - and meanwhile a stealthy transformation was being worked on the country, on Baghdad, even in the Mahalla itself.

He remembered the April evening it had struck him first. Strolling home from work that night, he had called at the cobbler's and picked up some shoes he had left to be mended. He had stopped to admire the shop that Yusuf was building on the ruins of the old dairy. He had gone to the patisserie to buy Sami some sweets and called in at the grocery where the good-tempered Jawad, now the plump father of five

124

children, still presided over his crammed and colourful store and gossiped gaily with his customers. In one small but significant detail these landmarks had changed and he had noticed it for the first time that night: behind their counters they all now displayed that talisman against evil, a portrait of Saddam Hussein.

By the time the war ended loyalty to the President, the Ba'ath Party, the state, was everything. To question them was to commit treason. A college caretaker who was in the Party could ruin a professor, a corporal outrank a lieutenant. They had closed their eyes as the web was spun around them and they woke to find the regime's hand at their throats.

Kamaran turned as he heard a splash and a shriek. Erin had jumped into the lake. She trod water for a moment, whinnying with cold as she waved to him. Then she struck out from the shore, her hair fanning out behind her as she swam into the broken path of the setting sun. He put a last handful of pine cones into the basket and walked back to the cottage.

They ate supper on the porch then took blankets down to the water and lit the fire. It was close to midnight and the sky shone with an odd greenish light, like a day for-night scene in an old film. A few pink clouds lingered behind the island but, beyond the circle of firelight, the water, the woods and the dewy grass had turned a deep, ethereal blue. Once in a while a peal of merry voices floated towards them from the other side of the lake. Other than that the silence was broken only by the crackling flames as the green twigs hissed and sputtered and little sparks snapped in the smoke like firecrackers.

Erin sat with her head bent towards the fire, running her fingers through her damp hair in an effort to dry it. She was already a little tipsy, and as she launched into the second bottle of champagne she started singing to herself. Kamaran lay back on the blanket and watched the burning pine needles swirl into the air as he listened to her wistful Irish ballads. He had nearly fallen asleep when he felt a cold touch on his hand. She was holding out a glass of champagne. He took it and sat up as she turned to face him.

'And so,' she said, circling her knees with her arms. 'The war with Iran started and what happened then? Were you in the army?'

Kamaran shook his head.

'But you knew men who were?'

'Of course. There was conscription.'

'But you weren't called up?'

'I was spared because of the work I did.'

Erin took a sip of champagne, her eyes still fixed on his.

'So what *did* happen - to you?'

'I carried on working. The foreign firms left when the war started but Baghdad was safe, they soon came back and they stayed until the money ran out. The secret police - *the mukhabarat* - asked me to spy on my foreign colleagues. I refused. I was expected to join the Party and I didn't. It became hard for me to find a job. Then, in the spring of eighty-eight, I was finally called up.'

'So that *is* why you left - because you didn't want to fight?'

'No-one wanted to fight by then,' Kamaran said with a sigh. 'Men hacked off their trigger fingers to avoid being sent to the front. So my… *decision* wasn't the noble gesture you might imagine.'

'But that's why you left?'

He didn't reply. She took another sip of champagne.

'You're being *discreet* again.'

Kamaran reached for a stick from the woodpile, conscious that she was still looking at him, and poked at the fire as he considered how to answer.

'You're a journalist, Erin,' he said eventually. 'You know about the slaughter of the Kurds in Iraq and I don't need to convince you of the ruthlessness of the regime. But,' he leant into the firelight so she could see his face, 'perhaps it's hard for you to understand what *fear* alone can do. I mean fear that makes you think about *everything* you say, because a careless word can spell death or prison and heartache for those who love you.'

'I'm sorry,' she said. 'I didn't mean to be flippant.'

127

'And I don't mean to be mysterious. But my secrets, as you call them, are not mine alone to keep.' He leaned back out of the light and took a swig of champagne, glad she couldn't see his expression.

'Don't you trust me?' she asked, after a moment. 'I'm only asking because I care about you - I thought you knew that by now!'

There was such tenderness in her voice that Kamaran felt tears start to his eyes. Hidden in the gloom, he was seized by a sudden longing to confess.

'I'd never repeat anything you told me,' she said, peering anxiously towards him. 'I promise.'

'Well then… I left because of a woman.'

'Oh!' Erin looked down and swirled the champagne around her glass. 'I see.'

'I left,' he went on, 'because when she learned I had been drafted she begged me to go. In the end she said she'd break off all contact with me if I didn't.'

'She must have loved you then.'

'She does. She did. But I doubted her. I thought she was hiding something from me.' He looked Erin squarely in the face. 'She's married, you see.'

'But not to you.'

'But not to me.' He grabbed the stick again and jabbed at the embers.

'And how long had it been going on, this affair?'

Kamaran winced.

'It wasn't "an affair". She was pure as a tear and we had loved each other *very* much, she and I, for a long time before -'

128

'Kamaran,' Erin interrupted. 'There's no need to defend yourself to me.'

'It's not myself I am defending.'

Erin's glass chinked against the bottle as she poured herself some more champagne. She threw her head back and drank it down in one long gulp.

'What's her name?'

He didn't answer.

'So what did you do?'

'I did as she asked. I crossed the border, illegally, hidden in a lorry.'

'Can't you go back, now the war is over?'

He shrugged, opening his hands in a gesture of helplessness.

'What would happen if you tried?'

'I'd be arrested the moment I crossed the border. At the very least they'd take my passport and I'd never get out again. The only other option is to go back to Jordan, to Amman, and try to buy some forged documents - a new passport or an exit visa for my own. '

'Have you got the money for that?'

'Yes. But what if they caught me? Anything I do may cause problems for my family. And so,' he threw his stick into the fire, 'rather than take that chance I wait, hoping for an amnesty, a revolution - a miracle!'

'And you've had no news from -'

'I've had no news of *anyone* for two years. They don't even know where I am. My grandfather is old but I don't want to take the risk of writing or phoning. Letters are opened, lines are bugged. As it is my absence may cause problems for them. The only way to protect them is to disappear. So that's my guilty secret,' he finished, looking up at her with a grim smile, 'and as you see, I'm a deserter - in every sense of the word.'

It was two in the morning when they went to bed. Erin, tired and tipsy, reached for Kamaran's hand as she got up from the ground. They walked along the path they had trodden in the grass and he took her arm to help her up the stairs to the cabin. The paneled room, lit only by the flame of a lantern, looked warm and snug. A double bed decked out with a patchwork quilt took up one wall. On the other side, beneath the window, there was an armchair and a small, uncomfortable looking sofa. They brushed their teeth together at the kitchen sink and Kamaran went back outside while Erin changed for bed.

A smudge of orange cloud, still visible on the far horizon, was eclipsed by the glimmer of their fire. Beyond it all was cold and blue. Faint wisps of mist rose like ghosts from the lake. Kamaran crouched down, poking the embers into life with a twig as he remembered their conversation. He felt no relief - no longed for absolution - because he had not told Erin everything after all. He had not told her the details of that fateful quarrel and his jealous accusations, nor what happened afterwards. Shame coursed through his body as he remembered the things he had said. From there it was one short, inevitable step to the argument's sequel. Remorselessly, in all its painful details, he was compelled to remember it once again as if, in reliving it, the outcome could be changed.

Two days after their quarrel - the day after he should have reported to the army - he had gone to ask for her forgiveness. As he hurried towards the house, distraught and anxious to make his peace, he had noticed a second trail of footsteps which dogged his own at every turn. A man in a safari suit was prowling a few yards behind him. Kamaran stopped. The man stopped. He crossed the road. The man crossed the road. He took a left, his chaperone did too. With hindsight he no longer even had the comfort of certainty. Was he really being watched? He would never know. At the time the fear had been enough. So, rather than lead this shade to the house, he had doubled back and headed in the opposite direction. He turned into a narrow street - an alleyway - his stalker on his heels. As the passage twisted he was blinded by a shaft of sunlight. A woman stepped across the glare and from her silhouette alone he saw that it was *her*. She carrying a box of cakes, her fingers hooked through the frill of ribbons that tied it, and it swung to and fro with every step. She stared at the ground as she walked towards him, her expression distracted and sad. Only as they were about to pass one another, close enough

131

to touch, did she see him. Her face lit up with its sweetest smile - full of joy, tenderness, forgiveness, love. It was too late to signal to her and Kamaran walked straight past her as if she wasn't there.

Time and again in the months they had been parted he had replayed this scene, hoping he would remember a glance, a gesture, a light in her eyes - something, anything, that would show him she had understood. Always he returned to the same crushing reality. He had left without any farewell and, unable to send word since, he was forced to accept that she must think him vindictive, indifferent, untrue.

He stood up and walked back and forth in the wet grass, trying to discharge the pain in his chest. For months he had clung to the hope that he would get a Finnish passport. He knew, now, that was never going to happen and he was faced, once again, with his own impotence: his fate, whether here or there, was in the hands of others.

An owl screeched somewhere in the wood and Kamaran turned to look back at the cabin. The slender birches in the wood behind it shone white in the gloom, the grassy path that led to the door was silvery with dew, and soft golden light spilled from the windows. It looked like a cottage from some European fairy tale. Through the curtains Kamaran could see Erin's shadow as she walked here and there, getting ready for bed. His heart was full. He felt exhausted by loneliness, the weight of his memories, the weight of his life. As he recalled Erin's face, so tender in the firelight, he was seized by longing. He need only take that silvery path and open the wooden door to step into a different life, a simple life, a life that held the promise of happiness.

He turned away and went back to the water's edge. Three pine cones glowed in the embers like fiery flowers. He kicked the ashes and watched the sparks take flight and disappear into the sky. Far across the lake, a bright patch in the eerie blue, he could see another blaze and the people gathered round it, capering stick-men against the flames. They had spotted him too, for as he stood there a plaintive cry drifted across the water.

'Hei! Hei! Hauskaa juhannusta! Hauskaa juhannusta!'

'As-Salaam-Alaikum Wa Rahmatullah,' Kamaran murmured, raising his hand in reply. Then he walked back to the cottage and went inside.

Erin was curled up beneath the quilt, her dark hair spread out on the pillow behind her. The room was filled with a fresh, sweet fragrance and Kamaran saw that she had picked a bunch of lilies of the valley and put them, with a candle, on a table by the bed. He shut the door gently, tiptoed to the sofa and sat down to take off his boots.

'Kamaran?' She was beckoning to him, her arm outstretched. 'Come here.'

He stood up and went over to her. Letting her take his hand he sat down on the edge of the bed. She looked up at him and he saw the sadness in her eyes.

'Do you like me?' she asked.

133

'I like you very much,' he replied.

'But... do you *like* me? Could you *love* me - in time?'

'I do love you,' he said. 'But there are many different words for love in Arabic. There's *hayam*, for example,' he shifted his hand so their fingers entwined, '*hayam* is a love like madness, like being lost in the desert and crazed with thirst. There's *ishq* which means two people entangled, like the branches of a vine. And then,' kissing her fingers he laid her hand back on the quilt, 'then there's *wid* - the love between friends.'

Chapter 14

On the afternoon of August the first, after a delay of two hours, the Paris-Amman flight finally trundled down the runway. A hush fell over the cabin as the aircraft lumbered into the air. Kamaran, who had a window seat, peered down through the scudding clouds. He had spent five hours at Charles de Gaulle airport, having arrived from Helsinki that morning, but it seemed that was to be the extent of his acquaintance with Paris. He could see nothing below but trees, meadows and roads. He sat back and closed his eyes, relieved to be in the air at last. Even the short delay at the airport had put his nerves on edge.

His mind was racing and he had barely slept or eaten since Erin had returned with a letter from Baghdad two days before. From the moment he had seen it the anguish and doubt that had tormented him since he left Iraq had been swept away in a flood of joy, and his life had been reduced to one simple imperative: he must return immediately to Baghdad.

His turmoil had started three weeks earlier when Erin first told him she was going to Iraq. She had left on the fifteenth of July and he had insisted on accompanying her to the airport, repeating his

135

cautions all the way: don't accept letters from strangers, they may be working for the secret police; remember telephones can be bugged, hotel rooms too; be careful what you say; be careful who you trust. He had made her memorise the address of the Old House rather than writing it down. Then at the last moment, fearful of putting anyone at risk on his account, he had changed his mind. He gave Erin the money for his grandfather and the gift he had bought for Leyla - a necklace with a little golden bird, a Finnish token of good luck. But the love letter which he had stayed up all night to write returned with him to his flat, to be re-read until it had lost its spell when he put it with a hundred others in the suitcase under his bed. It had seemed a momentous decision at the time. How infantile - how irrelevant - it all seemed now.

On July the thirtieth, at ten o'clock in the evening, Erin had returned to Helsinki. She phoned from the airport immediately she arrived. She had visited his grandfather, she explained, and he was well, but she had not met his cousin although she was living at the Old House now. That was the first surprise. Was she sure? She was sure. His cousin Leyla was living with his grandfather and she had left something with him before she went to work - a picture she wanted Kamaran to have.

Erin arranged to meet him the following morning but Kamaran could not wait and she arrived home to find him pacing up and down the street outside her flat. Half asleep, innocent of the thunderbolt she was about to deliver, she burrowed in her luggage and gave him a cardboard envelope. Inside was a photograph with a message inscribed on the back. As Kamaran read it he felt the blood drain from his face. He left a month's rent and the keys to his rooms with Erin the following morning, telling her only that he must return home without delay, and spent the next twelve hours at Helsinki airport, waiting for a flight to Jordan.

The click of seat belts and the flare of matches marked the end of the ascent. As the plane banked above a veil of feathery clouds, sunlight sliced through the windows and lit up the layers of cigarette smoke which drifted in the stale air. Some passengers pulled down the blinds, others stood up to retrieve bags or books from the lockers overhead. It would be another five hours before they touched down. Kamaran glanced at his watch and gave a sigh. He had transferred his paltry Finnish earnings to his savings account in Amman, but everything would be closed by the time they arrived. He had fifteen thousand pounds in the account - his life savings - and he had convinced himself that a well-forged passport, with the back-up of a generous bribe should he be caught, would secure his safe passage across the Iraqi border. Other than that he didn't allow himself to dwell on the risk he was taking. Everything would be alright since he was choosing to go back. The worst he could expect was a few weeks in prison. He had resisted calling home, nonetheless. He didn't want them to worry in the event he was detained. Neither did he wish to alert the authorities to his return with a conversation that might be bugged.

An unpleasant soupy smell woke him from his reverie. Two stewards were trundling a trolley down the aisle, dispensing trays of food. Kamaran forced himself to swallow some flaccid chicken and rice. By the time they landed in Amman he felt decidedly queasy. He caught a bus into the city, his stomach churning as they lurched through the congested streets. The terminus was in the centre near a number of large, unfriendly looking hotels. Nauseated and sweating, Kamaran asked the driver if he knew of a family-run place nearby. The man took pity on him and dropped him off at a little hotel a few blocks away. He was greeted by a gawky teenager with teeth like a mouse who showed him to a first floor room. Kamaran left his bags in the open doorway and ran to the bathroom to be sick.

All the next day he lay in bed struck down with virulent food poisoning. His world had shrunk to the limits of his stricken body and a fretful, nagging impatience that plagued him like the ache in his head. The family looked after him with reticence and delicacy, as if they were shielding him from some terrible news - which, as it turned out, they were. Even at the time their kindness made him feel tearful and wretched, as if he was about to die.

The patron's wife sent up tisanes of basil and mint, anise and chamomile, and tried to tempt him with flat bread and home-made lentil soup. Everything - the tea, the food, the marshy odour of the shower, the dowdy curtains, even the water he forced himself to drink - everything made him retch, leaving the bitter taste of bile in his mouth. The air-conditioning was broken and the breeze from the open window smelled thick with fumes. Outside, the city thrummed in the heat - a steady roar that rose and fell through the day like the snoring of a giant. Kamaran, feverish and befuddled, barely noticed it. For him the passage of time was marked only by the call to prayer at the nearby mosque. The beautiful sound, which seemed to beckon him home, tormented him with misery at his delay.

In lucid moments he gazed at the photo Erin had given him, which he kept on the table by the bed. It showed Sami and Leyla sitting on a sofa in the drawing room. Everything in the room looked just as it had always done. The ornate chairs still paraded along the window, keeping a stern watch over the chaise-longue. The rosewood table held court at one side and the Damascus desk, with its mother-of-pearl flowers, stood demurely on the other. Sami, it was true, had aged a little. The clownish hair that framed his face was now completely white, but Kamaran recognised his expression. His head bowed, as if he was peering over a pair of spectacles, he looked out at his grandson with a face that was both forgiving and grave. Leyla sat next to him, straight-backed as a dancer, black curls tumbling over her shoulders. Her wide-set eyes, dark as coffee beans and sweet as dates, gazed at him with a tender, enigmatic smile. Everything was just as he remembered - except for one remarkable change. For cradled between the two of them, her little legs too short to reach the edge of the seat, a white ribbon in her mop of hair, was a toddler who stared back at him with a lop-sided grin. Leyla, knowing him to be a fool, had obviously decided to take no chances. On the back of the photograph she had written six words:

This is your beautiful daughter - Haneen.

Part III - Majnun

Iraq 1990

Chapter 15

Leyla avoided the newspapers and television as a matter of course, and she left the Old House that morning oblivious to the tragedy unfolding around her. The sky had already turned a pitiless, Persian blue and she was grateful for the shade as she hurried along the alley, pinning up her hair as she walked.

The previous evening had been quiet, as usual. Sami still liked to climb to the roof in summer and eat and sleep under the stars. The hobbling pilgrimage took a little longer every year but he insisted on performing it alone, scorning the arthritis which obliged him to walk with a stick. They ate a light supper at seven, serenaded by the cooing of Ibrahim's pigeons. After tea Haneen played with her doll - the flaxen beauty Leyla had confided in as a child - who she fed, washed, scolded, and dragged about by the hair like an abused slave. Ibrahim came out at sunset and Leyla lifted Haneen over the wall between the roofs so she could watch him feed his doves. By half past eight, her cheeks rosy as pomegranates, the little girl was ready for bed. Leyla, her voice somnolent with heat, told her a story and fell into a fleeting slumber beside her. Then she and her grandfather sat on the roof and played bezique, which Sami had just learned, gambling for pistachio nuts and raisins.

After a fretful night Leyla woke at daybreak with the sense that something had happened. Already sweating in the heat, she hauled herself into sluggish wakefulness with the effort of a fat man climbing a ladder. She was still struggling to chase the fog from her mind when Haneen sprang into life like a jack-in-the-box and all other cares were swept aside. Sleepy kisses, a wriggled escape, the daily battle of the hairbrush, the trial of bowl and spoon, melon and dates disdained, white cheese deployed as war-paint then flung on the floor, more wriggles in the dance of the spurned flannel, impish giggles, devilish shrieks, a second get-away, the triumphant warbling of a little bird that has fled its cage - these charming routines ended with the usual guilty feints and ruses as Leyla tried to make good her own escape. Today, left in full command of her doting great-grandfather, Haneen had barely noticed her go, but Sami had sacrificed his weekly trip to the coffeehouse in order to look after her. Leyla's car was being repaired and as she hurried off to catch the bus she tried to side-step the familiar tangle of regrets - she had to work,

144

after all - and revisit the feeling that had possessed her on waking that morning.

It was still there. For three weeks she had pitched this way and that like a ship in a storm. Now where there had been turmoil there was calm and she knew in her heart that Kamaran was on his way home. It was a singular feeling - a stubborn instinct that had seized her at other times in her life. She had known, for example, immediately she fell pregnant. She had said nothing to Kamaran at the time but when he had left that day she had thrown out her cigarettes - cigarettes which, like an imaginary friend, had kept her company for fifteen years - and she had not smoked one since. She had known, too, that the mysterious creature blossoming inside her, refashioning her belly with the curves of a quince, would be a girl. Now she was so attuned to that exuberant little being that she sensed when her daughter felt tired, hungry or distressed, even when she herself was at work on the other side of the river. But that feral love, fierce as a tiger, had left Leyla with a superstitious fear of her own imaginings and when unhappy thoughts strayed into her mind she felt a frisson of terror.

She fumbled in her bag for her sunglasses, spilling pens and tissues onto the pavement as she turned into the scorching din of the street. Shadowy fears had flittered about her all night like ghouls that had lain in wait for the darkness. In the daylight, though her eyes were burning and puffy and her limbs heavy for lack of sleep, she had the strength to dispel them. As she climbed onto the bus she summoned the arguments she had made to herself, again and again, since Erin's visit: legions of de-mobbed soldiers still scoured the cities for work two years after the war had ended while the maimed, the scarred and the limbless haunted the streets and made everyone feel angry and ashamed. The regime, disgraced and bankrupt, an anxious eye on the revolutions in Eastern Europe, had loosened their grip on the economy and promised more liberties to follow. Exiles who had fled Iraq during the long years of war had returned in their thousands to Baghdad. Kamaran would come home and all would be well.

She pictured him standing in the courtyard - the angle of his shoulders, his foolish, cock-eyed grin, his ardent voice - and conjured their first embrace. From that moment sprung everything she longed for. They would escape to the country with Jiddu and live a simple life amongst the birds and flowers. Kamaran would rebuild the cottage in the date grove as lovingly as he had restored the Old House. They would play and laugh in the shade of the palms and lie close together on the roof at night, watching the slow procession of the stars. Wilfully, purposefully, Leyla banished the night's fears and wove together scenes of love and laughter, wrapping them about herself like a magic cloak.

By the time she got off the bus she felt calm and happy. Dry grass tickled her feet as she tripped across the parched lawn. It hadn't rained for weeks and the baked earth felt hard as cement. Dust coated every leaf and blade, rendering the garden the same pale ochre as the bricks of the museum, and her short cherry-coloured dress blazed in the sunlight like a splash of paint in a sepia photograph. She walked tipsily across the car park, the heels of her sandals sinking in the melting tarmac, and ducked into the shade of the building.

She had returned to work only two months ago and she still felt a thrill every time she unlocked the staff door. The treasures that filled the museum's vaults preserved the story of mankind's journey from nomad to citizen and she felt privileged to work there, like an acolyte in a hall of records. Her poky first floor office, blighted by strip lighting, ugly furniture and dingy paint, was a utilitarian hutch of the sort where hapless millions squander their days, dreaming of escape. Yet in this drab setting Leyla lived the fabulous life of a fairy-tale queen, consorting with woodcutters, shepherds and magical creatures one minute, merchants, scribes and priestesses the next.

She shut the door on the heat and noise of the city and paused for a moment as her eyes adjusted to the shade. She had arrived early, as usual. There was no-one about and she decided to walk through the galleries rather than go straight to her office. The halls were hushed and still. Their denizens had been undisturbed for hours and Leyla cherished the fancy that she might turn a corner and find the stone lions cavorting in some wild dance, or discover that everything had changed places during the night. Her solitary footsteps echoed in the still rooms. She stopped and slipped off her sandals. The tiles felt deliciously cool against her bare feet and she slid along the smooth floor without a sound, save the silky rustling of her dress. Rays of dusty sunlight poked like angels' fingers through the high windows and bathed the rooms in golden light. The cool floor, the lichen coloured paintwork and chalky walls, the statues of alabaster, marble and clay, made her feel as if she was wandering through a sunlit grotto.

She stopped before a series of reliefs. Carved into the honey-coloured stone some four thousand years before, amidst a familiar landscape of date palms, reeds and swirling water, were scenes that could still be found today. A fisherman steered his boat between tall rushes. A farmer tended a vegetable plot in an orchard that flourished beneath a grove of dates. A woman baked bread in a clay oven that she, too, had called a 'tannur'.

Leyla lingered before this last scene and studied the woman's gestures. Her arms were outstretched as she flipped a ball of dough from hand to hand, just as Aunt Rabia had taught Leyla herself to do. Sometimes, like an astronaut contemplating Earth from space, she was left giddy by the vast reaches of time, the footprints of empires and civilizations that spanned back to the beginning of history. These homely skills, passed like a magic thread from mother to daughter, father to son, for four, five, six thousand years bound her to her country and consoled her when she felt alone.

Cloistered in her office, Leyla saw no-one all morning. Her task was to illustrate and catalogue a collection of artefacts that had been donated to the museum. Today she was working on a number of seals. Worn like beads on a string, these tiny cylinders of jasper, carnelian and lapis lazuli were engraved, as if by nimble-fingered sprites, with miniature scenes that unfurled when the seal was rolled in wet clay. The first revealed a huntsman and his dogs chasing wild boar in the marshes, the next, tableaux of feasting and music and the third, a heraldic menagerie of jaunty stags, rampant lions and winged horses. Bent over the desk, her magnifying glass in one hand and a pencil in the other, Leyla did her best to capture the artists' handiwork.

By midday the office smelled of scorched paper and putty and sweltered like a *hamam*. The hum and whirr of the desk fan did little to stir the dusty air and Leyla felt hopelessly sleepy. A bead of sweat rolled off the tip of her nose and splashed onto the magnifying glass. She wiped it clean on the hem of her dress and put it down, sending little rainbows dancing across the wall. Merry voices rippled in the hot air outside and she got up and went over to the window. A troupe of school children burst out of the shade of the museum and stampeded across the parched gardens, kicking up dust like a herd of colts. Leyla decided it was time to go home.

The Tigris glittered in the sun as the bus crawled over the bridge. Some boys were swimming from the far shore, splashing in the water like ducklings. A haze of smog shimmered over the embankment making the traffic lights quiver and flex, and fumes washed through the open windows as they lurched away from the river. Amidst the drowsy hum of traffic Leyla caught a procession of other sounds - the rattle and thwack of a sidewalk game of table football, snatches of music, a policeman's whistle, the cries of a peddler selling *sherbet al-tamur-hindi*. They had reached the suqs. The sun was burning a hole in her back and she felt thirsty. She decided to get off and walk.

She bought a cup of tamarind ice and stirred the sour-sweet slush with a straw as she wandered towards the fruit stalls outside the main suq. Despite the heavy traffic the market looked deserted and a sense of vague foreboding prickled in the hot air, like dust before a sandstorm. A waiter emerged from a shady chaikana, clinking two glasses together to attract passers-by. He took one look at the empty sidewalk and returned once more to his cave. The pavement glistened like a sandy beach and Leyla could feel the baking concrete through the thin soles of her sandals. The bright awnings and umbrellas over the stalls seemed to have drooped and withered in the glare. Here, too, the merchants had abandoned their chorus of bargains and blandishments and wilted in the shade like so many songbirds limp with heat. Leyla bought some grapes and early figs and headed home, pursued by a trio of wasps.

It was a relief to get into the shade of the alleyways but as she wound her way towards the old Mahalla, she felt her face stiffen into a mask of defiance. The gossip that had once kept the community in line had been upstaged by more sinister voices, but Leyla had no doubt her story was recited as a cautionary tale behind closed doors, and some zealous busy-bodies flaunted their indignation in public. There was the swarthy, pinch-faced electrician whose glare, all fire and brimstone, declared that stoning was too good for her. There was the nosy boutique owner, with the brassy hair and neon blouses, whose weapon was a more forbearing look. 'There is much I *could* say,' her snooty gaze implied, 'but *some people* have the decency to keep things to themselves!' And then there was the pharmacist, Um Warda, a glowering she-devil whose poisonous grimace had been honed at Leyla's expense.

Someone had hosed down their doorstep and the damp, uneven ground was steaming in the heat. She turned a corner and a flight of pigeons scattered out of the shade and wheeled back to Ibrahim's roof, the clap of their wings bouncing like applause between the high walls. She could already hear the metallic clatter from his workshop and she caught the whiff of cinnamon and tomato paste from the bakery, which sold *laheem bi ajeem* rather than the crusty samun rolls which had been the rage in Kamaran's day. Another twist in the alleyway revealed the familiar landmark of Jawad's General Store - still overflowing with packets and tins of every hue, still guarded by the sacks of marbled beans that stood sentinel at its door. As she neared the shop Leyla heard Um Warda's shrill, hectoring voice and she hurried past, her head held high.

Her heart beat a little faster as she walked away. Baghdad was full of widows and fatherless children and it would be possible to disappear elsewhere. But she refused to leave her grandfather alone and no amount of tittle-tattle or slander would ever convince her that she had sinned, or even made a mistake. From the first glimpse of her baby, a miraculous being already in full possession of a character entirely her own, the gossips had lost the argument. The day that Haneen had graced her with her first, charming toothless smile they had lost it again, and they continued to lose it every day because she was utterly in love. Now, incredibly, that silky little creature was eighteen months old and was already walking - or rather running as the momentum made her less likely to topple over. *Pit-pat-pit-pat-pit-pat-pit!* Round and round the gallery she trotted, unsteady as a drunk. The drumming of her feet beat out a glorious chorus to her new-found freedom and she accompanied it with little cries - the 'zzz, zzzz, zzzzz!' of a blue bottle, or the trilling 'rr, rr, rr!' of a very small frog. She had already mastered the art of eavesdropping and she learned new words every day, shouting them out like a clever little parrot: 'More! 'nuff! 'tato!' and, of course, 'youma!' and 'Jiddu', though not 'baba' - not yet.

'Leyla *aini! Shaku maku?*

Leyla looked up to see Yusuf waving from the alley to the right of the square. He was wearing a white T-shirt and a jaunty cap which gave him the look of a sailor in a Hollywood musical.

'Come and see!' he called, beckoning to her. 'Come and try my new recipe!'

The cheerful, illiterate boy who had once paraded his white duck around the square, now the father of three little girls, had discovered his vocation. After twenty years of scraping and saving he had transformed his parents' dairy into a pristine ice-cream parlour. He made all the ice-creams himself and they were so heavenly that people drove across the river to try them. Each week he concocted some tantalising new creation and he always asked Leyla for her opinion. Today, like a master showman, he had cast chaste carrot and sweet orange with racy ginger and perfumed cardamom.

'Have you been busy?' she asked, digging her spoon into the sorbet. 'There was no-one about in the suq.'

'Hmm,' Yusuf growled with a pointed look which Leyla didn't understand. 'That's hardly surprising, is it? But I expect people will come out later. They'll need something to cheer them up. So what do you think?' he asked, watching her anxiously as she took her first taste. 'Is it too sweet?'

'It's perfect,' she answered as the zesty flavours melted on her tongue.

'Thank you aini!' he cried, throwing his cap into the air. 'It's taken me days to get it just right - but I can tell by your face you really like it! You see? Ice-cream makes people happy. It's happiness on a spoon!'

He gave Leyla three portions, heaped in wafer shells and adorned with fruit. At the last minute she got one for Kamaran too.

By the time she reached the house the fruit was sliding off its perch and sticky orange rivulets were trickling through the box and onto her fingers. She hurried across to the kitchen and put them straight into the freezer, wafers and all. Then she rinsed her hands, pulled a bottle of rosewater from the fridge and splashed her face and neck. Her hair had come loose and she twisted the stray curls together and pinned them up as she walked slowly back into the courtyard.

The house was silent and still. A discarded picture book had fallen under the swing- seat. The flaxen doll lay face-down beneath the tree, her flowered dress smeared with dust. One red sandal, all of four inches long, was floating in the basin of the fountain, along with a soggy hunk of bread, and there were dark splashes on the dusty tiles. The watery trail - a damp sock, a beaker, a red ribbon - led across the courtyard to the foot of the stairs. It was clear from the evidence that Haneen had gained the upper hand.

Leyla walked quietly along the gallery, listening for voices. She heard none. When she got to the door of the drawing room she hesitated for a moment, clinging to the faint hope that Kamaran might be inside. The familiar scent of rose tobacco wafted over her as she stepped into the room. Sami, wearing a rumpled white *dishdasha* rather than the suit he normally donned on Thursdays, had nodded off in his armchair. Haneen was sprawled on the sofa beside him. There was no sign of Kamaran.

Leyla went over to her daughter. She was sound asleep, her arms and legs flung out like a starfish. Whispers of breath from her open mouth set a flicker of hair rising and falling onto her cheek. Leyla tucked the stray lock behind her ear and kissed the damp curl of her hot little fingers. She could see silvery marks below her eyes - the traces of tears shed in protest, no doubt, at the sleep that had subdued her. When Leyla looked up Sami had opened one eye and was watching her like a drowsy owl.

'Has she worn you out, poor Jiddu?' she asked, kissing his hand.

'No. We've had a splendid time - though she wouldn't eat a thing. It's too hot.' He reached for his stick and cursed as he knocked it to the floor. 'It's a damn nuisance, getting old!' he muttered as Leyla passed it to him. 'Shall we have a bite of something, while little *simsimiyah* is asleep?'

Leyla carried a tray up to the drawing room - a picnic of juicy tomatoes, white cheese and olives, followed by the sorbet from Yusuf's shop. Sami ate slowly and Leyla tried to keep pace with him, watching him tenderly. He had grown thinner in the last few months and his beaky nose and arched eyebrows lent a look of permanent surprise to his face, framed as it was with a shock of white hair.

'What is it?' he asked without raising his eyes from the plate. 'What are you gawking at?'

'Just you my Jiddu,' she answered. 'Your dear face.'

He grimaced and continued eating, lifting his hand carefully from the plate to his mouth. A piece of tomato dropped onto his dishdasha and he glanced up to see whether Leyla had noticed.

'Did anyone phone today?' she asked, looking away.

'No, little pigeon.'

'No word from Kamaran?'

'No, Kashkash, no.'

Leyla sighed and moved onto the sofa to sit next to him. He patted her hand and she leant her head against his shoulder, just as she had when tired as a child.

'Coo coo ukhti!' It was Ibrahim, come up to the roof to give his pigeons their supper. He hailed Haneen as he always did - with lines from an old Baghdad nursery rhyme which sounded like the cooing of a dove. 'Coo coo ukhti! *Wein ukhti?'*

The little girl wriggled from Leyla's lap as his head popped up above the wall. Leyla smiled when she saw his kindly face, which always made her think he should be a running a magic shop or walking through the streets showering gold coins in his wake.

'Hello simsimiyah!' he said, his thick moustache spreading across his cheeks as he smiled at Haneen. 'Do you want to come and say hello to the pigeons?'

Leyla hurried to finish her chores while Haneen played. Then she brought Sami's nargeela up to the roof. She lit the charcoal, fanning it into life, and sat down as her grandfather puffed at the pipe to kindle the tobacco. Her hair was damp with sweat and she kept the palm-leaf fan as she flopped into her chair, batting it to stir the air about her face. Sami slipped off his sandals and lifted the hem of his dishdasha to catch the breeze.

'Lord!' he sighed, gazing at the mottled skin on his feet. 'What a useless bag of bones I've become! Give me the fan, Kashkash. You look worn out.'

'I'm fine, Jiddu,' she protested. 'And you know I wouldn't last a week without you. I don't spoil you half as well as you deserve.'

'If we all got what we deserved,' Sami remarked. 'Who would escape a thrashing? Now give the fan to me and let me look after you for a change!'

They sat quietly for a while, listening to the soothing bubble of the nargeela and Haneen's happy voice chirping amidst the coo and flutter of the pigeons. From the streets below Leyla heard two sets of footsteps converge into a single march, with a lively *'masa' al-khair'*, as two men passed each other in the square. A languid stork flapped back to the old nest across the alley and a flock of swifts spun high above the houses, squealing with shrill, excited cries. Someone was beating eggs or cream. The chimes of the whisk mingled with the sound of mothers calling suppertime, the chink of china and glass and the querulous voices of tired children, calmed by stories, songs and jokes. Then, from the nearby mosque, Leyla heard the crackle of a megaphone and the evening call to prayer, tender and forgiving, floated across the rooftops.

She climbed up the steps so she could see over the wall. Ibrahim was sitting by the coops, smoking a cigarette, and Haneen was busy with her favourite occupation - trying to catch a pigeon. She tottered about amongst the flock, her arms outstretched, and gave a happy shriek each time a bird fluttered into the air.

'Haneen *babati*,' Leyla called. 'It's almost bed time - and please don't frighten the poor doves!'

'My own children are just the same,' Ibrahim said. 'They can't resist it.'

Leyla stayed where she was, balanced on the top step. The sky was pale at the horizon but darker above like an unevenly dyed cloth, and already sprinkled with stars. A lazy yellow moon, almost full, peeped through the palm trees like a lantern. Perched high on the steps, Leyla could feel the breeze stirring from the river. Skeins of fragrant smoke drifted from Sami's *nargeela* and mingled with the smell of sizzling garlic that rose from the courtyard of Ibrahim's house. She lifted her hair to

159

cool the nape of her neck and smiled as Haneen, tired of running around, bent down and chattered to the birds. Their snowy feathers and the little girl's white jellabiya had taken on a pink hue in the sunset, as if they were made from the petals of a rose.

A shutter banged open in the alley behind her and someone turned on a television, the volume at full blast. Leyla paid no attention. She was watching her daughter as she pranced amongst the doves, waving her arms in some private dance while they fluttered and bobbed around her. Then a blare of martial music burst over the rooftop. A strident announcement bristled in the hot air like static, and the bright visions Leyla had nursed all day scattered, a mirage, as spectres of a darker hue took wing and reeled about her, like mocking birds around a dying beast.

Chapter 16

Kamaran, too sick to venture from the hotel, languished in bed for days and did not hear the news. On the evening of the fifth day he managed to eat some soup. He slept soundly all night and was woken by the morning *adhān*. The yearning cry soared above the hills to mingle with another, then a third, far away, which sounded faintly in the pauses like an echo. *Prayer is better than… Prayer is better than…. Prayer is better than sleep!*

He got out of bed and walked across the room to test his legs. They were a bit shaky but he felt hungry rather than sick and he resolved to go out as soon as the shops were open. He could not bear the thought of another hour's delay. Drawing back the curtains he looked out over the city. The hillside, still dark against the dawn sky, was sprinkled with lights and he could already hear the hum of traffic. He took the photo from his bedside table, pulled a chair to the open window and sat down. His head felt clear for the first time in days. As he studied the picture of his daughter Kamaran marvelled, once again, at that other change. He had been reprieved. Nothing else mattered. For the first time in two years he could think of Leyla without pain. Like a miser unearthing a

161

forgotten hoard of gold he devoted himself to his memories as he waited for the day.

He had left London at the age of twenty seven imagining, after a student romance and two affairs, that he knew the sweet and salty savours of love, the bitterness of parting. But when he returned to the Old House three years later, he felt as if he had crossed vast deserts to reach his sweetheart's encampment and found nothing but ashes and a ring of blackened stones. Leyla, married just three weeks before, was gone.

Her husband Adnan was fifteen years her senior. A professor of archaeology, handsome and charming, he courted people as a matter of course and collected them as others might collect records or books, for his own amusement and pleasure. He made a great show of friendship to Kamaran when they first met and invited him often to his elegant house - a stylish villa with a lush garden set amidst the greenery of Al Mansour. There he exhibited his young wife like a prized bauble. Modishly dressed, made-up, perfumed and poised, Leyla did her best to play the hostess at his glamorous soirees.

From the start Kamaran felt gauche and surly in Adnan's company. It took him several months to admit the cause of his resentment, which was simple. This smooth-talking Ogre had kidnapped, bewitched and enslaved the savage little girl that he adored. He

162

soon found a pretext for his dislike. Adnan fancied himself an artist and amongst the pictures he flaunted on his walls was a voluptuous charcoal nude, an erotic homage to a former lover. That he had not taken it down in deference to his bride was enough to make Kamaran loathe him.

As the months went by he saw other distressing proofs of vanity and neglect, and so, for six years, he watched the marriage unravel in a kind of dumb show. Three longed for pregnancies ended in miscarriage and Leyla was left to grieve alone as her husband spent more and more time away - two months in Kuwait, another two in Syria, five in the north as he supervised a dig at the site of a proposed dam. Kamaran looked on in anguish as Leyla was diminished, belittled by her husband's slights and gossip of his of adulteries.

Every now and then they had shared precious evenings with Sami in the Old House when Leyla chatted and laughed with something of her old abandon. But Kamaran, convinced that his love was blameless, remained blind to his own heart until he went to see her at work, on a dig near Nasiriyah. There, out of her husband's orbit, he found her once again in her natural state - tanned, dusty, her sleeves rolled up, her hair wild from the wind.

In a long white tent syrupy with evening sunlight Kamaran watched, his head on his arms and half asleep, as Leyla tidied away her day's work. When she had finished she stopped in the doorway of the tent

163

and looked out over the desert, her curls a fiery halo in the sunset. Shaking the sandal from one brown foot, she brushed a stone from the pale arch of the other. With a languorous yawn, she stretched and turned towards him, her hands clasped above her head. Small damp patches marked the armpits of her shirt, which had ridden up to reveal a waist the colour of honey, and Kamaran was suddenly aware of the creamy skin of her wrists, untouched by the sun, the moist curls that stuck to her neck, the sweat glistening on her collar bone. He shut his eyes as she walked towards him, her leather sandals slapping against her feet. He caught the delicious, musky smell of her body, heard her sigh, felt her breath, and then her fingers tickled the nape of his neck. When Leyla's colleagues came into the tent a little later they found them huddled together on a bench, giggling like two naughty children.

Whenever they met after that Leyla smiled up at him with the candour of a little girl waiting for a kiss. She looked so eager and lovely Kamaran could barely stop himself from throwing his arms around her, or flinging himself at her feet. He tried to keep away. The separation was too painful to bear. So he disciplined himself to love her as a brother, the guardian Reem had appointed before her death, cherishing every moment of her company and plundering it for memories like a thief.

One April evening in the seventh year of her marriage Leyla had sought refuge with her

164

grandfather. But Sami was away - a rare visit to some ancient relative. When Kamaran came back to the Old House, as he did every weekend, he found a suitcase in the courtyard and Leyla curled up on his bed in the kabishkan, where he still chose to sleep. The wings of her nostrils were pink from crying, mascara smudged her cheeks and the humiliation in her beautiful eyes made him want to weep. He stood for a moment, battling against his first impulse which was to track down Adnan and punch him in the face. Then he went to fetch rosewater and cotton wool and sat beside Leyla on the bed. With the delicacy of a painter restoring a peerless work of art, he wiped the traces of make-up from her skin and gazed at her, enraptured by the sight of her naked face.

They parted that night chaste as priests, Leyla sleeping in the room her parents used to have. At two in the morning Kamaran was woken by the creak of the door. Still dressed in jeans and a T-shirt, she came into the kabishkan and stood for a moment by his bed. Without a word she lay down beside him, her head a little below his. He put his arms around her, breathed in the smell of her hair, and tried to master his desire to kiss her by imagining they were sharing a bed, just as they had as little children. Leyla's ethereal, girlish form vanished like a troublesome sprite the minute he tried to summon her and he recalled, instead, a hundred long forgotten thrills. The excitement of

165

hiding in the Kuwaiti chest, their hot limbs pressed together, the darkness filled with the marshy scent of the henna Rabia used to wash her hair. The warmth of her breath upon his neck as he lay with his head on her bare chest, listening to her heart beat. The times when they gorged themselves on sweetened mulberries and he licked the gritty sugar from her cheeks. The squeamish pleasure of pushing his fingers, sticky with syrup, one by one into her mouth. The dares they made to suck each other's toes. The bed times when she let him brush her hair. The tickling, the chasing, the wrestling, the hugging, the tumbling like two kittens in the dust - every memory, it seemed, was charged with a joyous intimacy that had not faded with the years.

When he woke in the morning Leyla had left his bed. They spent the day together - cooking, eating, talking - and neither of them mentioned what had happened. The next night she came to him again. This time she rested her head on the pillow next to his. They lay together in the darkness until the half moon peeped above the alley and Kamaran pulled open the shutters. Leyla kept her eyes closed, pretending to be asleep. As the moonlight crept across her face he watched over her, dizzy with love. Then she opened her eyes and looked into his - and they surrendered themselves to bliss.

The memory of that tentative first kiss was so exquisite that Kamaran sighed out loud. The sound recalled him to the present. He had not thought it

166

possible, after that longed for consummation, that he could love her more. But now Leyla had borne him a child and the intoxicating vagaries of romantic love had been upstaged by a feeling that was wilder, keener, deeper than before - a visceral urge to be near them and to protect them both. He stood up as a scooter whined around the corner and pulled up on the other side of the road. The rider got off. Accompanied by a polite tinkling of keys, he unlocked the door of the chaikana opposite the hotel. The day had begun.

By the time Kamaran had showered and dressed the sun had risen and the din of the rush-hour reverberated between the rocky hills. He felt a thrill of pleasure as he stepped out into the balmy morning air. The white buildings, tumbling down the valley like dice, were shrouded in a rosy haze. It was going to be a hot day.

He turned right after the mosque and the buzz of traffic faded away as he wound into the side streets, where the merchants were setting out their wares. Mounds of glossy aubergines, sacks of nuts and pungent spices, packets of rose petals, golden tins of tea - the bright produce spilled from the shops like treasure from a cave.

'*Balak! Balak!*'

A man trundling a hand-cart piled high with rings of bread hurried along the uneven street, the scent

167

of warm dough and sesame trailing in his wake. The earthy smells, the haphazard strings of light bulbs looping overhead, the lovely calligraphy of the battered signs, the babble of voices and tinkling spoons as old men chatted outside the tea shops - everything seemed as familiar as an old friend's face. But as Kamaran emerged into another main road he was confronted with the arid hills, the cypress trees and white stone buildings. He was still far from home and he felt like a deep-sea diver who, seeing the first glimpse of sunlight in the water above him, finds he is desperate for air.

A crush of taxis, cars and lorries barged and beeped their way down the street, already quivering in the haze. Three waiters in emerald shirts darted like dragonflies amidst the traffic, serving shots of coffee from a roadside stall. A plump matron in a hijab sat behind two brass coffee pots and a pyramid of sugar lumps on a makeshift counter. Kamaran asked her for a coffee with cardamom to soothe his stomach. He sipped at the thick spicy brew with a blissful sense of recognition. Then he remembered the cash he had exchanged at the airport was in a trouser pocket at his hotel. He had nothing but Finnish Markka in his wallet.

'I'm sorry,' he said, beckoning one of the waiters. 'I've just arrived from Europe and I completely forgot - I haven't got any dinar. Is there a bank nearby?'

'You're Iraqi aren't you?' the waiter replied. 'It's on the house, brother. What's ours is yours.'

'There's a bank just across the road,' called the matron with a sour look.

A peanut vendor and an old man selling herbs stood on either side of the entrance, barking their wares like two dogs in the night. Kamaran hurried between them and the lively clamour of the city died away as the heavy door swung shut behind him. The bank was dark after the sunlit street and the tap of his heels echoed in the chilly silence. A pimply cashier, young and slight as a schoolboy, sat at the desk. He was counting under his breath and now and then he tossed his head to dislodge the greasy forelock that dangled over his eyes. His fingers blurred with movement as he flicked through a wad of dollar bills and the leathery smell of money - sweat, dreams and desperation - drifted from the booth as Kamaran stopped before him. The boy glanced up gratefully when he indicated he would wait, but as Kamaran put his cheque-book and passport on the counter the young man slid the pile of notes to one side with a sigh.

'If that's an Iraqi passport, sir, it may present a problem,' he announced, tugging at his fringe. 'I can't give you a penny in fact. It's the new resolution.'

'The new… what?' Kamaran asked.

'The new resolution. The United Nations passed it yesterday.'

'The United Nations?' Kamaran laughed. 'I think you must be mistaken!'

'A mistake it might be,' the clerk replied with an injured look. 'But, God forgive me, I can't give you any money.'

Kamaran decided the boy was an idiot, or was enjoying a prank at his expense, and he asked to speak to the manager. The clerk got up with a sigh and re-appeared a few moments later, followed by a thickset man in an ill-fitting suit. He gave Kamaran a baleful look as he neared the counter, picked up his passport and repeated, with evident satisfaction, that the bank was unable to give him any money.

'It's the new law. Security Council Resolution 661,' he added, as if this settled the matter. 'It was passed yesterday.'

'I've got no idea what you're talking about,' Kamaran protested. 'I've got *thousands* of dollars in my account and all I want now is enough for my hotel bill and a plane ticket to Baghdad. But I can take my custom elsewhere if you prefer.'

'You can try,' the manager replied. 'And you'll get the same answer everywhere you go. You won't be flying to Baghdad either,' he added, shoving Kamaran's passport back across the desk. 'If you persuade your army to withdraw we'll be delighted to serve you. In the meantime your money is

170

staying where it is.' He gave Kamaran a nasty look, turned on his heel, and walked away.

'Forgive him,' murmured the clerk. 'His daughter's in Kuwait City.'

'I don't understand,' Kamaran said. 'What's happened?'

'What's happened? All Iraq's foreign assets are frozen as of today - and that includes the money in personal accounts. It's because of the invasion.'

'Invasion!' he cried. 'What invasion?'

'*What* invasion?' The clerk gaped at Kamaran as if he was the village idiot. 'The *Iraqi* invasion - the Iraqi invasion of Kuwait!'

Chapter 17

The cashier was happy to explain the whole sorry story. He embellished it with details of his own which Kamaran - his heart filled with shame and sorrow for the people of Kuwait - was too stunned to grasp. The blow, it seemed, had fallen in the early hours of August the second but the crisis had been brewing for weeks.

'Months in fact,' the boy went on, relishing the novelty of being an expert on the subject. 'First the Emir wants his war loans back. Then Saddam says they're pushing down the oil price and drilling from your wells. They have meetings and missions and who knows what but one thing leads to another and five days ago - bang!' He flicked his fringe from his forehead for dramatic effect. 'The Kuwaitis heard about it on the morning news, they say, and when they saw tanks in the streets they thought it was their own army. But the Emir had gone, like salt in water, and it was all over by the end of the day. The Americans jumped in, quicker than you can say "oilfields", and now this! They've banned all trade with Iraq, frozen their assets, Kuwaiti accounts have been stopped too and,' he gave a theatrical sigh, 'to cap it all, I'm the one who has to sit here and tell people they can't have their cash! Believe me,' he murmured with an afflicted look, 'I'm not enjoying it at all.'

Kamaran made him repeat this chronicle three times and then plagued him with impossible questions. How could an oppressed people be held to account for the crimes of the tyrants who tormented them? On what basis, having profited from eight years of bloodshed with Iran, did 'they' impose this blockade after only four days of war with Kuwait? How could he, Kamaran, be held liable for the invasion when he was not even in the country at the time? And why, having fled one murderous war, should he be reduced to penury because his masters had embarked upon another? If the issue had been a matter of ethics he would have left the bank a satisfied man because the clerk listened patiently to his objections and agreed with him on every point. But he still refused to hand over any money. In the end he called the manager again. Kamaran spotted the gloating leer of victory in the man's face as he sauntered towards him and he strode away.

Unable to swallow the fact that his savings had been seized in the name of the law, he went to another bank, and then another and another and another. In every one he heard the same rotten tale, sugared over with references to the United Nations and Security Council Resolution 661, as if every cashier in the city had been trained in international law. In the fifth bank, as he listened to the officious

173

jargon that people use to dress up the awful things they do to each other, he finally understood. He had fallen into the maw of a machine more capricious, even, than the arcane mechanisms of the Finnish immigration system, and as implacable as the spidery apparatus that awaited him in Iraq. Resistance was futile and for the sake of his own sanity he must forget the fifteen thousand pounds he had worked so hard to save. He exchanged his Finnish Marka and left the bank with sixty two dinar in his pocket.

In the days that followed Kamaran felt like a leaf caught in the wind, blown hither and thither as a tempest raged around him. He left his passport at the hotel as security for his unpaid bill and paced the burning streets until he found a job on a building site. Here he toiled until his back burned the colour of coffee, hoping all the while the storm would blow over. He spent the first two nights at a mosque and then decamped to a sordid room he shared with five vagrants and the reek of ammonia from the latrine. Cockroaches scuttled across his face in the dark and his mattress felt skinny and bony as an African cow. Exhausted by his labours, he slept like a child. No sooner had his head hit the lumpy bolster than he was woken by the crackling megaphone at the nearby mosque. By the time the last echo of the call to prayer faded into the dawn, he had reconciled himself, once again, to his changed circumstances

174

and was already hurrying back to the patch of rubble where he worked.

In the evenings he went to a coffeehouse. There he watched the news with a handful of Iraqi exiles who clustered around the television, pensive and glum, like patients who had just learned they had cancer and were waiting to hear the prognosis. Sleek warships slipped into the shallow waters of the Gulf and the vast docks at Basrah, idle and deserted, scorched in the sun like the ruins of an abandoned city. Across the Arab world young hot-heads marched in the streets, waving pictures of Saddam Hussein and burning the stars and stripes for the cameras. In Baghdad, Party stooges chanted patriotic slogans under the steely watch of the mukhabarat, and this grainy footage was intercut with glossy tableaux of American soldiers in battle-dress and gas masks, posed against the backdrop of the Saudi sun. During the interminable discussions that followed, western politicians and diplomats spouted homilies about moral crusades and a new world order, but to Kamaran it sounded like the same old same old - a turf war between the well-heeled mobsters who plunder the planet in the name of all that's holy, lining their Swiss bank accounts with loot, while the poor and humble are made to pay the price. The stench of oil leaked from their every word and it was clear they were spoiling for a fight.

Meanwhile, Amman was over-run with eager journalists and a flood of frightened, penniless refugees. Night after night a forlorn caravan of trucks and buses filed from the border laden with a human cargo: Indian waiters, Filipina maids and other skivvies who had fled the chaos of Kuwait, Sudanese students and a million Egyptian labourers from Iraq, and the wandering Palestinians who drifted across the region like tumbleweed across sand. From the snootiest hotel to the meanest flop-house, every room in the city was soon taken. Makeshift encampments of sacking and blankets, plastic shacks and alleyways of cardboard sprang up in car parks and vacant lots, and thousands of fugitives found themselves trapped in the no-man's land between Jordan and Iraq.

In the third week of August, in an attempt to stem the tide, the Jordanian authorities announced they were going to close the border. The thought of getting stranded in Amman was more than Kamaran could bear. He decided that the time had come to throw himself on the doubtful mercies of the ruffians who made a living from selling forged papers to Iraq. His miserable wages hidden in his right boot, he joined the coterie of hoodlums who loitered near the coach station and tried to distinguish the bona fide crooks from the informers who lurked in their midst. Eventually he found a knavish youth who, for ten dollars, led him through a web of narrow streets to the lair of a 'travel agent' with a sideline in forged passports and visas for Iraq.

'Can't help you,' the man announced cheerily as soon as Kamaran had paid the boy. 'Not now...' Breaking off he watched a blue-bottle, which had been buzzing round his sweaty face, scurry across the desk and gorge itself on a smear of jam. He had a politician's smile - all teeth and no eyes - and Kamaran couldn't help feeling the belly he had squeezed behind his desk had grown fat at other people's expense.

'But I've got to get home *now*,' he said.

'Think about it,' the man went on, his fingers crawling stealthily towards a fly swat. 'Smugglers, racketeers, diplomats, all those foreign news types hollering to get in - they see spies everywhere they look. Got you!' he added, slamming the swat on the table.

'It's a risk I'm willing to take.'

'If they catch you with forged papers they might break your bones until you squeal. And that, my friend, is a risk I'm *not* willing to take - not for the money you've got.'

'Then what do you suggest I do?'

'Stay put until it all blows over.'

'I can't. I've got to get home.'

'Then you'll have to try your luck with the passport you've got and face the music.' He sat back and stared at him with a shrewd smile. 'You're a draft dodger, aren't you?'

Kamaran didn't reply. The man lit a cigarette and blew a stream of smoke from the side of his mouth, watching him closely the while.

'I can arrange a lift to Baghdad if you like. The border police don't bother as much with cars as they do with buses and taxis. But the driver won't wait if you get pulled in for questioning.'

'How much?' Kamaran asked.

'Cheap as chips,' he replied, 'for you.' He took another drag on his cigarette. 'Change what cash you've got into dollars. If you're lucky you'll get some poor sap whose mother has got cancer or something, and you'll be able to grease your way through with a bribe. Prices at home have gone sky high. In a few months the Iraqi dinar won't be worth the paper it's printed on. Everyone wants to get their hands on some dollars. And if *that* fails,' he added, stubbing out his cigarette with a snigger, 'you can tell them you've come back to fight for your country like a man.'

Kamaran left Amman the next day in a scrofulous pick-up truck. More rust than paint, it was the property of an old man who had the flattened nose and scarred cheeks of a prize fighter and who gave his name as Abu Kadir. Kamaran rode in the back, perched on a pile of blankets and wedged between boxes of fruit and ice they were taking to the border to sell. There was only one passenger seat and he had no chance of squeezing in next to the driver's accomplice, a beady-eyed giant with a thatch of black hair. The cab was strung with fairy lights and prayer beads and graced by a doe-eyed portrait of Imam Ali which bobbed above the rear-view mirror. Kamaran remembered how Rabia had appealed to him in moments of stress and he wished he had the faith to do the same. *'Ya Ali! Help me now!'*

The houses on the hillside, white as knucklebones in the sun, were lost in the haze as they left the city behind. They emerged onto a glittering plateau of black stone where the only verticals were the road signs that counted down the distance to Iraq: three hundred kilometres, a hundred and fifty kilometres, ninety kilometres. By then the crust of stones had gone, leaving them on a plain of sun-baked mud. The closer they got to the border the more traffic they saw, all of it heading the other way, a motley cavalcade of cars and taxis, lorries crammed with refugees, and gleaming oil tankers which thundered by in a storm of dust and smoke.

They stopped in the last town before the border - a meagre flyblown place which seemed to have been embalmed in the heat - and bought some rancid falafel and three cans of warm cola. By the time they got to the frontier the sun was setting. The black-haired giant unloaded his wares from the back of the truck and said his farewells, and Kamaran sat in the cab next to Abu Kadir for the drive through customs.

A flaming sky framed the sprawl of buildings and the ground, an ashy monotone by day, glowed suddenly red. Kamaran felt his heart beat a little faster as they slithered along the sandy road. It was as if the fear that had stalked him when he fled the country two years before had been lurking in the desert, waiting for his return. A crush of vehicles was queuing to pass through the customs shed into Jordan and a frantic mob had gathered round the long concrete benches, brandishing their transit papers, each man convinced he had a special case. They were all heading west, however, and the beleaguered officials waved Kamaran and Abu Kadir onward with barely a glance.

It was only when they passed into the no-man's land beyond that Kamaran grasped the scale of the exodus. Clouds of dust choked the air and a weary, shuffling horde stretched as far as the eye could see, their dim forms receding into a sepia fog. Dark-faced, white-robed men, bent double beneath bales and boxes, pushed their way through the dense throng. Orange and white taxis had become marooned in its midst and overloaded cars nudged through the dust like tortoises, carrying their homes on their roofs. Pots and pans, upturned chairs, mattresses and table-legs poked indiscreetly from modest tarpaulins. Round-eyed children nestled close to their mothers in the cars beneath, or pressed flushed faces to the window. Abu Kadir cursed under his breath, beeping his horn, as they lurched through the crowd. Above the churning engine Kamaran could hear another sound, like the commotion of a flock of geese on a lake at dusk. It was the incessant, babbling rise and fall of thousands of voices, pierced now and then by a shriller note - a shouted name or a child's cry, flung into the air like the call of a lost bird.

By the time they reached the other side the last of the sunlight had faded and the fugitives were bedding down for the night, their flimsy bivouacs dwarfed by the darkening desert around them. A greenish glow issued from the compound on the border ahead. Kamaran's heart began to pound as they drove into the light.

Their bags were searched, their passports taken and they were left sitting in a waiting-room under the watchful eyes of a portrait of Saddam Hussein. A clammy breeze snaked in through the double doors which opened onto the compound. The only other exit led to an office, the domain of a dour official in a brown suit who came out and summoned them one by one. A woman in a black abaya sat slumped on the floor to one side of this door. She glanced around her, with a terrified, abject look that made Kamaran's skin crawl, and jumped to her feet whenever the door opened as if she was attached to it by invisible strings. Five soldiers huddled in a cloud of smoke in the opposite corner, playing a noiseless game of cards. A few solitary travelers waited alone, their faces marked with that mix of compliance, fury and dread that people feel when their fate is in the hands of a bureaucrat. Someone had been eating hard-boiled eggs and the sulphurous smell merged with the

181

faint but unmistakable whiff of nervous sweat. The only sounds in the room were the buzz and crackle of a dying fluorescent light, the slap of the playing cards and the gritty footsteps of the guards patrolling the forecourt outside.

Kamaran and Abu Kadir sat one chair apart, facing the office. Neither of them spoke. Kamaran shut his eyes and tried to calm his breathing. Each time the door opened his stomach did a somersault. The minutes crawled by. The guards outside changed shifts and a whistling soldier strode into the room and went to join the card game in the corner.

Eventually Abu Kadir was called. He emerged ten minutes later. Kamaran was next. He stood up as the old man sauntered towards him and tried to catch his eye. Abu Kadir glanced at him and looked away, stuffing his passport into his breast pocket, and as Kamaran stared at his sly old face he realised, too late, that he had been betrayed.

Chapter 18

It was a desolate complex of concrete and grit where no tree grew. The mossy odour of the river and the stink of the canals at low tide sneaked into the compound on a flaccid breeze and whispered of the world that lay beyond. Inside, the serried rows of bunks and lockers, the passageways and halls were all painted drab tan and green, and the unadorned labyrinth echoed with the hoarse shouts of the officers who strode about trying to marshal the garrulous crowds. The conscripts, still dressed in civilian mufti, presented a defiant riot of shape and colour and the barracks rang with that unsettling noise - the bird-like commotion of myriad voices that seemed to loop and swirl round Kamaran's skull.

For three days he sat amidst this chattering throng, crammed together like battery chickens in a hutch, and every hour more men arrived. Plump merchants in dishdashas and sandals, stocky tradesmen with calloused hands, soft-skinned teenagers in jeans and T-shirts, pallid bakers and delicate clerks - they walked into the hall carrying jars of dates and photos of their families and tried to stay aloof from the sweating host around them, as if hoping someone would realise they had no business there and send them home.

The garrison was completely over-run as the army struggled to keep pace with the draft. They had run out of beds and food and the military police gave up trying to patrol the camp perimeter. A few daredevils, unable to buck the mercantile habits of a lifetime, slipped through the fence and sneaked back from Basrah with food and cigarettes they hawked to the highest bidder, and newspapers which were auctioned, bartered, passed from hand to eager hand, then torn up and peddled as toilet paper.

Kamaran stayed put. His interrogation at the border had been brief but terrifying and he could not risk any infraction of the rules. On the fifth day he was dispatched to a boot camp where, with the fortitude of a slave, he endured six weeks bullying and humiliation. In October he was assigned to a unit in the reserves. He left the garrison in a convoy the following day, with a number, a haircut and a gun.

The midday sun hit the metal floor of the truck like flame from a welder's torch. Kamaran dropped his kit bag, unbuttoned his shirt and leant over the tailgate, brushing at his neck to dislodge the shavings that stuck to his skin like the whiskers of a prickly pear. In the building behind him two barbers were still harvesting mounds of black hair as the regiment started moving out from the yard. Beneath the uniform sea of khaki, of helmets, knapsacks, webbing, guns and tired brown faces, they were a motley bunch. Mutton and salad, the officers called them - family men and boys too young to have finished their military service. Kamaran wedged himself into a corner of the truck as they clambered aboard in a storm of dust and thundering feet.

'*Shlonak ?* A soldier with wistful eyes and a gentle face, freckled by the sun, sat down beside him. 'We're in the same squadron, along with Sadiq here,' he said, nodding at the man to his left. 'But I don't recognise you…'

'I was only assigned to the company yesterday,' Kamaran explained.

'Well you are welcome, brother!' the man said in a sing-song voice as he shook Kamaran's hand. 'My name is Jamil. That poor kid climbing on now is Hassan and *that*,' he added as a swarthy officer, built like a buffalo, flung his bag into the truck, 'is the platoon sergeant - Sergeant Abbass. But you'll know us all soon enough, I suppose!'

'Do you know where they're sending us?' Kamaran asked.

'No,' Jamil replied. 'But not to Kuwait, *insha'Allah!* They say the regular army's being shipped there to replace the Republican Guard. As for us conscripts - God knows best! When were you called up?'

'He wasn't. He was arrested.' The sergeant had planted himself on the bench opposite and he was staring at Kamaran, his eyes glittering with malice. 'I've seen your file *soldier*,' he sneered. 'And I'll be watching you.'

They were sent to join the reserve divisions in the province of Muthanna, where the Arabian Desert laps at the Euphrates. Halfway between the river and the Saudi border lay two settlements, As Salman and the village of Al Busayah - the headquarters of the VII Army Corps. To the east a silty wasteland, the grave of a long-dead river delta, swept all the way to the Gulf. To the north-west was the *Sahara al Hijara* - a vast tract of broken rock, scored with indistinct lines like the letters of some forgotten alphabet. To the south an ocean of red dust rolled into the Empty Quarter, where fiery winds scoured the rocks and sand snaked from place to place with a whispered lullaby until every stone was worn to a zero.

This vast desert, the domain of the Bedouin, was criss-crossed by invisible paths that linked an oasis here, a patch of brush there, in an ancient constellation of footsteps. But to Kamaran and the other conscripts it was *chol* - a dun-coloured wilderness that lay beyond the civilised horizon of the city - and there was no way out. One tarred road went north from As Salman to the river, a second led towards Al Busayah. This dwindled to a dirt track as it headed east, winding between rocky outcrops and plunging into a deep gully before it reached the village. For at this point the land dropped away in a series of steep cliffs and *wadis*, gouged out by savage flash-floods which surged towards the distant Euphrates. Between the gullies lay salt flats, covered in a crust of wind-blown sand, which quickened into treacherous quagmires when it rained. It was here that Kamaran's battalion was deployed, south of the rest of their division, in the midst of the wilderness.

They might as well have been entombed by the French Foreign legion in a desert fort built to house the damned - except there was no fort. There were no supplies either. The stranglehold of the blockade, the pace of the draft, their isolation, the wild terrain - it was all against them. Everything they needed had to be trucked in and mostly it wasn't. Water was hoarded like silver but an inexorable slush of marshy lentils, or soup made from bones and onions, slopped onto their plates at every meal - and it was a lucky man who fished out a lump of gristle or rancid fat. Sand conspired with grease to make an abrasive sludge that could cripple an engine in minutes. They lacked tools and spare parts. The heavy machinery had all been sent to the regular army in Kuwait, and the emplacements for guns, the networks of trenches and foxholes, had to be chipped out of the vitrified sand with picks and spades - but there weren't enough picks and spades.

At day-break the sun rose like a beast from its den and the horizon vanished in a haze of dust. By ten Kamaran could have fried an egg on the rocks - if he had one - and a dry wind filled the air with dancing grit that burned his skin like sparks from a fire. Still they dug and scraped, raising a cloud of fine sand which settled in his hair, leached moisture from his eyes and nose and cloaked the sun in a red cloud. By eleven the desert glittered like broken glass and moving objects - trucks and men - vanished in a smoky shimmer or rose to float above the ground, only descending at dusk. Then the red eye closed again and the heat sauntered off to explore the vast darkness above. For an hour or two the jangle of mess tins, whistling, shouts and laughter drifted across the stony ground, as if the sun's inmates were celebrating their brief, illusive freedom. By midnight the desert was cold and silent as the grave. Wrapped in his threadbare blanket on a bedroll as thin and lumpy as gruel, Kamaran found himself longing for the dawn.

Some of his comrades shivered through the frigid nights dressed in flimsy cottons. Others, like him, sweated into scratchy woollen khaki in the furnace of the midday sun. Camouflage fatigues had been dealt out in exotic combinations that mingled desert and woodland, jungle and scrub, along with steel helmets, berets, or nothing at all to put on their heads. Even within Kamaran's squadron no two uniforms matched and two of their number had left the barracks with nothing sturdier than a pair of plimsolls. A myopic enemy taking aim from a safe distance might mistake them for an army but - as the company major soon discovered - there was barely a soldier in sight.

Day after day they toiled, carving out a system of trenches which looked like the unearthed burrow of a desert rodent. Their bunkers were little more than caves scraped in the ground. They shored up the walls with sandbags. A sheet of canvas held down with rocks masqueraded as a roof and in each of these dugouts, no bigger than a tomb, three men lived. They spent long hours digging wind-blown sand from the trenches, cleaning grit from their guns and fighting a losing battle with the desert for their vehicles and equipment. In their free time they played football and cards and tore pages from their books so they could share them out and read the chapters in relay. They scoured out their mess tins with grit, cleaned their clothes by leaving them in the sun, used their helmets as shaving basins and checked each other's hair for lice. They prayed together, cooked and ate together, worked together and went to sleep together, curling close to fend off the desert cold. By the end of a fortnight Kamaran could recognise every man in his unit from their footsteps, their snoring or the shape of their hands.

He shared his dugout with Jamil - the tender-hearted soldier with the wistful eyes who had befriended him on the first day - and the glowering thuggish youth, Hassan. Hassan swaggered about, spitting obscenities to make up for the comical fluff that sprouted above his lip where a moustache should have been, and drove them both to distraction with his moaning. He moaned that the Republican Guard lived the life of kings, their shelters lined with swag from Kuwait. He moaned that the major had a bunker with wooden revetments, electric light from the generator and a cot while they had to sleep on the ground like dogs. He moaned because nobody got leave although they were entitled to a week every month. He moaned because their mail was delivered late and had always been opened and pillaged for facts that were entered into their files. He moaned about the heat and he moaned about the cold. He moaned that he was tired and he moaned that he was bored. He moaned about the food and the tea and the blankets and bedrolls and bugs and the howling of the jackals in the night. He moaned about everything they had to endure as if he alone suffered and he never stopped moaning, taxing Kamaran's goodwill until he didn't know if he wanted to smash Hassan's skull with a rock, or weep with despair because he knew he was just a frightened boy trying to be tough.

In the bunker to their right lived Ali, a shy pastry cook, Sadiq, a bearded taxi driver with the bulbous nose and hearty laugh of an avuncular djinni, and a man they nick-named Private Onion on account of the tear-jerking songs he inflicted on his comrades. The platoon lieutenant was billeted to their left. A commissioned officer who conducted himself with the gracious authority of a wise mullah, Lieutenant Ismael never ate until he knew every man in his unit had been fed. He was courageous and loyal, honest and clever, handsome and tough, and he had all the makings of a hero except for the sadness that consumed him when he thought no-one was looking, and the fact that he was slyly over-ruled by his own second in command - the major's favoured henchman and Kamaran's scourge, Sergeant Abbas.

The major had been told to dig in and await orders but there were no orders. There was no intelligence either, just uneasy rumours that rippled through the ranks like Chinese whispers. A formidable army was gathering against them in a grand alliance of enemies old and new. Canadians, Danes, Egyptians, French, Greeks - they had an enemy for every letter of the alphabet, some of them from faraway lands which no-one had ever even heard of. But mostly and as usual, the Amrikiyeen were the villains of the piece - accompanied by their fawning side-kicks, the Brits - and they were armed with bombs that sniffed out human warmth like ghouls and deadly missiles aimed with the glance of an evil eye. Worse still, these fearsome weapons could be unleashed by soldiers sitting safely out of range many miles away and still hit their target, more or less, incinerating men where they stood without them ever seeing who it was who wanted to kill them, or giving them any chance to fight back.

Their own arsenal, on the other hand, was a clapped out hotchpotch of vintage Russian scrap from the sixties. In short, in addition to everything else they lacked, it was clear to Kamaran that there was no chance whatsoever they could win this war. Fortunately, if he was to believe his comrades, there was not going to be a war, just a thrilling side-show of rousing speeches, cliff-hangers and brinkmanship followed by the surprise twist of a peaceful resolution - the story that emanated from General Headquarters in Baghdad and was passed down the chain of command to the junior officers.

The only person who thought there would be a war - hoped there would be a war - was Sergeant Abbas. While the rest of the company lounged in the shade of a canopy made from camouflage netting and played cards and smoked, Sergeant Abbas dropped Kamaran's platoon miles from their position in the heat of the midday sun and told them to find their own way back. He sent them on patrol on moonless nights so dark they couldn't see the ends of their own noses. He ordered them do bayonet practice as if they were about to fight for freedom from the Turks. He constructed a fiendish obstacle course and made them clamber over sandbags and crawl on their bellies under coils of barbed wire while he fired blanks in the dirt around them, and he watched Kamaran all the while, willing him to make a mistake. When he did, Sergeant Abbas made him do extended drill with a pack full of rocks and he made him do it at the double, or he ordered him to squat for twenty minutes in a contorted pose that became intolerable after five, telling him all the while that he was a lily-livered, yellow-bellied, treasonous gobbet of scum. Regardless of what the rest of his handsome savage's features were doing, his eyes never lost their demented gleam and wherever Kamaran went and whatever he did he could feel those eyes upon him, watching him like a cobra, waiting for the moment to strike.

Chapter 19

There had been a heavy dew overnight but all that remained of it was a briny tang that hung in the air as they trudged along, kicking up puffs of dust. The land to the south of the camp dropped away in a choppy sea of ridges and troughs, littered with boulders. Sadiq had been appointed corporal of Kamaran's squadron and he played his part to the full, bending low as he dashed from one bit of cover to the next. They were carrying their entire kit - rifles, bayonets, ammunition, tools, bottles, mess tins and gas masks - and the five of them rattled like a rag and bone man's cart as they followed him across the rough ground. It was hard going. Kamaran's steel helmet cooked in the sun. Trickles of sweat ran like beetles down his neck and soaked his woollen shirt. The scratchy fabric, rubbed by the straps of his kit bag, chafed his shoulders with every step and his boots, which were half a size too big for him, scraped at his heels.

Sergeant Abbas had dispatched the whole platoon on a field exercise. Their squad had orders to attack and take possession of the 'watchtower'- an outcrop of rock in the middle of a sweep of sand - which was being defended by the other sections in the platoon.

The sergeant had issued them with blanks for their rifles and he was following the whole exercise through binoculars from the camp. As they plodded down towards the rocks they spotted their opponents sitting together in the shade of the escarpment, where he would not be able to see them. Sadiq flung himself to the ground. The others, worn out, looked on as he crawled behind a drift of feathery plants.

'Why - they're not even hiding!' he protested. 'They might at least have made an effort... they're playing *cards!*'

'Let's sit down for a bit, too, eh?' Jamil suggested. 'War's a young man's game!'

Kamaran shrugged his kitbag from his shoulders and unstuck his sodden shirt from his back. His socks had gathered in wrinkles under his feet. He sat down to undo his laces as his comrades let their bags clatter onto the stones and dropped to the ground around him. It was such a relief to get off his boots that he peeled his socks off too and sat barefoot, wiggling his hot toes in the air and trying to ignore Hassan who had already started his litany of grumbles.

'He did it again this morning,' he announced as he unscrewed the lid of his water bottle. 'Didn't he, Kamaran? Didn't he?' He took a swig of water. 'He did it again, didn't he Kamaran?'

'Who did what?' Kamaran asked.

'Sergeant Fuck-face,' Hassan replied. 'Big fucking camel spider - big as my hand! Threw it into our foxhole and I swear it fucking chased me down the trench!'

'They're ugly creatures, it's true,' said Jamil. 'But they don't bite, remember? It was probably more frightened than you were.'

'He gives me the creeps.'

'He only does it because he knows he'll get a rise, Hassan,' Kamaran said. 'You shouldn't take it personally.'

'But why doesn't he like me?'

'I don't think the poor man likes anyone very much,' Jamil replied. 'But look! These are *harmal* plants!' He broke off a dried seed-pod, shaped like a shepherd's heart, and crushed it between his palms. 'My mother used to hang it in the house against the Eye,' he said, sniffing at the seeds. 'You can burn it like incense. We should collect some because it's good against lice and things... there you are, Hassan! We'll chase all the bugs away!'

They set off again five minutes later, leaving Kamaran to put on his boots. By the time he got up the rest of the squadron were fifty yards away, crossing the flat sand that lay between them and the watchtower. The ground around them glistened like a beach after the tide had gone out. The outcrop looked like an islet in the sea and the five men, silhouetted against the glare and shadowed by their own dark reflections, appeared to be walking on water.

As Kamaran scurried after them the silver glimmer ebbed back and the air seemed to ripple and bend. The only sound was the clink and scrunch of his footsteps on the loose pebbles and the jangling of his pack. He took off his helmet and swept his sweaty hair away from his forehead. A hot breeze licked his neck and face. A few wormwood bushes grew amongst the stones, their leaves still verdigris when everything else had withered, and they released a spicy green smell as he brushed past. The breeze, the aromatic scent and - most of all - the silence, made him feel suddenly elated. He realised it was weeks since he had been alone. He made no effort to catch up with the rest of the squad, enjoying his brief moment of freedom.

A sharp crack snapped and bounced across the rocks. His comrades ducked to the ground in earnest and started zigzagging forward, still tagged by their shadows, as gunfire erupted from the high ground behind them. Kamaran turned. A shaggy silhouette, flickering and warping in the heat, seemed to glide along the crest of the ridge. The others were still bolting across the sand like a drove of hares. A third salvo exploded in the hot air and was answered by a burst of gunfire from the outcrop of rock. Puffs of dust sprung up from the stones ten yards away, at the foot of the bank where Kamaran stood. The second and third units were making up for their former apathy by firing rounds of blanks willy-nilly across the sand, answering the fire that came from the rocky ground behind him.

Everything seemed to slow down as a bullish figure emerged from the glittering haze above the ridge. Slowly and purposefully, Sergeant Abbas raised his rifle and took aim. Another volley burst from the outcrop and, once again, Kamaran was caught in the crossfire. He heard whistles and pings as bullets ricocheted amongst the rocks, sending pebbles careening into the air. As he ducked something hit his forehead. Reeling, he slipped on the scree, his bag jerked at his shoulders, and he tumbled five feet onto the rocks below. For a moment he thought he had been shot. Blood was streaming from his forehead and he was completely winded. He could barely move his head as the sergeant came pelting down the slope towards him, his boots crunching and grinding on the stones. Kamaran tried to move back, flailing in the dust as he closed upon him. A towering shadow against the blazing sky, Sergeant Abbas threw his gun to the ground and fell on his knees at Kamaran's side.

'Adil!' he cried, gripping Kamaran's shoulders in his brawny hands. 'Adil!'
Kamaran shook his head, gasping for air. Lost in some other time and place, the sergeant took Kamaran's face in his hands and gave a low moan which made goose-pimples shiver down his neck.

'Adil!' he sobbed. 'Adouli! My friend, my brother! Stay with us - don't die! Adouli, Adil!'

Kamaran looked on, transfixed, as tears trickled down the sergeant's cheeks, leaving dark tracks on his dusty skin. A tall figure shimmered over the rocks above them and Lieutenant Ismael jumped down, sending a cascade of pebbles tinkling down the bank.

'Sergeant Abbas.' He put his hand on the sergeant's shoulder and gave it a shake. 'Sergeant Abbas!'

The sergeant looked up at him. Like a cloud passing over the sun, the expression of his face darkened and he jumped to his feet and saluted.

'Go back to the base,' said the lieutenant quietly.

The sergeant stared down at Kamaran and his eyes narrowed. Then he turned and stumbled away. Kamaran sat up and he and the lieutenant watched him as he trudged back towards the camp, shaking his head like a bull tormented by flies.

'Sergeant Abbas fought at the battle of Fish Lake in nineteen eighty-seven,' Lieutenant Ismael said after a moment. 'Out of an entire company of a hundred men, only the sergeant and the major survived.'

Sergeant Abbas stopped bullying Kamaran after that but he wanted him out of his sight. He gave him extra sentry duty and for the next month, in addition to his normal chores, Kamaran did four hours watch for every eight hours he had off. Intended as a punishment for having lagged behind his squadron in the field exercise, the solitude it gave him came as a relief.

The patrol section stretched around a stand of thorny trees - a scrap of land he came to know more intimately than any other and which, featureless and barren at first sight, he soon discovered to be rich and variable. Hour by hour the landscape changed hue - a dull cumin under a leaden sky, bright as turmeric when a storm threatened, cinnamon pink at dusk. In the evening flaming clouds trailed from the horizon and glowed like embers that turned to ash as darkness fell. Sharp reports echoed amongst the rocks as stones shattered in the cooling air and the stars blazed at eye-level all around, the dark earth curving beneath them like a pregnant belly.

Here, away from the hubbub of the camp and the chatter of his comrades, Kamaran tried to make sense of what had befallen him. The rift in his life was so brutal that his own past seemed like a distant dream. The army was an endless round of boredom and privation beyond which he could dimly remember the transit camp in Basrah and his labours on the building site in Amman. The months he had spent in Helsinki belonged to some other world, his friendship with Erin too, as if some other Kamaran might still be there, haunting the snowy streets. The only vivid recollections he could muster, polished from use, were the blissful moments of love he had shared with Leyla.

He longed to write to her but, fearful of compromising her in any way, he dared not even scribble the unsent letters that had given him solace in Helsinki. Instead he tried to conjure her in his thoughts, willing her to think of him and to know that he was near, and he gazed at the picture she had sent him, gazed at their daughter, filled with yearning and joy. Confounded by love and faced, for the first time, with the prospect of his own death, Kamaran found himself contemplating the world with the clear sight of a child, to whom a glimpse of the humblest creature or flower is a magical encounter.

In the still depths of the night it seemed to him that he could feel the earth spinning, and he understood, as never before, the lonely splendour of our strange planet. For even in that wilderness there was life, tenacious and abundant. Animals the colour of stone crept about, their tracks blurred by the fur that protected their paws from the hot sand. A family of hedgehogs emerged at the same time each evening, followed by a pretty little sand fox who appeared, as if from nowhere, and trotted gracefully across the stones. At dusk a nightjar swept above the sparse trees with a soft *kroo-kroo* which rose and fell as it turned its heard from side to side, and at dawn a solitary bird hovered far above the camp and tumbled out of the sky with a haunting warble which sounded like a flute. Drifts of rock-rose and prickly bushes clung to the shale. Long, hairy roots crawled through the dirt like centipedes, and the *Kaff Mariam* plant

201

clenched twiggy fingers round its ball of seeds, waiting for the rains that would coax them open to offer up new life like a prayer.

In November the rains came, washing the dusty foliage clean and gathering like a mirage on the silty ground. Majestic thunder-storms blew in from the Empty Quarter, rumbling and crackling overhead as veins of lightning groped through the clouds. Within days grass hazed the pebbles with green. Great flocks of sand grouse set upon the pools of rain and rose like steam as the sun came up, to spread in smoky trails across the pastel sky. Feathery shrubs burst into bloom and the air smelled sweet as a mosque sprinkled with rosewater. The saltbushes turned ochre, red, and brown, like heaps of spice strewn over the desert, and tiny flowers decked their gnarled fingers as if the rain had persuaded an ancient queen to wear her rings once more. Then the temperature dropped suddenly and they woke to find a hoar frost had fallen, tracing white ferns on their mess tins and coating the thorns with new prickles of ice.

By now three hundred thousand foot soldiers were entrenched along a front line that stretched inland from the Gulf. Across the border in Saudi Arabia, the whisper went, their enemies had mustered a vast army. The ruckus of men and machines had churned up the fragile surface of the desert and unnatural dust storms raged across the barren land, turning the skies black at midday. Cooped up in their dugouts, cold, hungry, bored, resentful, the men began to mutter they were caught between the hammer and the anvil in a conflict that could only be lost. Their numbers dwindled as soldiers failed to come back from leave, and whole units deserted in the dead of the night.

In the first week of December Lieutenant Ismael summoned the platoon together after the morning roll call. He had two bits of news. The first was that Private Hassan had one week's compassionate leave to visit his sick mother in Baghdad.

'The other news, comrades,' he said with a frown, 'is that all further leave is cancelled from today. Last week the United Nations Security Council passed a new resolution. They have demanded we surrender our claim to the nineteenth province of Iraq - that is Kuwait. There is a deadline - January the fifteenth - for us to do so. If we have not withdrawn our forces by that date then, I regret to tell you, there will most certainly be war.'

Chapter 20

'Dearest Kashkash,' he wrote. 'I hope that
you, our lovely daughter and dear Jiddu are in
good health and this letter finds you well. I've
struggled in my heart to know if I should
send it, for reasons you'll come to
understand. I left Helsinki as soon as I got
your message and with only one desire - to
come home to you. We had no inkling, then,
of what was about to happen and I couldn't
bear to be parted from you any longer. But
happen it did and here I am, in the army -
though not in Kuwait. We're somewhere in
the southern desert. That's as much as I can
say. This letter comes with Hassan, a soldier
in my squadron. He's not the messenger I'd
have chosen but he has every incentive to
deliver it because I'm paying him. Please send
some token back with him so I can be sure
you have received it.

It's strange to be writing to you, knowing
that you'll see these words. I've written you
so many letters I had no hope of sending. In
Finland's white summer nights and the dark
days of winter, I was always thinking of you.

At work, at 'home', in the streets, in parks, on buses, I was always writing to you. Drunk on memories of you at night, waking to find I was alone - and yet I prayed for dreams of you. If I glimpsed in some passing stranger an expression or gesture that reminded me of you I found myself staring at them, following them, hungry even for this poor shadow of remembrance. Amidst the squalid jobs, the prying of officials, the petty humiliations, the loneliness of being 'an immigrant', it was my love for you that kept my soul alive.

All our sorrows, my darling, have been of my making. I understand now why you urged me to go. You knew if I guessed the truth I'd never have left you and you didn't want our child to lose her father as you and I, in different ways, lost ours. I'm impelled to write now, not with the wretched prayer you'll forgive me once again but so you'll know that - for all my foolishness and despite this third disappearance from your life - I never have and never will stop loving you.

At times in Helsinki I couldn't resist the temptation to re-write our past - saying the things I should have said, imagining how things might have been. If only we'd known the war was about to end. If only I had had the strength to remain your friend - your brother - without desire or jealousy, loving you as you deserve to be loved. If only we had met again sooner. If only we had never been parted. If only your mother and father had been saved. Everything springs from that first betrayal and my own childish weakness and lies, for which there never can be remedy. And so I found myself, time and again, harking back to those early days when we were innocent.

Do you remember, Kashkash, when Aunt Rabia took us to Khadimain? That first sight of the mosque - its golden domes high above us, the minarets braced to part the city on either side like the gateway to another realm? I remember you said it looked like a fairy palace floating on a cloud. And as if that apparition of beauty were not enough, our discovery that every surface was ornamented with tiles, showering the courtyard in petals of blue and gold? The splash of water as people washed themselves for prayer, the adhān winding into the dusk like a rope to heaven, the tickly feel of the carpets beneath our bare feet, the smell of dust and rosewater as we bent to pray.... We were so inspired we made vows of piety to each other which lasted at least five days! And afterwards all the families picnicked in the courtyard and shared dainties with their neighbours. We gobbled up the feast which Rabia had cooked while the piping calls of the other children twittered round us like a choir of little birds, and then you and I chased a flock of doves that scattered into the sky as the lamps strung between the minarets became a spangle of yellow stars.

Do you remember the screens of camel thorn your father used to put in the windows in summer, and how we would splash them with water so their fresh, clean smell scented the house? Do you remember the merchants who strolled the city in autumn crying *'tuk al sham!'* How we would pester Jiddu for money and run after them in the street? The blissful taste of those sugared mulberries eaten with a thorn and served on a leaf?

Do you remember how we could never wait for the persimmon fruit to ripen? We'd always pick some early and protest they were delicious, even though the sourness dried our mouths and made us spit? And then, after the first frost, the leaves would drop and the fruit would go red and black, and I'd climb into the branches and throw them down to you so we could gorge ourselves on that spicy apricot mush, which seemed to us the food of kings!

Do you remember making *kleicha* biscuits at Ramadan? You and I cut out the pastry with a tea glass and carved patterns on the top with the point of a knife? And we'd nibble scraps of dough till our faces were covered with sugar and flour and we felt quite sick? And after they'd been cooked at the bakery Rabia would stash them away with our presents, somewhere out of reach, and we'd spend hours hunting for them, beside ourselves with excitement, unable to wait?

Do you remember how we'd go from house to house with Yusuf and the other children, knocking on the doors for treats? *'Majeena, ya majeena* throw us a coin!' And Poor Jasim the Cobbler would always shower us with water from the roof and we'd dance around, delighted, shouting up at the stars: *'Ya* how he's soaked us! The pinch-fist has soaked us!' These little things are the things I thought of - trying to piece my memories together, fragment by fragment, sense by sense, so vivid and free and full of joy.

Or I pictured the moment I saw you for the first time in eighteen years. You were standing on the gallery, framed by a beam of sunlight, your hair springing back from your head as if you were at the prow of a ship. I couldn't see your face but, as I came towards you, you tilted your head to one side like a bird - and that gesture, so familiar, so beloved, made my foolish eyes brim with tears.

Now I see you, your chin on your hands, your beautiful eyes filled with shame as you hint at your husband's subtle cruelty and lies. It's hot and humid, the air like a sponge in our mouths and heavy with the smell of jasmine. Your curls stick in damp tendrils to your neck, white flowers cascade behind you and some have fallen, like stars, in your black hair. You bite your lip and smile at me, trying not to cry. We're both dismayed at what has just been said. I reach out and catch a tear from each eye on my finger. 'My Tigris, My Euphrates,' I say. You laugh at me and look away but we both know what will happen if our eyes should meet. I sit there, scarcely able to breathe, willing you to look: look at me, look at me, look at me... but you won't.

I don't have the words to tell you how you make me feel. I long to hear your voice. I long to make you laugh again. I long to see you, to breathe you in, to touch your skin. When I think of you, *truly think* of you, my whole body sings. You once told me you felt like a corpse in your husband's embraces. Now I understand what you meant. Time has stopped for me. I'm like a wraith - eating, walking, talking in the present, a body forsaken, my soul always with you. Baghdad always. Happy always. Always you.

My thoughts are racing. My mind jumps from one thing to another, too fast for me to catch them, too fast to write them down. But time is short. Please tell Jiddu I regret the pain - the shame - that I've caused him. I know, too well, what a poor return it is for the kindness he has always shown to me. I don't ask for his forgiveness because he knows how much I love you and his heart is too big to condemn anything that springs from love.

And to our beautiful baby girl, what can I say? I see from her photo that she's her mother's daughter. But though she looks just as clever and wise as I'd expect, I doubt if she can read as yet. So tell her for me, in whatever way you can, that she has a father who loves her, who longs to see her, who wants with all his heart to protect her. I hope she'll live in happier times than ours and that our country, with all its riches and the kindness of its people, will provide her and all our children with the peace and good fortune they deserve.

Leyla, I will do everything I can - everything I must - to return to you. I am *determined* to survive this war. But the possibility remains that I may not.

It's a strange feeling to envisage that our modest hopes, the simplest of our dreams, the unassuming life we longed for, may be cut short and never realised. That's why I've hesitated to write. I thought, if I should die, it might be better for you to have remained in ignorance of my return - to know nothing of me, to dismiss me instead as faithless, feckless, a coward. But every soldier fears an unmarked grave and I couldn't conquer my own longing to reach out to you.

The thought that I may die fills me with sorrow, of course. But that sorrow is just a measure of my joy - the happiness I know will be ours when I return, the censure and hardship you'll endure if I do not, the sadness of our little daughter growing up without the shelter of a father's love. But what I need you to know is this - I no longer have any regrets. From the moment I saw that photograph I could not have wished anything else for my life than to have given you the child you longed for. I feel myself blessed to have known such beauty and such love - and these are the only things that matter in the end. If I die, I'll die thinking of you. If there's any world after this, any way in which a spirit can return, know that I'll be watching over you and our beautiful

211

daughter, fulfilling in death, if not in life, the promise I made to your beloved mother all those years ago. Only one thing has tormented me - the fear that you might doubt my love, or that you would never know the things I tell you here. If *I* am sure of that - that *you* are sure of me - I can face anything.

Leyla - my sister, my comrade, my lover, my friend. Leyla - your name alone is a caress. It is the heartbeat that courses through my life. Leyla, Leyla - my sickness and my cure.'

Chapter 21

The days dragged by, the week elapsed and Hassan did not return. Two weeks passed, then three, and then - on the twelfth of January - they were given the order to move.

It was a chilly overcast morning and a fine drizzle, little more than a fog, swathed the landscape in spectral shades of grey. Phantom figures swarmed about in the gloom and paled to a smudge on the horizon. The clammy air was thick with fumes, disembodied shouts, the cough and splutter of cold engines and the whine of wheels spinning in slicks of mud. Despite the dismal weather, despite the fact they were hungry and damp, the men walked with a sprightly step and merry shouts and banter rang out in the misty air. As the days passed and the deadline ticked ever nearer, conflicting rumours had swirled through the ranks, swaying them this way and that like grass in the wind. They had all heard about a peace conference in Geneva three days before and, from the moment they had been ordered to pack up that morning, the story doing the rounds was that they were going home.

They worked in chains to load the trucks, like sailors loading a ship. Buckles, spoons, mess tins, pots and pans, clinked and jangled as they handed the bags down the line and from a distance it sounded as if a flock of sheep had wandered into the trenches. Some soldiers milled about by the trucks when they had finished, chewing crusts of bread and stamping their feet to keep warm. Others gathered round a half-hearted fire where they were burning scraps of rubbish. Jamil and Sadiq squatted to one side, brewing up tea in the embers. Someone had thrown plastic onto the flames and acrid smoke hung in the air, making Kamaran's eyes smart as he walked over to join them.

The tea was weak and scabbed with flakes of ash but it was hot. Kamaran clasped his hands round the tin cup, trying to warm his chilled fingers. Through a veil of white smoke he could see the major and his staff studying a map spread out on the bonnet of a jeep. Kamaran had been trying to catch a glimpse of Lieutenant Ismael all morning, hoping his expression might give some clue to their fate. He and the other officers watched intently as Sergeant Abbas jabbed his finger at the map. The smoke cleared but all Kamaran could read from the lieutenant's face was that he seemed as solemn as ever. The major looked on distractedly while the men loaded the last of the baggage onto the trucks. His features, too, bore their habitual look - the stern demeanour of a man determined to overcome all obstacles or die in the attempt. His head squatted on his shoulders without the convenience of a neck and

214

- as Kamaran watched - he marched off down the column of lorries, his whole body swiveling as he looked about him like a shark deciding which way to attack.

'So is it true, do you think?' Jamil asked. He shook his cup over the fire and drops of tea hissed in the ashes.

'We'll know soon enough,' Kamaran replied.

'Do you think so?' he murmured. 'They never tell us anything'

'They might not have to tell us. There's only one road. If we head north there's a chance it's all over. If we head south, they're sending us to the front.'

It took less than two hours to break camp. By the time they had finished it was raining hard. Pleased with their handiwork and happy to be on the move, they bumped off across the stony ground to a chorus of cheers and whistles. The entire platoon had to squeeze into one lorry. Kamaran got in last and tried to brace himself against the tailgate as they lurched over the rough ground. Within a minute the plume of smoke from the smouldering fire was all he could see of the trenches behind them.

The carefree mood of the morning ebbed away as they slithered and bounced along the dirt track. They had to stop to dig a baggage lorry out of the mud and everyone grumbled as they heaved and pushed, getting spattered with grit. Half a mile later they came to a halt again and the driver turned off the engine. Above the patter of the rain they could hear a constant, gravelly drone like the churning of a cement mixer. They had been brought to a standstill by a long convoy of trucks, joining the trail ahead of them from a position to the east. Eventually they nosed their way into the crush and jolted onward towards the road. Near the highway the convoy came to a stop yet again. As the growl of engines died away Kamaran heard another sound - an unmistakable rumble. He pulled himself to his feet and craned his neck to see over the heads of his comrades.

Immediately in front of them a jeep had got stuck in a patch of boggy sand. An irate, red-faced officer was shouting in turns at the driver and the hapless men who were trying to shovel dirt from under its wheels. The mud beyond was scored with tyre marks, already filling with rain, as a snaking cavalcade of lorries tried to edge onto the highway. Through the cloudy air, thick with mist and the smoke of burning diesel, Kamaran could see the road was already clogged with vehicles. Baggage trucks, ambulances and lorries crawled forward, bumper to bumper with beetling troop carriers and an array of combat vehicles and artillery which trundled along, their tracks clattering on the tarmac. A howitzer had broken down in the middle of the road, adding to the jam. Vehicles from their own infantry brigade had got mixed up with units of the

52nd Armoured Division and, as Kamaran watched, a column of tanks loomed like ghost ships out of the murk and split in two, taking over both lanes of the road. Drizzle and smoke reduced everything to grainy shades of grey, giving the whole spectacle the eerie look of an old newsreel. The grisly procession stretched as far as the eye could see in both directions before vanishing into the mist - and it was heading south.

In a welter of fumes and noise, their uniforms turning dark with the rain that dripped in swollen beads from their helmets, they crept forward until they too were sucked into the convoy and found themselves rolling forward at a steady speed. From ahead and behind they could hear nothing but the roar of engines, the hiss of tyres on the wet road and the relentless rattling tread of the tanks. The desert dropped away as they headed south and at each descent they glimpsed the column of armour rolling before them, as inexorable as the cogs on a wheel. A few straggling vehicles had beached on the sandy verge. Their crews bent under open bonnets, tools in hand like mechanical dentists, or lay in the dirt, dwarfed by the their machines, as they tried to repair the links of a broken track.

About fifty miles south of As Salman the armoured units rumbled off the highway, heading southeast. A short while later, they bumped off the road themselves and cut out across the open desert. Soldiers from another brigade were already hard at work throwing up entrenchments in the stony ground. Clouds of ochre dust puffed into the damp air and everywhere they could hear the chink of metal hitting rock, as if they had stumbled into a giant quarry. Two signalmen ran alongside them for a few yards, unrolling a spool of wire like boys bowling a hoop. An entire company stood in formation, amidst a jumble of boxes that had been left to get wet in the rain, while a morose warrant officer paced up and down before them waiting for someone or something to arrive. Elsewhere soldiers were already queuing to get their rations from the quartermasters' vans, heaving baggage from the lorries and lugging sandbags across the stones. Beyond them the desert stretched to the horizon - a featureless carapace of stone and sand, laid out beneath a lowering sky. A few rocks punctured the yellow plain like bones, as if mother earth had starved to death, and the men that crawled about its surface looked no bigger than flies.

By the time they came to a halt dusk was falling. To the east and to the north, spangles of yellow pricked the gloom as soldiers lit their stoves to cook the evening meal or shone torches across the darkening ground. Starred by the rain, the glistening chains of light stretched for miles as if an entire city had decamped to the desert for the night. Chilled, hungry, tired, their limbs aching after the bone-rattling journey, they climbed out of the lorry and looked about them in dismay.

The position had been occupied before, though drifts of sand now choked the trenches. Their officers had told them the base was a three day walk from Saudi Arabia. They had been travelling due south all day, however, and Kamaran calculated the border couldn't be much more than ten miles away. They were, in fact, on the front line. But in place of the defenses the words 'front line' suggest, they found themselves looking at a puny maze of trenches no better fortified than the holes they had scraped in the rock three months before. Narrow and completely straight, they offered no protection from the flanks, and the heaps of spoil on either side meant they would be visible from the air. A swathe of barbed wire, some ditches filled with oil and a shallow belt of unconcealed mines were all that stood between them and their foes.

Chapter 22

'Get up! Get up! Get up and get out!'

Kamaran was dreaming - a restless, panicky dream. It took a moment for the shouts to penetrate his sleep. He opened his eyes. Dressed only in a T-shirt and shorts, his skin prickled with goose-pimples as he sat up, pulling his blanket to his chest. His back ached and his hands felt raw. They had spent the last four days digging - digging in guns, digging out foxholes, digging away the tell-tale banks of mud along the trenches. The previous afternoon they had all got drenched in a downpour. An icy wind had chased the clouds away and they had draped their sodden uniforms on a line strung between two piles of sandbags, in the hope they would dry overnight. They had gone to sleep curled close together but Jamil was gone and Kamaran felt chilled to the bone.

He scrambled up and cursed as his feet touched the freezing ground. Tugging on his unlaced boots he shuffled to the doorway. The trench was still in shadow. Jamil was standing on the fire-step opposite the dugout. His black and white blanket draped over his shoulders, he looked like a Navajo chief as he looked out over the wilderness, his head framed against a red dawn sky.

'What's happening?' Kamaran asked.

'I don't know.' Jamil turned to look at him and blew into his cupped palms, his breath white in the frosty air. 'Do you think it's started?' he asked timidly. 'I heard the officers' call a while ago. Sadiq and the other corporals have gone over to HQ. And that's Sergeant Abbas shouting. What d'you think? Perhaps it's started… but you'd better get dressed *habibi!*' he added, glancing along the trench. 'Here comes the sergeant now. I'll get your things.'

He clambered out of the trench and hurried over to the line. The drying clothes had a sinister look, like a disemboweled scarecrow or something hanging from a gibbet. Outlined like a shadow puppet against the bloodshot sky, he unhooked them one by one.

'Look out!' he called as he threw Kamaran's socks, trousers, and jacket into the trench. 'They're frozen solid!'

The clothes were heavy, stiff as a biscuit and covered in sand. The fabric scrunched in rigid pleats as Kamaran tried to soften them up. He worked his feet carefully into his trousers, keeping the legs straight to avoid touching the icy cloth, but they crinkled like sandpaper behind his knees as he crouched down to do up his boots.

'Get up! Get up! Get up and get out!'

Kamaran hurried to join Jamil outside as a beam of light flickered along the trench. Ali and Private Onion, half-naked, shivering and bleary-eyed, were already standing outside their dug-out. They stood to attention as Sergeant Abbas stopped before them, followed by a corporal from the number two squadron who was clutching a mound of clothes in his arms.

Shoving the two soldiers out of the way, the sergeant ducked behind them. A monstrous shadow loomed over the trench as he shone his torch around their bunker. They heard a rattle and two kitbags flew out of the doorway and landed with a crash in the dirt. He stepped out and handed the flash-light to the corporal. Then he opened each of the bags in turn and held them upside down, shaking out the contents with brisk, efficient snaps as if this was something he did every day. A copy of the Qu'ran, cigarettes, letters, a magazine, a razor and a heap of crumpled clothes lay in the mud. He picked through the first pile, pulled out a red jumper and a pair of jeans and threw them at the corporal, who stared at the ground throughout, dodging the glances of his bewildered comrades. The next heap was searched in the same way and a pair of black trousers, a Manchester united T-shirt and a denim jacket were added to the corporal's pile. When he was sure that he had taken every garment other than their uniforms, the sergeant grabbed his torch, shone it into the bunker and checked it one last time. Satisfied, he turned away. The yellow light flicked along the uneven floor of the trench. Then he stopped in front of Kamaran and shone the beam directly into his face.

'Good morning, *soldier!* Baring his teeth in a ferocious smile, sergeant Abbas leant into the circle

222

of light. 'Leyla, Leyla!' he whispered. 'My sickness and my cure.'

Delicate pink clouds streaked the sky which had lightened to a chilly, eggshell blue. The frosty desert, shimmering rose and white, looked eerily beautiful, like the setting of some winter fairy tale. A splash of lamplight spilled from the major's bunker and the clatter of the generator rang out in the crisp air as they traipsed towards the company headquarters.

A trail of objects peppered the ground between the trenches and the muster point - penknives, worry beads, watches and photographs that had fallen from the pockets of their confiscated clothes. The men collected them as they walked, stooping to gather them up like so many birds pecking for worms in the frozen ground. Kamaran's heart was pounding and he could feel his jaws clamp tight as he pondered the sergeant's words. Nothing he had written could identify or endanger Leyla - he had made sure of that. But, however the sergeant had come by his letter, one thing was certain. Leyla had not received it - and that knowledge filled him with despair.

Lieutenant Ismael strode over to them as they filed into position. He looked more than usually sombre and there was something brusque about his movements as he turned to stand with his back to his men. They watched in silence as corporals from the various sections added bundles to a growing pile of clothes. The tangle of fabric - red, yellow, turquoise, green - looked gaudy against the frost and it struck Kamaran that he had not seen so many colours since he left the transit camp at Basrah. The major had come out of his bunker. At his signal Sergeant Abbas picked up a jerry-can. The heady smell of gasoline drifted on the crisp air as he sloshed petrol onto the heap of cloth. The major lit a twist of paper and dropped it into the clothes. For a moment blue flames danced above the mound, then the fabric caught light and black smoke coiled into the air.

As they stood watching the blazing pyre a transit van bumped along the track towards them, leaving dark tyre marks in the frost. Two military policemen jumped out and marched over to the major, their footsteps crunching on the hard ground. Lieutenant Ismael turned round and took a step towards Sadiq, who stood in the first row of the platoon.

'You'll have heard,' he said, 'I am sure, that two men from the second platoon deserted last week. They were picked up in the desert two days ago. And,' he glanced at Kamaran and Jamil, 'Private Hassan is with them. His papers were for transit to Baghdad. They captured him near Suq Ash Shuyukh, trying to get into the marshes. He has been in the military prison at Al Samawah for the last four weeks.'

'What's going to happen to them?' asked Jamil.
The lieutenant frowned and shook his head.

'Their shame is great,' he murmured as he walked away.

A bitter wind blew across the plain. Flames danced about the bonfire of clothes and flakes of black ash flittered across the white ground as the men were bundled from the van. Their hands were tied in front of them, the laces had been taken from their shoes, and their feet were bare and red with cold. A lance corporal from the second platoon, thin, bearded and dirty as a tramp, was led out first. His friend shuffled after him, a grubby bandage wound round his head. Then came Hassan. He walked with a nonchalant swagger, like a cocky schoolboy being marched off to the headmaster, as if determined to play his part to the last. One of his shoes slipped off and he hopped about with a clownish smile. Squatting down in front of him, the guard wiggled it back onto his foot and led him to where the other two prisoners stood, in front of a dense coil of barbed wire. One of the military policemen - an officer with a pale, weary face - read out the sentence, his breath puffing out in the chilly air. Then he walked over to the condemned men and offered them all a cigarette. They sucked on them eagerly, lifting their cupped hands to their lips as if in prayer. Hassan even blew a smoke ring, still looking about him with his clownish, insolent smile, as the officer recited a prayer for the dying. It was only when they tied the other prisoners to the wire that he seemed to grasp what was happening.

'No! No!' he shouted suddenly, as the officer stepped in front of him. 'Don't touch me! Let go of me! Let *go*!' He tossed his head like a frightened horse as the man tried to secure his blindfold. 'Let go of me! Let go! You're hurting me! What's happening? What are you doing? Let *go*!'

Even as he struggled, the firing squad took up their positions, two men for each prisoner. Hassan's protests rose to a scream, drowning out the final benediction, as one man knelt to shoot at his heart and the other, standing, aimed at his head. A salvo of bullets rattled in the cold air and the prisoners disappeared behind a fog of milky smoke. When it cleared they were slumped over like marionettes, held up by the wire. Blood and clots of flesh spattered the frosty ground around them. Kamaran stood in shocked silence at what they had just witnessed. Then he heard a strangled, desolate cry.

'*Youma… Youma!*'

It was Hassan, calling for his mother. With a scowl, the major nodded to Sergeant Abbas. The sergeant strode over to the bodies, drew his pistol, and shot Hassan in the back of the head.

The war started the following day.

Chapter 23

In the early hours of January the sixteenth heavy ground fog rolled into Baghdad, making ghostly silhouettes of trees and buildings and covering the Tigris in a chill white shroud. The muddy odour of the river mingled with petrol fumes in the damp air as a caravan of cars began to leave the city. By dusk nearly a million people had fled. The traffic withered away and the deserted streets rang with the squeal and clatter of metal shutters as merchants closed up their forsaken shops and went home. An eerie silence fell with the darkness, as if the entire city had decided on an early night.

On the rooftops soldiers dozed by their anti-aircraft guns or paced about, clapping their arms round their shoulders to keep warm, their breath misty in the cold night air. There was no black-out. From above, the city looked like a giant circuit board divided by the sinuous Tigris. Baghdad's monuments and mosques were floodlit, spangles of bulbs looping between the minarets. The bridges cast glimmering arcs across the inky river and the glow from the tower blocks chased the stars from the clear sky. In Karada and Sa'adun Street a few juice bars and restaurants stayed open, splashing the pavements with gaudy colours. But the roads were silent and, in the residential quarters, dark. Here and there a solitary light shone from a window - a student studying late or parents tending to a wakeful baby.

At the edge of the old Mahalla, Ibn Hussein had forgotten to turn off the sign that now read 'Pastries as Li   as an Eastern   reeze.' Yusuf had been persuaded to leave his precious ice-cream parlour and had gone with his wife and daughters to Hillah. Ibrahim and his family had decamped to a shelter. The bakery had been shut all day. Even Jawad had closed his store early, looking sadly at the dwindling stock on his once abundant shelves. No-one stirred in the square but, long after midnight, stars of light still sneaked through the shutters of the Old House where Leyla was sitting alone.

She had put Haneen to bed upstairs as usual, Sami had retired at ten and the house was quiet and still. Her footsteps echoed as she made her way across the courtyard. She stooped to pick up a cloth mouse with burnt ears which Haneen had dropped by the fountain, and went into the kitchen to make some hibiscus tea. She had left a saucepan soaking in the sink and she decided to scrub it out while she waited for the kettle to boil. As soon as she turned the taps the pipes began to cough, grumbling at being asked to work when everything else was at rest. Leyla turned them off again lest the noise should wake her daughter.

She poured her tea and went back across the courtyard. When she got to the stairway she put her glass on the fourth step, crouched down and opened a low wooden door. Under the stairs was a pantry, or rather a large cupboard which Rabia had used as a storeroom.

It had seemed like an endless cavern then, and she and Kamaran had often used it as a setting for their adventures. Urns of tomato paste had stood guard along one side of the door, jars of pickles and jam had glinted like jewels on the other. The date press, stored at the back, had filled the cave with the fertile, musty smell of ripe fruit. Beyond it the darkness had seemed to recede forever, an underground passage to a thrilling world, home of treasure, bandits and unpredictable djinn.

It was this cupboard they had decided to use as an air-raid shelter, should the need arise. Leyla had cleared it out earlier that day and stacked blankets, cushions, a basket of food and Haneen's favourite doll along one wall. She added the cloth mouse to the pile. Then, leaving the door open, she picked up her tea and climbed the stairs.

Light blazed through the stained-glass windows of the drawing room and rays of colour rippled across her face as she walked along the gallery. The chandelier tinkled in the draft when she opened the door and silvery discs shimmied across the walls. The room felt cold and smelled faintly of dust and acetate. Old photographs and darkroom contacts lay strewn across the rosewood table - the contents of a battered suitcase she had found in the cupboard under the stairs, along with a stack of ancient seventy-eight records and a wind-up gramophone. She picked up a sheaf of pictures and sat down at her grandfather's desk.

Most of them were portraits Yona had taken in the days he and Sami had run a studio - publicity shots of famous singers with the staid, melting good looks of a more innocent age. She flicked through them, pulling out the street scenes of old Baghdad and putting them in a different pile: a horse-drawn omnibus on Rashid Street, a public scribe wearing a fez, a man rowing a round quffa boat, crammed with passengers like a brood of chicks in a nest. Stuck face down to this last picture was a small photo with a frilled edge. Leyla peeled it off carefully and turned it over.

It was a snapshot taken on a picnic at Babylon by the famous statue of the lion. For a split second Leyla felt as if she had tumbled back in time and she and Kamaran were capering around the statue again, as Sami directed them in a series of dramatic tableaux. The smell of the sun-warmed stone, the drowsy humming of the bees, the grass tickling her bare legs - she could feel them all. But even as she tried to grasp them her memories scattered like dry leaves in the wind. She tilted the desk lamp and bent over to study the picture more closely. Little Leyla, her face in a theatrical scream, was about to be devoured by

230

the lion. Kamaran, wielding a stick, was coming to the rescue. As she looked at his heroic pose and her own merry face, Leyla felt a surge of such bitterness she almost tore the photograph in two. She sat for a moment, battling with her anger and the unwonted self-pity which filled her eyes with tears.

Standing up, she crossed the room to light the heater. It filled the air with a steady hum, as if there was a wasps' nest in the eaves, and made her aware, suddenly, of the silence outside. She gathered a second pile of pictures from the table. They smelled musty and she sneezed as she sat down, conscious of the creaking of the chair. Her hand scuffed the desk with a hollow knock and the pictures rustled as she turned them over. She could hear the tinkle of her earrings as she moved her head, her own breath. Every noise seemed preternaturally loud and gave her the unnerving feeling that she was being watched. Getting up again, she went to the record player and put on some music to mask the silence and keep her company in her task. Then she went to the sofa and lay down for a moment, feeling suddenly tired. By the time the first song was over she was fast asleep.

She was woken by the crackle of the stylus. That unnerving feeling, the sense that she was in the eye of some malign presence, was now so strong it drew her to the window. Nothing moved outside except for a thin cat. It disappeared, briefly, into the shade of the tree and slunk back into the lamplight, intent on some mission on the other side of the square. Then it stopped suddenly, looked up, and raised its paws to bat the air. Leyla watched, bewildered, as flecks of silver flitted through the lamplight like the sparkly snowflakes of a winter pantomime. This, she later discovered, was anti-radar chaff. She had no time to ask what it might be because at that instant red and yellow tracer fire sprayed from the rooftops. An ear-splitting clatter erupted above her, echoing and booming in the alleys. She leapt away from the window, caught her foot on the leg of a chair and landed with a thump on the floor. She could already hear her daughter calling for her. Haneen, barefoot in her little jellabiya, her mop of curls awry about her sleepy face, trotted into the room as Leyla scrambled to her feet. She stopped in the doorway and held out her arms for the safety of her mother's embrace.

Leyla reached her as the first bombs hit. A long, rumbling explosion made the whole house judder and was followed by a musical tinkle as glass petals tumbled from the window and broke on the floor like brittle tears. It was all Leyla could do to stop herself grabbing Haneen and diving with her under the table. Instead she scooped her up, holding her close to her chest, and ran along the gallery. The door to Sami's room was shut. She flung it open and called to her grandfather as another blast rumbled through the house, making the floor of the balcony

232

quake. Leyla shifted Haneen to her hip and steadied herself with her free hand as she scurried down the stairs. She turned on the light in the cupboard, sat Haneen inside and told her to wait there. The little girl began to cry. As Leyla reached the bottom of the stairway she turned to see her daughter toddling after her. Kissing her cheek she put her back in the cupboard and shut the door. She heard her screams as she ran back up the stairs. Sami had hobbled out onto the gallery without his stick. Leyla took his arm and together they limped down the steps. He bent awkwardly to get through the low door. Leyla ducked inside as another blast crackled above them and a rush of air slammed the door shut behind her.

After that the explosions came thick and fast, each one followed by a tinkle of glass as the windows in the Old House shattered, one by one. Squalls of hot air rushed under the door and the light, a bulb strung from the ceiling, swung and shuddered and cast jittery shadows on their frightened faces. Haneen started to cry again. Leyla hugged her, rocking her to and fro. So they sat, for hours it seemed, until the bombing stopped. In the sudden silence they could hear nothing but the thump of their own hearts and the rasp of their breathing. Then the light went out altogether and Haneen, who was frightened of the dark, began to scream.

'It's alright, little pigeon,' Leyla said, trying to sound calm. 'The bulb has broken, that's all. I'll go and get another one.'

'No youma *no!*' Haneen wailed. 'Don't go 'way!'

Leyla crawled out and felt along the wall for the light. Nothing happened when she flicked the switch. She could just make out the red glow of the sky and she stumbled her way across the courtyard to the kitchen. The light there had gone too. Somewhere, she knew, was a tall white candle, wreathed in ribbons, which she had bought the week before for her daughter's second birthday. She found the stove and groped for the lighter but knocked it to the floor. Cursing, she crouched down and fumbled on the ground. At that moment the anti-aircraft fire started to crackle again. Another explosion shook the house and sent plates crashing into the sink. Leyla ran back across the courtyard as the sky turned white above her.

At every blast the bombing seemed to get louder, closer, like the footsteps of a monster staggering towards the house. As the frenzied attack blundered towards its bloody climax a new noise, more fearsome still, sounded in the lull between the explosions - the steady, menacing drone of aircraft. It sounded as if they were circling right above them, on the roof. Then, amidst the tumult, they heard a savage, piercing shriek.

'Whatever's *that?*' Leyla cried.

Haneen began to whimper as the macabre screams slithered in the darkness above them.

'What is it, Jiddu?' Leyla cried again. 'What *is* it?'

'Calm, Kashkash, calm,' Sami said.

'Why it's the cats!' she groaned after a moment, her own voice rising to a wail. 'It's the cats - it's the poor, poor cats!'

She felt her grandfather's hand on her elbow. He reached down her arm until he had her fingers in his and started to pat her hand.

'Do you remember Ibrahim's rhyme about the pigeons, little Haneen?' he yelled above the din. 'If you can say it with me and youma we shall go to Jawad's store tomorrow and I'll get you some of those nice sweets. A whole bag of that sugared aniseed they call... what *is* it those naughty boys call it?... What's that little pigeon? I didn't hear.'

'Mouse poos!' shouted Haneen.

'No!' Sami exclaimed. 'Those naughty, naughty boys!'

Then, beating time with his fingers against Leyla's hand, he began to chant.

'Coo coo ukhti!
Wein ukhti? Bil Hillah.
Eysh takul? Bajilla.
Eysh tishrab? Mai Allah.
Wein tanam? Bab Allah.'

First Leyla, then Haneen joined in, while the uproar raged in the darkness around them. Between the explosions the little girl's voice piped and trilled, diligently repeating each line as though, if she was very good, she might weave a spell to protect them from the terror above.

Chapter 24

A whisper of daylight, tinged with ash, crept under the cupboard door. Leyla's throat burned, her mouth felt dry as old leather and she could hear nothing except a shrill whine, as if some mosquitoes had taken up residence in her ears. Her left leg had gone completely numb. She had to lift it with her arms in order to reach over and push open the door. She could just make out Sami's sleeping form in the gloom. His head had drooped on his chest and his open mouth was dark in his pale face. Haneen was asleep in his lap, sprawled like a rag doll with her arms flung out behind her. Leyla sat for a moment, wriggling her toes and rubbing her calf as currents of pins and needles tingled up her leg. She crawled out and got to her feet cautiously, as if she was walking for the first time after a long illness.

A cold grey light dropped like drizzle from the square of sky above her and all colour had been washed from the world. The bed of amber earth beneath the persimmon tree had vanished and its filigree branches were traced in white. The friendly green of the swing-seat, Haneen's blue tricycle, the patterned mosaic of the fountain, the old clay tannur - everything was shrouded, like some new Pompei, in a fall of ash.

Leyla's ears were ringing. She couldn't hear her own steps as she walked to the kitchen, leaving a trail of footprints behind her, nor the flick of the switch as she tried the light again, to no avail. The kettle made no sound when she knocked it against the sink and the tap didn't squeak when she turned it. A dribble of water trickled silently into the spout and dwindled to a slow, mute drop. Leyla twisted the tap to full but still there was no water. She poured herself a little juice and swilled it round her dry mouth. There was a painful pop when she swallowed. Wriggling her jaw about to unblock her deafened ears, she retraced her footsteps across the courtyard and climbed upstairs to the roof.

She let the door swing open. Dreary light seeped through a sallow mist onto another field of ash. The air reeked of petrol and burnt plastic, and here, too, there was an uncanny silence. She hesitated for a moment, steeling herself to go and look at the city.

'Leyla, aini, is that you?'

It was Ibrahim. His head popped up above the wall as she walked towards him and she felt her eyes well with tears at the sight of his familiar, friendly face.

'You're alright, thanks be to god!' he said, putting his hand to his heart. 'Your grandfather and daughter too?'

Leyla nodded.

'How was it in the shelter?' she asked.

'Terrible!' he replied with a grim shake of his head. 'More than a thousand souls crammed inside. The

whole building was shaking. Everyone screaming…
crying. We thought we would all be buried alive. And
here?'

'The same,' she said. 'Could you spare me a
cigarette? My nerves are shot to pieces.'

'Of course aini!' He climbed onto the top step,
pulling a pack of Sumer from his pocket. 'A coffee and
a smoke will help you cope, as my dad used to say.'

'I just tried to make some tea but there's no water.'

'No…' He leant towards her, cupping his hands
round the lighter as she lit her cigarette. 'There's no
electricity and no telephone either. My wife is frantic
with worry for her parents. She just tried to call them
but the line is dead.'

As they stood in silence, smoking, Leyla heard a soft,
rolling *booroolacoo* and she realised why the roof had
seemed so quiet. A single white pigeon, its wings
beating with a plaintive whistle, fluttered out of the
smoke towards them. Ibrahim held out his arm. As the
bird alighted on his outstretched hand his kindly face
screwed up and he started to sob.

'Ibrahim!' Leyla exclaimed. 'What is it? What's
happened?'

'Forgive me, aini,' he said after a moment. 'Forgive
me. It must have been the shockwaves - the pressure
of the explosions.' He shook his head. 'It hurts my
eyes to see it!'

Leyla climbed onto the top step and peered over the
wall. Petrified amidst an expanse of dirty, windblown
ash, some on their backs with their feet curled in the

239

air, others with their wings outstretched as if they had fallen mid-flight, all of them dead, lay Ibrahim's flock of pigeons. She watched him hobble back towards the coops, the prodigal bird fluttering its wings as it clung to his hand. Then she turned to look out over the city.

To the south the tall towers of Dorah power station had keeled over, like the columns of an ancient temple. Clouds of tarry smoke barreled from the nearby refinery, fanning out and blurring the whole sky with a pall of soot. Beyond the muddy sea of rooftops a tall building had been sheared in half and spewed cables and wire like the severed limb of a giant robot. But across the river the lines of high-rises on Haifa Street marched, unbroken, into the mist. In place of the sweep of smouldering rubble Leyla had feared to find, she saw a sky-line which, at first sight, seemed largely unchanged. It took her a moment to grasp what was wrong. The sun drifting in the smoke above the horizon, small and cold as a tin coin, was the only point of light. The sparkling threads of street lamps, the starry spangle around the mosques, the gay shop signs, the homely golden glow from the windows of the houses - all had been snuffed out.

'We're finished!' Leyla murmured. 'Finished!'

Baghdad's power stations had been wrecked in the first ten minutes of the war, pitching the whole city into darkness. On the third day the national grid had to be turned off and the flow of clean water died with it. By the fifth, the radar system had been knocked out and they were left blind. After that, jets shrieked and circled about them day and night as if the Mongol warlords had unleashed their grim riders to lay waste to the land once more. Strike by strike, blow by blow, bomb by bomb, the things essential to their survival were destroyed. Like survivors of a tsunami which washes away, in brief seconds, any sense of order or meaning in the world, the people of Iraq gazed, stunned, at the useless debris of their former lives.

Between the daylight attacks an unearthly silence settled over Baghdad, broken only by the keening air raid sirens. Petrol was first rationed and then gone and the grumble of engines and claxons faded away. The jaunty music that blared from the kebab shops, the crackling speakers that heralded the call to prayer, the lively hubbub of five million busy people and the hum and rattle of their machines, all died away. But at night the sky roared like a foundry, showering metal and fire on the streets below. The earth shuddered with the thud and crash of falling masonry. Palm trees burned like matches, dogs whimpered, cats screamed, and the birds on the riverfront started flying upside down and turned drunken somersaults in the air.

On the first afternoon Leyla rummaged in the storeroom for the old Ala'ad Din stove. It lay amongst a tangle of dusty junk, wedged between a tin tub and Kamaran's old bicycle. When she tried to light it she discovered they had no kerosene. She cleaned the tannur instead, carried two old wooden stools downstairs and smashed them with a sledge-hammer to make a fire. By the fourth day the old Kuwaiti chest, the furniture in the drawing room and Sami's library of antique books were the only things left in the house to burn. Leyla went out in the morning and spent three hours hunting for kerosene, arriving back in the Mahalla at midday.

A trickle of fluid gathered in the gutter as she drew near the square. It was viscous and dark red and for an instant she thought it was blood. It turned pink, then green as she turned the corner. Yusuf, back from Hilla, was standing in the doorway of his shop with a broom in his hand, sweeping a sticky puddle into the street

'Melted! Ruined!' he cried when he saw her. 'All of it gone! Quince and almond, rose and pomegranate, pistachio and mint...' he shook his head sadly and Leyla heard his lament start up again as she walked by. 'Melted! Ruined! All of it gone!'

They attacked a bus depot in broad daylight and killed fifty people. They bombed the Nuclear Power Station outside Baghdad. They hit flats and shops by the river again and again as missiles went astray. The police uprooted the eucalyptus trees along the embankment and used them to camouflage the bridges, but the Allies bombed all the bridges anyway and they dangled over the Tigris like broken ribs. The Rasafi Cinema burned to the ground, killing six Egyptian workers who were sleeping inside. Bombs razed an entire street of old houses in Battaween and left an ochre haze swirling in the air, and every time someone was killed - it seemed to Leyla - their songs and jokes died with them so the city hummed with the haunting silence that is left as a note decays.

More people fled the Mahalla each day, a refrigerator strapped to the car roof, a gaggle of aunties and cousins crushed inside. They drove out of the city in a trail of sparks, their axles scraping the road, stopped to barbecue the thawing meat from their freezers, and pushed on to discover the destruction was as bad, or worse, elsewhere.

By the end of the second week everything was scarce. Reckless thieves braved the nightly bombardment to siphon petrol from abandoned vehicles and sold it mixed it with water, so ailing cars hiccupped along the roads in clouds of steam. There was no fuel for deliveries - not even the government rations which had kept the wolf from the door. The markets were empty, the shops boarded up, the banks closed.

Piece by piece, Leyla sold her dowry of gold jewelry to buy things on the black market. She sold the necklaces that Sami had given to his bride and Evin had bequeathed to her. She sold her antique bracelet of filigree silver and turquoise - a birthday present from Kamaran. The only things she would not part with were her mother's pearl earrings and the lucky charm Kamaran had sent from Finland, which she wore like a talisman to call him home.

For an hour each morning she queued at the standpipe for water. Then she left Haneen with Sami or Ibrahim's wife and prowled the streets on Kamaran's bicycle, ignoring salacious whistles and the mutterings of the devout. She peddled three miles to get candles, another for matches and a fifth for toothpaste and soap. She raced across the river chasing rumours of sweet lemons, peddled back again on the whispered promise of oranges from Diyala, and returned empty-handed. The sweetness of fruit paled to a distant memory, the smell of fresh bread, too. Milk, cheese, eggs and meat became legends from a bygone age and the bright colours of the vegetable suq haunted them like the memory of a rainbow in the fog. Pasta, chickpeas, lentils, rice - all the food they ate was brown or white and it had to be cooked with kerosene as precious as oil of attar made from the Caliph's own roses. Sugar was as prized as frankincense, flour as dear as saffron, and each grain of rice might as well have been a pearl plucked from the deep by slaves worth a thousand cowry shells apiece. Leyla bargained like a harpy for every morsel, drop and crumb, beating down the prices in her own private war. Then she rode back, turning away from the frantic women who begged in the streets, hardening her heart to their woebegone faces lest pity drove her to surrender her spoils.

They had abandoned the cupboard under the stairs. The cramped cold nights left Sami's bones stuck together, he said, and - bombs or no bombs - he wasn't going grovel like a rat in a hole. Instead they slept, ate, lived in the drawing room. They draped the Persian carpet over the big table, lined the floor with cushions and told Haneen she had a tent fit for a Bedu princess. In the daytime, if the bombardment was on the other side of the river, Sami cranked up the old gramophone they had found in the storeroom. Playing riotous music to mask the noise of the explosions he taught Haneen to dance the *chobi*, whirling his worry beads round his head and stamping his feet with the jerky movements of a marionette. Or he sang along to his favourite melodies, teaching his great grand-daughter love songs in his warm, croaky voice:

'To you, my black-eyed love, I'll never say adieu.
I'll feast on your cheeks, as white as geymar.
She tosses me bread from behind the tannur,
One crumb from her hands is food for a year!'

'We didn't have electricity when I was a boy, either, little Simsimiyah,' Sami told Haneen one night. 'And it was wonderful! Country folk hung lanterns on their palm trees to light wayfarers to a warm bed and even in the city you could look up and see the twinkling stars. We didn't have any televisions, we had story-tellers so you could make up your own pictures in your head. All our letters were delivered by a man on a horse. There were no noisy, smelly lorries, just boys leading little white donkeys with a dot of henna between their ears and saddle bags as wide as the alley. And at the day's end the little scamps leapt on their backs and raced the poor beasts home so you had to jump against the wall, quick as a grasshopper, as they came galloping by! How my baba used to curse them! But in those days all the houses were like ours, with courtyards and windows to shade the alleyways, and you could walk from the river to the old town wall without being scorched in the sun. There was only one bridge across the Tigris - the bridge of boats - and there was always a crowd on it selling sweetmeats and tea. Al Khark was full of orchards and in the spring the whole town was sweet with the scent of orange blossom...'

'What sort of boats? Haneen asked.

'Oh, the prettiest little boats - each with a different colour sail and a name to match.'

If the dogs started barking, or the muezzin called a warning from the nearby mosque, the three of them crawled under the table. Then Leyla encircled Haneen in her arms and tried to distract her with stories about talking fish and golden clogs, poor thorn sellers and clever little girls, and the adventures of the foolish mullah and his ass. Between the night raids they were left in utter darkness. Haneen,

246

exhausted, slept. Leyla bent over her, nuzzled her silky hair, smelled the tarry smell of her woollen jumper, stroked her soft face with her fingertips, and tried to shelter her from harm with the strength of her love.

By the fourth week rats the size of cats scurried between fattening heaps of rubbish in the alleyways. The stench got tangled with the greasy smoke from the burning refinery, the reek of drains, the rotting meat in the slaughterhouse, and a thousand and one other pestilential smells from the dying city. Desperate looters descended on abandoned houses and bombed shops and stood bartering in the wreckage. Dirty children hawked matches, cigarettes and kerosene, or scampered over the ruins like mountain goats, rubble clinking under their feet as they searched for shrapnel or scavenged for wood.

A mood of anarchy and riot fomented in the lawless streets. Men famed for their piety became embittered atheists overnight whilst the godless recited fervent prayers as bombs thundered around them. Informers who had denounced neighbours, colleagues and friends kept a fearful eye behind them when they ventured from their homes. There were murmured reports of a rebellion in Basrah and the towns of the north. Islamists envisioned the advent, at last, of a religious state, communists, a fair one, capitalists, a prosperous one, pacifists, a peaceful one, idealists, an ideal one. Children dreamed of a life without school, teachers of a country without ignorance, and everyone began to whisper the Amrikiyeen were coming to Baghdad. Party cronies who had requisitioned houses, land and women plotted their escape. Bitter graduates schooled in London and Washington vowed they would never utter an English word again, and merchants with an eye to the main chance wrote signs in anticipation of the invasion: 'Coca cola and Kentucky Kitchen here.'

In the middle of February a sandstorm swirled through Baghdad, followed by a downpour which left sooty teardrops on the buildings and a charred smell in the air. No matter where the wind blew it carried a sour, sulphurous odour which lingered in their hair and clothes. Leyla felt as if her skin was caked in an unwholesome, chemical sludge that lodged everywhere, even under her broken nails. They were all grubby and gaunt, their hair was dull with dust, and Haneen began to wheeze and cough.

Leyla tried to find her medicine but the pharmacies were either shut or empty. She stuffed sacks and old clothes into the broken windows to try and keep out the chilly, dust laden air. She made her daughter sit with her head over a bowl of steaming water to try and clear the filth from her lungs, and she listened anxiously to the gurgling breaths and sharp, barking coughs that kept the little girl from sleeping and tried to gauge whether they were getting worse. Then the sky cleared for two days of peerless spring weather and she seemed much better.

On the second afternoon Leyla left her with Ibrahim's family and set off in search of kerosene. She arrived back in the Mahalla at five and called in at Ibrahim's house. The children were playing a complicated game about sorcerers and tigers in which Haneen, the youngest, was the principal hostage. She looked rosy-cheeked and excited and she pleaded to stay with her friends. Leyla left her for another hour and went back to the Old House.

As she pushed Kamaran's bicycle into the courtyard she heard strains of music coming from the drawing room. The restless, sweeping strings resolved into a stately pulse and she found herself marching in time as she climbed the stairs to the gallery. It was an old song - *che mali wali* -a haunting lament about a wronged and forsaken woman. She stopped by the drawing room windows as a sinuous feminine voice, rich and sweet, coiled into the air.

Peering through a glassless flower in the broken screen, Leyla saw that Sami had thrown open the shutters of the middle window. Shafts of winter light flooded through the broken glass, suffusing the dusty air like a spotlight and spilling onto the wooden floor. Aside from an armchair, the shelter they had made and the cascading chandelier, the room was bare. They had been forced to burn all the furniture and nothing remained but the shadow it once cast - a row of neat squares by the window, the scalloped lines of the Damascus desk. Years of sunshine had bleached the boards around the place where the carpet had been, leaving a dark rectangle like a stage in the middle of the room, and on this stage Sami was dancing.

He was standing with his back towards her, leaning on his stick, and swaying slightly from side to side. As the tender, sensuous voice spiraled above the strings he raised his arm in a fluttering arabesque and turned a slow, shuffling circle. His white hair was matted with dust, his eyes were shut and his clownish face, pale as his dishdasha, was ecstatic. Round and round he tottered, circling his bony hand in the air, his gestures halting but eloquent like the dance of a clockwork toy or a puppet with only one string.

As Leyla came into the room he opened his eyes and held out his hand. She stepped onto the stage to join him and for a while they danced together, smiling shyly at their unschooled steps and laughing at the comical flourishes they made for one another. Then Sami twirled away and left her the floor. Leyla shut her eyes, gave herself to the music, and danced for her grandfather as she had never danced before.

Like a child, without restraint, she tried to express what was in her heart. She danced for the two rivers, Tigris and Euphrates, and for the place where they mingle amongst thickets of tamarisk and palm to slide to the sea in a broad reach of mossy green. She danced for the whispering marshes, home of the Ma'adan, their islands of rushes and ornate houses woven from reeds. She danced for the waterfalls and mountains, the streams singing into the valleys, and the Kurdish girls in bright dresses like flowers in the fields. She danced for the wide deserts and their star-spangled skies, ruined temples and cities, priestesses and queens. Then she opened her eyes and stood aside for Sami to dance again, and as she watched her eyes brimmed with tears.

She cried because the music filled her with longing and the only man she had ever wanted had abandoned them. She cried because she hoped that wasn't true. She cried because her grandfather had seen so much he loved destroyed. She cried because Haneen, just two years old, had already suffered what no parent would wish their child to endure in two lifetimes. She cried because the music was filled with dignity and their dignity was being ground into to the dust. She cried because - even in the midst of these ashes - they were honouring, with their strange dance, everything that was beautiful. She cried because Sami was dancing as a gesture of defiance, and most of all she cried because she felt, somewhere in her heart, that he had chosen this dance, this tune, as a kind of swan song.

'Little Kashkash,' he said as the music came to an end, 'come here and help me sit down. My old bones are done for!'

Leyla held his arm as he manoeuvered himself awkwardly into his chair. He slumped over, breathing heavily, as she knelt on the floor at his side.

'Jiddu, Jiddu!' she murmured, kissing the mottled skin on the back of his hand. 'This nightmare can't last forever. It'll be spring soon. The air will smell of blossom again and we'll eat white cheese and cucumber and play bezique on the roof as we used to do… '

Sami did not answer. For as Leyla stopped speaking they heard the patter of light footsteps on the gallery and Ibrahim's oldest son careered into the room.

'Um Haneen!' he cried, gasping for breath. 'Youma asks you to come - come quickly! Little Haneen is ill!'

Chapter 25

At the start of the war, in one of the many presentations delivered to the world's media, the American General Colin Powell was asked to explain the Allies' strategy against the Iraqi army. 'Our strategy to go after this army is very, very simple,' he replied. 'First we're going to cut it off - and then we're going to kill it.'

For Kamaran and his comrades the war was like a horror movie come to life. Hunted by a savage and invincible foe, they discovered they could neither fight nor flee but must wait, in darkness, for the blows. As they heard the roar of enemy planes above them on the first night, the boom and flash of fire from their own trenches cheered their spirits and gave them the illusion of protection. The cannonade only made them the target of attack and they soon realised that their anti-aircraft guns might as well have been pea-shooters. By the third day, wheels shredded from rocking on the stony ground, long snouts nosing the air, their hulks lay abandoned in the drifting sand like the bones of some blundering prehistoric animal. That afternoon low clouds gathered above the desert like a prayer mat. Three nights passed without a single raid. On the sixth their position was bombed again and from then on they were attacked, day and night, for five weeks - and the only fire they heard was enemy fire.

At night the boom and crack of explosions sounded like the collision of planets adrift in space. Earth and air burned. Fireballs streaked through the clouds with a rumble like thunder, or a rash of white sparks prickled the darkness until the sky burst into flame and hailed cluster bombs over the desert, marooning the troops below. When they were not under attack themselves, tremors from the barrage along the front rattled their mess tins and sent sand whispering onto their heads like the threat of things to come. By the time they heard the shriek of the jets it was too late to hide. On clear days they could see the bombs falling as the planes tore above them, as if their sharp wings were slashing open a bloody seam in the sky.

From the second week trucks and tanks were picked off one by one, erupting in huge explosions which flung hot shrapnel into the trenches. Veteran soldiers, who had sheltered in their vehicles in the last war, joined the gunners and conscripts huddling in the muddy foxholes. The convoys that ferried provisions across the desert dwindled away. The Allies bombed the bridges on the Euphrates again and again and blew up the fleets of lorries stranded along the river bank. The stuttering, wild-eyed drivers who made it to the front told garbled tales of their ordeal, like survivors of a shipwreck whose companions had been eaten by sharks.

Once they knew the Allies were targeting vehicles, the soldiers refused to linger near the trucks. Instead they stripped out the batteries and headlights and used them to light their bunkers. Many men refused to leave the dugouts at all. Others, crazed by fear and lack of sleep, wandered about the open ground as the jets screeched overhead. They all wrote the names and addresses of their families on their arms and, for safe measure, on their ankles too. They became deaf and shouted at each other rather than speaking, their voices hoarse with dust. They slept with their boots on and wore cumbersome layers of clothes in a futile bid to fend off the cold. They stunk and looked filthy. Their dusty faces were pallid as sheep's cheese and haggard with fatigue. For between the air raids the thud of distant drums and siren voices troubled the night. 'Your only sanctuary' they sighed, 'is across the Saudi border where bombs and famine stop.' Rumours of mutiny spread amongst the troops. Death squads scoured the roads for deserters but men ran away every night, and it was plain that those who stayed did not intend to fight. They stopped cleaning their rifles. They left belts of bullets to rust on the machine guns. They moved boxes of ammunition out of the trenches, abandoning them to the rain and sand.

By the fourth week the army was forced to requisition civilian vehicles in a vain attempt to get food to the front. The troops eked out the remnants of their meagre rations and collected rainwater to drink. The wire for their field telephones had been cut by artillery. All communiqués had to be sent by messenger, but petrol was scarce and anything that moved was attacked. Their officers tuned their radios to the BBC or gleaned information from The Voice of the Gulf, unaware the station was run by the Americans. With no communications, no intelligence and no orders, they hunkered down and remained positioned against an attack from the south, through Kuwait. The main assault, when it came, would strike two hundred miles to the west and up through the southern deserts of Iraq, in a flanking movement that encircled the army and trapped them between the Euphrates and the Gulf.

At times, it seemed to Kamaran, the natural order had unravelled and was in league with their foes. Clouds exploded into flame and the ground erupted beneath their feet. The night burned and roared and seeded the horizon with a hundred fiery suns that brought no light. Smoking pyres shrouded their days in perpetual gloom and poisoned the air with dust and fumes, like the atmosphere of a dying star. Time itself seemed to buckle and warp. Whenever Kamaran summoned the strength to leave the bunker between raids he found the same dismal scene, as if they had been cursed to re-live, time and again, one day. Men wandered about the trenches like sleepwalkers, lost to the world, their faces cracking into grisly unwitting smiles. Or they fell asleep with their eyes open, rambling in the grip of nightmares until they were roused by their own cries. Then the listless hours of boredom, hunger and cold seemed, to Kamaran, as boundless as the desolate wilderness around them.

But the instant he heard the swelling crackle of a jet, or the ominous drone of the B52s, everything fractured into distinct, vivid images like the motions of a dancer lit by a strobe. A canon thrown from an exploding tank hung, improbably, in midair. Jamil's face, livid with fear, shouted at him soundlessly as he careered along the trench. Kamaran - who had knocked his head whenever he came into the bunker before the war started - developed a new balletic grace and flew from the fire-step to the back of their foxhole in one nimble leap.

Then the ground began to quake as shockwaves rumbled through the desert. Shells whistled and burst overhead, and every explosion was followed by the rattle of shrapnel on the stones, the thud of falling boulders and a sustained hiss as sand showered from the sky. Even then - when it seemed the earth itself would split open and engulf them all - Sergeant Abbas prowled about the heaps of spoil outside and fired his rifle into the sky, a deluded slave challenging goliath to a duel. He never seemed to rest. Fearsome, dark and shaggy-haired as the mythical Tantal who slept with its eyes wide open, he paced about the trenches making sure that no-one else escaped. The company had already lost nearly half its men. Twelve had been killed, another five injured and the remnants of two squadrons deserted in the middle of the night. The major, who would be held accountable for their flight, didn't have the manpower or the transport to try and round them up. Sergeant Abbas took it upon himself to guard the trenches, and wherever Kamaran went he could feel his eyes upon him.

One morning in the third week of February, a swarm of helicopters thundered over their position and shrouded them in whirling clouds of dirt. That evening they heard a new sound to the east - the pulsing thump of artillery. It seemed to quicken and swell as the night wore on, like the pounding footfalls of an army on the march. The major sent a runner to the nearest brigade to request reinforcements and another to the headquarters of the VII Army corps. The first man never returned. The second made it back a day later after driving without lights throughout the night. Even before he left the major's bunker, word got round that the General had refused to send help without orders from Baghdad.

It had rained steadily all morning. The low clouds, which meant air raids were unlikely, had turned desert and sky to the colour of muddy water. All along the trenches men gathered in little knots, braving the drizzle to mutter about the news. Eventually Kamaran spotted the messenger himself, flanked by a gaggle of soldiers who scurried along the soggy banks of spoil as he picked his way along the trench. A skinny wretch called Mahmoud, he was dressed in a cotton uniform sodden with rain. Shivering and bewildered, he refused to say anything about his journey until he had been given some food. Kamaran found him a scrap of bread, stiff as shoe leather, and a blanket. He squatted at the back of their foxhole, the rug drooping from his thin shoulders, and gnawed at the crust while his impatient comrades jostled outside, peering at him as if he was an exotic captive from a far off land.

He stunk like a jackal and Kamaran stood outside the dank bunker to wait with the others in the rain. They all fell silent as Mahmoud got to his feet and poked his pale face out of the doorway. In addition to the dispatches, he said, he had two other bits of news. The first was that Saddam Hussein had ordered a retreat from Kuwait.

'You see!' Jamil cried, turning to Kamaran with a happy grin. 'We'll all be going home in one piece and you shall see your baby at last!'

A few questions revealed that Mahmoud had no idea when the order had been given, or even if the rumour was true.

'What was the other news?' Kamaran asked.

'The other news?' he echoed with a baffled look. 'Oh yes! A battalion of the 45th Division surrendered yesterday to the Americans.'

'That's ridiculous!' Sadiq protested. 'The 45th are at As Salman. They must be seventy miles north of us, way behind the front!'

'I'm just telling you what they were saying,' the man repeated with a shrug. 'It was the 1st Battalion - the whole lot of them, their commanding officer too.'

The soldiers pressed him with more questions and he answered with the same bemused look, scratching under his blanket the while as the lice on his thawing body began to move.

When the crowd had dispersed Kamaran left the dugout. The air stank of dirty bedding and rotting sandbags, and the queasy smell of rancid, boiling water hung in the drizzle as he made his way along the trench. Four or five soldiers were huddled together in the next bunker. They fell silent as he passed by. Sergeant Abbas was standing to one side of the doorway, shaking out his blanket. The clink of mess tins and the first notes of a plaintive song rang out from the foxholes behind them.

'Like wheat sown between river and bank was I left stranded, they neither blessed me nor bade me farewell…'

'I wish that bastard would give it a rest!' the sergeant muttered as he watched Kamaran walk by.

The water-logged soil crumbled like a dunked biscuit as Kamaran climbed out of the ditch. The sky was smeared with yellow fog as if something noxious was burning over the horizon. Looking back he could see the rings of trenches and the black wires trailing between the observation posts, like veins in the sand. The burnt out carcasses of two jeeps - which had once been kitted out with radios - dug their noses into the ground, as if they had been trying to burrow their way to safety when they were hit. A trail of sooty craters punctured the earth beyond them and the rusty, oxidised hulks of three troop carriers lay nearby, like the wreckage of some army that had perished long ago.

Kamaran sat down on the lip of a crater and watched the spitting rain pock-mark the puddles. He had eaten nothing since three spoonfuls of rice the night before. His stomach was cramping with hunger, his muscles were stiff and his hands and feet were numb with cold. Rain drummed on his helmet and ran in little rivulets from its brim. He held his head back and opened his mouth to catch the drops. He wanted to make sense of the messenger's stories but he felt so confused and exhausted he found it impossible to follow his own train of thought. He fumbled in the breast pocket of his jacket and pulled out the photograph that Leyla had sent him, as he did whenever he was alone.

As he gazed at the picture he tried to invoke the feeling that had gripped him when he first saw it seven months before - that joyful determination to return home, whatever the risks. To be warm, to be clean, to taste something sweet - even these simple pleasures had become an unimaginable paradise. Sleepless weeks of fear and hunger had erased every recollection of delight leaving only an instinct to survive, and that was fading. Like a prisoner glimpsing sunlight through the bars of his dungeon, he looked at the picture to remember there was another world for which he wanted, passionately, to live.

It was then that he heard the engine - a lazy drawling above the clouds. He jumped up, his heart thumping, slipped and fell sprawling on the muddy ground. Twenty yards away his comrades dived for cover and the landscape emptied suddenly, as if everyone had blown away. The plane, invisible above the clouds, circled lazily overhead and droned off. As Kamaran got to his feet, wiping the mud from his chilly hands, he became aware of a pale flicker in the murk above him. Scraps of paper were fluttering earthwards, soggy as butterflies beaten by the rain. Men clambered from the trenches, catching in the air as the leaflets fell around them. One landed at Kamaran's feet and he stooped to pick it up. The damp paper stuck to his hands and he unfolded it carefully so it didn't tear.

'WARNING!'

He read.

'This position will be bombed tomorrow.
Flee and save yourselves, or remain and die.'

Chapter 26

The bombardment on the night Haneen fell ill - the fortieth night of the war - was the most violent Baghdad had seen. Slashes of light sliced through the shutters of the Old House with each blast, cutting stripes in the darkness. As the raids gathered force the sky above the courtyard turned white. The empty drawing room was showered with snowflakes and stars as flash after flash burst through the glassless lattice of the gallery window. Leyla lay along the length of the wall under the table, shielding Haneen with her body, and stroked her hair. The little girl was feverish and every breath she took cost an effort. In the silence between explosions, as her chest heaved up and down, Leyla could hear a high-pitched whine like the rusty hinge of a shutter squeaking in the wind.

She prayed for daylight to come and the barrage to stop. But a brew of burning oil, dust and fog eclipsed the dawn and the blitz that had rocked them all night raged on throughout the morning and into the afternoon. Haneen refused to eat. It was all Leyla could do to coax her to drink. As the day wore on her temperature increased. By three o'clock her pulse was fluttering like the wings of a moth and her hair was soaked with sweat. Sami, throwing an overcoat over his dishdasha, went out to see if he could raise a neighbour with a car and petrol to drive them to the hospital.

Gathering a blanket, a bottle of water and Haneen's cloth mouse, Leyla carried her daughter down to the courtyard and waited in the cupboard under the stairs for her grandfather's return. Haneen lay in her arms, limp as a wet feather. She was still wearing the dress she had put on to go and play with her friends. The lace round the neck trembled with her laboured breathing. Her skin was pale and she seemed barely able to open her eyes. Her face, normally alive with mischief, had settled into an unchanging mask as grave and tender as the countenance of a stone angel. Leyla brushed the damp curls from her forehead and rocked her gently to and fro. Suddenly Haneen started to pant and whimper - a frightened whimper full of protest and surprise.

'Haneen, babati,' Leyla murmured, kissing her fingers. 'It's alright, youma's here!'

Even as she spoke every muscle in her daughter's little body cramped and stiffened and she stopped breathing altogether.

'Haneen - Haneen!' Leyla cried, her own voice shrill as a child's. 'Haneen, my love!'

Haneen's eyelashes flickered. She gave a great sob and her eyes rolled back in her head. Her body went limp again and her legs and arms started to tremble and twitch.

'Jiddu! Jiddu!' Leyla screamed. 'Haneen, my baby!' She loosened the buttons at the neck of her dress and cradled her head until the convulsion stopped. For a moment she sat, petrified, her heart thumping like a drum; the next she had leapt out of the cupboard, her unconscious daughter clasped in her arms, and was fumbling at the door with shaking hands.

The square was deserted. Leyla threw the blanket over her shoulders and wrapped it round Haneen, trying to screen her from the cold air which was thick with ash and dust.

'Jiddu!' she called, turning to face each corner of the square. 'Jiddu! Jiddu!'

There was no answer and no sound, except the distant rumbling of an air raid and a siren's wail. The nearest hospital was a mile and half away. Leyla cut back through the alleys and headed for Rashid Street in the hope she might be able to flag down a passing car.

As she hurried through the dismal, shuttered lanes, Haneen cradled in her arms, Leyla had the same sense of estrangement she had felt when she crawled from the cupboard on the first morning of the war. Smoke and dust drowned the streets in an amber fog, and this sinister light seemed no more remarkable to her than the explosions that crackled and rumbled like a thunderstorm to the east. The only thing that existed for her was the desperate love she felt for the little creature in her arms. Everything else, including her own thoughts and actions, seemed to have slipped out of time. It was as if the stitches that bound each second to the next had unravelled. Leyla had to muster all her strength to fight through these fractured moments, and would only re-enter the living world when she had delivered her daughter to the sanctuary of the hospital.

As she neared Rashid Street the lane stopped abruptly. The homes on either side had vanished. For two hundred yards there was not one house left standing and no trace of what had struck them, save a series of craters, like giant footprints, in the middle of the road. Steel shutters had twisted like crisps in the heat. Intimate clutter - scraps of sodden fabric, a purple dress, a bird cage and a scattering of shoes - stuck out of the rubble, the tell-tale traces of a mass grave. Leyla turned back and took a different road. Here too the ground was strewn with debris and the windows had all been blown out and stared blindly across the street. Her arms were aching. She hitched Haneen a little higher so that her head was resting on her shoulder and picked her way through the wreckage, oblivious to the glass scrunching under her feet.

She emerged near the riverfront. A pitchy cloud of smoke, warping with the wind, had blotted out the remains of the day and trapped the entire city in an ominous yellow half-light. She heard the whine of a car but it was heading the wrong way. Drifts of rubbish in the gutter came to life as it sped past, sending scraps of paper hopping into the air like scavenging birds. A scrawny dog was digging in the garbage. It stopped for a moment, pricking its ears, and then scampered, yelping, towards a narrow side street.

A deep boom shook the ground and the blast seemed to rumble across the river and sweep up the road like a wave. On the far bank a volcano of flame and ash mushroomed into the sky, casting capricious shadows across the buildings and lighting the waters of the Tigris an angry red. An air-raid siren began to howl, too late. There was a second explosion, a third and a fourth. With each blast a new ball of fire and ash belched upwards, lighting other pillars of smoke that rose from the city beyond, as if the earth itself was on fire. Leyla pulled Haneen's head against her shoulder, turned tail and ran. Another column of smoke and fire erupted into the air ahead of her, towering above the rooftops like an angry djinni. She threw herself into a doorway and crouched in the corner, sheltering Haneen with her back as flakes of fire started falling from the sky.

A missile had exploded between two high rises and both towers were now on fire. Tongues of flame licked up through the broken windows on the lower floors, chasing plumes of smoke into the sky.

Black figures rushed about in front of the blaze, slinging something at the buildings as if they were stoking the flames. An old man in a dishdasha, beside himself with grief, hurled himself again and again towards the doorway of the flats. He was restrained by a fireman who caught him in both arms. Each time he was caught he took his feet off the ground, like a child tired of walking, until his captor put him down. Then he tried to launch himself, once more, into the burning building. Leyla turned her face away. Sparks and ash eddied around her and she felt a rush of air suck her down the narrow street. A second fireman was trying to direct a disorderly chain of men who were passing buckets of water, hand over hand, from a standpipe somewhere out of sight. Leyla could see they were shouting but she couldn't hear their voices as she passed by. Their cries, the clang of the buckets, the slop of the water - all were drowned beneath the roar and crackle of the blaze, which sounded like the thundering of a massive waterfall. She pulled the blanket over Haneen's head as she hurried past, her feet sinking slightly into the melting asphalt. Then, breaking into a run, she hastened on her way.

Night was falling by the time she reached the hospital. As she crossed the forecourt the air was shattered by a metallic clatter. A deafening, hammering roar unspooled across the concrete and

269

seemed to come from the building itself, which glowed suddenly with a sickly greenish light. As she neared the entrance Leyla was overtaken by two children pushing a prostrate woman in a handcart. An ambulance careered through the gates, its siren lost in the din of the generator, and nearly knocked them all over as it screeched to a halt. She heard a cry as the porters opened the back door and started unloading their freight. The first pulled out a corpse and dragged it away, leaving a smear of blood on the ground. The second jumped out, a small body bundled in a blanket in his arms, and ran into the building.

Leyla shifted Haneen's weight to free her left arm and pushed open the main door. A sickly smell - the smell of a butcher's shop - washed over her as she stepped inside. Along one wall lay a row of bodies covered with blood and dust, as if the graves had opened and spat out their dead. On all sides she saw faces filled with pain and grief. A woman sat on the floor, her cheeks streaked with blood and tears, cradling a boy who was unconscious or already dead. A little girl staggered in giddy circles and screamed as she clutched at her ears. At her feet sat an old, old man who shielded his face with one hand as he rocked back and forth - and all these people, too, seemed beyond reach and lost in a private nightmare of their own.

In the dim light beyond them, a host of shadowy shapes moved hither and thither in an agitated dance, like horses that sense a wolf is near. Leyla stood still until she saw what she was looking for. A man with a white coat ducked quickly out of an office and disappeared through a set of double doors. She pushed her way through the panic-stricken throng and followed him out. As the doors swung shut behind her she felt the scrunch of grit underfoot. The doctor was already half way down a long corridor, lined with a march of broken windows. She slipped as she set off after him and saw there were drifts of sand on the floor, blown in from the storm the week before. At that moment another air-raid began and all the lights went out.

On and on she wandered, through a labyrinth of dusky passageways, until she heard a rumble of carts like the close of day at the suq. Two porters pushing a woman on a trolley dashed past her, leaving the smell of burnt meat in their wake. Leyla hurried after them and found herself at the beginning of a long ward. A doctor emerged from a bay to one side and strode off, his white coat flitting like a ghost in the gloom. She was about to cry out when a second doctor strode after him, calling his name. She was carrying a lantern and they bent their heads together in the circle of light, reading the label on a phial of medicine. The first doctor looked stern and unsympathetic. The other had a placid, tender face and was very young. They both looked up in surprise as Leyla stopped beside them.

'No, no - that's the last one,' the man said, passing the phial to his colleague. Without a glance at Leyla he hurried from the ward.

'Can I help you sister?' the second doctor asked. Leyla felt grateful tears start to her eyes. For a moment she was unable to speak.

'It's my daughter, doctor,' she said at last. 'She's had a high temperature all day. She's barely conscious and she's struggling to breathe.'

The woman lifted her lantern and pulled the blanket from Haneen's face.

'When was she admitted?' she asked.

'She hasn't been admitted.' Leyla said.

'Then you need to go back to reception and register with them.'

'She had a fit. *Please* look at her. I've just walked through an air raid to bring her here. You can see how poorly she is.'

The young doctor nodded distractedly.

'You need to go back to reception, as I said,' she repeated as she began to walk away. 'I'm sorry but there's nothing we can do until then.'

'Can't *you* look at her now?' Leyla asked, falling into step beside her.

'What do you expect me to do, sister?' the young woman replied without slowing her pace. 'I can't give you medicine if that's what you want. We don't have enough drugs for the sick and wounded here.'

'But you can see how ill she is!' Leyla protested. 'She's struggling to breathe - you can hear her!'

'Yes - she and half the children in Baghdad. What do you expect with all this smoke?' The doctor stopped suddenly and wiped her eyes with her hand. 'Forgive me, I'm very tired. The whole place is alive with infection and there's little we can do for children who are ill. If you want my honest advice I would take her home.'

'Just look at her,' Leyla said. 'I beg you.'

The young woman gave a sigh.

'Come with me,' she said.

Leyla followed her into one of the bays. In the glow from the lantern she saw three cots without sheets and three small bandaged bodies. Three black-clad women, swathed in abayas and holding bags of saline aloft, stood vigil by the beds, their arms raised as if in some unanimous gesture of protest or despair. They turned to watch as the doctor cleared some papers from a table by the door. Leyla laid Haneen down and took the doctor's lantern. The little girl's face was pale as milk and her chest shuddered with every ragged breath. As the doctor took her pulse she opened her eyes for a moment and gazed up at her mother with faraway, bloodshot eyes. Leyla kissed her little hand then lowered the lantern to watch the doctor's face as she bent over her daughter with a stethoscope. When the brief examination was over the doctor took the lantern back. Leyla wrapped

Haneen in her blanket, gathered her in her arms, and followed the young woman outside.

'Her temperature *is* high,' she said, lifting the lamp so Leyla could see her face. 'But that in itself is nothing to worry about. The fit was probably a febrile convulsion. Young children sometimes have them with a high fever. They're alarming for the parents but not generally dangerous.' She cleared her throat and took the lantern in her other hand. 'It does sound as if she's got a lung infection, though. I suggest you take her home, keep her quiet, and give her plenty to drink. I'm sorry there's not more we can do to help,' she added, 'but now I really must go.' She took a step forward.

Leyla stepped in front of her, blocking her way.

'But surely if she's got an infection she needs medicine - penicillin or-'

'We don't have any penicillin.'

'Some other antibiotic then. Surely you -'

'We've run out of antibiotics.'

'Please!' Leyla said. 'I-'

'You've heard of the blockade, I presume?' the doctor snapped, cutting her short. 'Come to the dispensary if you don't believe me. We're tearing up *sheets* to use as bandages!'

'Please!' Leyla said again. 'She's my only child.'

The doctor looked at her with a little shake of the head.

'Where do you imagine these bombs fall? Every time you hear an explosion people are burned,

274

injured, killed. We're burying the *dead* in the hospital garden!'

'There must be *something* you can do!'

'What?' the doctor cried. 'What? What is it you think I can do?' She stared at Leyla for a moment, her eyes ablaze. '*Every* machine we have stopped working on the first night of the war. Incubators, monitors, blood, vaccines - *all* ruined. I have given blood *three times* this week - as has every other doctor in the hospital!'

Leyla stared at her aghast as, her free hand waving in the air, her voice growing higher and higher, the young woman went on.

'When the air-raids start we must turn off the generator and then we have no lights, as you can see. We have no clean sheets. No water. Our surgeons stand in pools of blood and operate by *candlelight* and now we're running out of candles. *Shall I go on?* There's a woman in labour upstairs with a compound fracture in her thigh, there are two more who need emergency caesareans and there are people arriving *every* minute who need operations if they are to live. But we are running out of anesthetic. What is it you suggest I do? You're an educated person. Do you want to help me decide who lives and who dies? Me, I'm just a doctor, I'm not God!'

'Please,' Leyla whispered. 'Please help my baby!'

'I would help her if I *could*, my sister!' the doctor cried. 'But all I have is advice. *Go home*. Give her

275

plenty to drink and keep her cool. God willing, she will survive. There's nothing I can give you but my prayers.' With that she stepped to one side and walked away.

As Leyla turned to watch her go the tears she had choked back all day streamed from her eyes. The light from the lantern splintered into a hundred stars. Then a door swung shut and she was left in darkness.

Chapter 27

In the dark hours before daybreak on the twenty-fourth of February the Allies launched their invasion. Shadowed by a gathering sandstorm, they punched through the defences along the Saudi border and rumbled north.

The shell-shocked foot soldiers in the Iraqi trenches, wielding machine guns and rifles as if they were expecting the Ottoman Army to march over the dunes, stared aghast at the chimera that burst from the fog. A new brood of predators, half beast and half machine, had spawned in the toxic air. Squat, fire-breathing robots scuttled over the sands, savage birds and monstrous insects wheeled in the storm above them, screeching for blood. As the ironclad legions sped north, Iraqi troops - blinded by the sandstorm - didn't know what was afoot until their foes fell upon them. Every position told the tale of a doomed and frantic flight. The tyre marks which scarred the mud led inexorably to the charred carcass of a truck or tank, some still ensnared in their own camouflage nets, and the scorched earth around them was littered with kit bags, helmets, boots, broken rifles and dead men. A hundred thousand mutinous soldiers defied their Generals, abandoned their trenches, and started the long walk home. Famished, out-gunned, bewildered by the savagery of the assault, most of those who stayed tried to surrender. Ten thousand were taken prisoner on the first day.

The night before the invasion the desert shook with the boom of artillery, quickening as the minutes ticked by like the pounding drums of a marauding tribe. Kamaran sat with his knees drawn up and his right hand clasped against the photo in his breast pocket, while his heart slammed into his ribs like a bird trying to batter its way out of a cage. As the barrage gathered force gasps of foul air swirled around the dugout. In the livid glare of the explosions he could see the leaflets the Allies had dropped that day, flapping and hopping about the trench in the wind as if they wanted to hide. Still he tried to imagine the riot of machines as an earthquake or volcano. The reality, that it was the deliberate work of men, possessed him with a sense of such terrifying evil it stripped him of all reason. Jamil, curled up on the ground beside him, began to pray, the pitch of his voice rising at each new blast as if he was practicing his scales.

'Oh please God let it stop, let it stop, let it stop! Oh please God let it stop, let it stop, let it stop!'

Sometime after midnight the cannonade died, briefly, away. In the sudden quiet, above the soughing wind and the hiss and bubble of the rain, Kamaran

278

heard swift footsteps in the trench outside. A slim form ducked into the dugout and a low voice whispered in the darkness.

'Kamaran? Jamil? You're leaving.'

It was Lieutenant Ismael.

'How?' Kamaran asked.

'Sadiq has got one of the trucks working. They're all ready to go, everyone but the sergeant. They're only waiting for you, Jamouli too. Are you coming?'

'What about the other platoons?' Kamaran asked.

'They'll follow our example,' the lieutenant replied. 'In sha'Allah. Are you coming?'

It was a wild, wet stormy night. Ragged clouds and smoke raced over a gibbous moon and the rain spattered Kamaran's neck as, bending low, they hurried along the trench. Every ten yards or so the plink of raindrops on tin and canvas broke the regular patter of the shower, and the lieutenant stopped to shepherd more men from the bunker below. To the east the sky was aglow, as if a city was burning over the horizon, and the wet sand was slicked with red. Dim, hunch-backed shades slunk forward in the rusty light and stopped every time the clouds cleared the moon, fearful of being seen. For hours, it seemed, they moved forward in this strange, slow dance, still as statues in the marbled moonlight, beetling shadows when clouds eclipsed the sky.

By the time they reached the end of the earthworks there were twelve men in all. Against the red sheen of the flat sand beyond, Kamaran could just make out Sadiq's silhouette and the shape of the lorry parked behind him. They clambered out in pairs and waited to run across the open ground. Kamaran and Jamil climbed out last and Kamaran turned back to help the lieutenant from the trench. At that moment the sky lit up again, the air buckled and the shockwaves of a huge explosion nearly threw him off his feet. Flashes of white and orange flickered across the wet sand and he saw a bulky figure scale the mound of spoil behind them, his rifle shooting into the air. For an instant the darkness returned. Then something popped far above them, a hundred white fires exploded out of the desert to the west, there was a blinding flash and Sergeant Abbas was standing in their midst. As the glare faded the soldiers began to back away from him towards the truck.

'Steady boys, steady,' he growled, reloading his rifle. 'Remember the army!' He looked from one soldier to another, but still they backed away. Then he saw Kamaran.

Even in the gloom Kamaran could make out the ghastly smile which crept across the sergeant's face as he aimed his rifle.

'Get back you motherfucker!' he snarled, planting himself between Kamaran and the lorry.

Kamaran raised his hands in the air but he kept on moving, circling the sergeant like a matador circles a bull, until he was no longer blocking the way to the truck. Then he turned and walked away.

'Come back!' the sergeant roared, walking after him. 'Come back! You're a disgrace to your country!'

A salvo of bullets peppered the dirt at Kamaran's feet. He stopped and turned as another flash lit up the sky and Lieutenant Ismael scrambled from the trench.

'Stand and fight!' the sergeant screamed again. 'Stand and fight or I'll -'

He never finished the sentence because the lieutenant cracked him over the head with his pistol. Sergeant Abbas staggered forward, like a drunk trying to stay on his feet, and fell on his face in the dirt. For a moment everything was quiet, save the sighing wind. Then the wheeze and sputter of an engine rang out in the stormy air.

'They're ready to go, Sir,' Kamaran said.

The lieutenant had dropped his gun and was on his knees beside the sergeant. Rolling him onto his back, he peered anxiously at his face.

'They're leaving, Sir,' Kamaran said again, as the truck slithered to a halt beside them.

The lieutenant looked up at him and shook his head.

'I took my oath willingly. It's different for me.'

'Kamaran, Kamaran!' Jamil cried, as the driver revved the engine.

The truck began to slip away.

'Go, you fool!' the lieutenant said. 'Get out while you can!'

At sunrise they were still south of As Salman. Leaving the highway, they cut east into the desert. The barren landscape gave them nowhere to hide and the truck kicked up a plume of dust which lingered in the damp air. Frightened of being attacked from the skies, frightened of stumbling onto their own positions, ignorant of the enemy closing behind them, they chose to stop and wait for darkness to fall. They built a rough bivouac of rocks half a mile from the lorry and spent the day huddled inside it, trying to sleep as sand lashed about them.

At dusk they set off again, looking for a trail marked on a British Army map from some fifty years before. They dared not use their lights. As the night wore on the storm grew worse and they crawled across the rocky, pitted wastes, barely faster than they could walk, until the truck came to a gliding, silent halt. They had run out of petrol. The songster Private Onion and a young soldier with a sprained ankle decided to stay put until daylight. Kamaran and the others, taking only a compass and their water-bottles, set off on foot.

To the north lay a chain of wadis that would lead them to the Euphrates. Their goal was to reach the shelter of these ravines before the sun rose. When the wind blew a hole in the clouds they stumbled on in the moonlight. The rest of the time they couldn't see the rocks beneath their feet and they bunched together like ponies, sheltering their faces from the cold wind.

By the time they had walked three miles, Kamaran's boots had rubbed huge blisters on his heels. Every time they stopped he tried something different. Jamil offered to swap boots with him but that was worse and at the next halt they swapped them back again. Kamaran re-threaded his laces and bound them tight around his ankles. He loosened them again and tried to shove his feet forward to lessen the chafing at his heels. He ripped the pockets from his trousers and wedged the folded fabric under his feet. Nothing worked. With every step the leather ground sand into his socks and scoured at his heels, flaying them by degrees. The edge of his sleeves, wet and crusted with grit, tried the same trick on his wrists. His sodden jacket seemed to grow heavier and heavier on his shoulders, and he began to feel he was being hag-ridden by devilish djinn.

Towards daybreak the wind picked up, the clouds thinned and his companions hurried ever faster across the stony ground. Kamaran shuffled after them, trying to ignore his lacerated feet which, with every step, begged him to stop and lie down. His thoughts began to dance. Fragmented recollections shuffled this way and that in a mocking sequence he could neither master nor understand. A captain who had been killed in a sunset raid lay spread-eagled on the sand, his face changing colour with the sky as dust swirled about him. A little sand fox, its ears pricked up, trotted across the stones. Five men trapped in a burning tank shrieked with the gale.

Jamil's garbled prayers and the laments of Private Onion rustled and rang in his mind until he fancied he could hear all the voices of the dead, sobbing and moaning as they whispered their mournful stories to the desolate hall of winds. Then everything grew muddled once again and seemed to spring from the pain in his feet, which pleaded with him to stop and lie down.

At daybreak they found themselves on a cliff above a rocky ravine, breached along one side by patchy, windblown dunes. The pebbled desert behind them crept all the way back to their own front line. Ahead lay quicksand and twisting wadis, hazed with green. They stopped and rested for a while, waiting for the sky to lighten so they could pick their way down through the boulders to the shelter of the gorge.

Kamaran sat with his head on his knees and worked his hand under his jacket, touching his fingers to the photo in his pocket. Lost in a weary stupor, he had just agreed with his feet that they would go no further when he heard a low, soft whistle. He looked up to see a ragged line of birds trailing across the stormy sky. His first thought was that they were sand grouse, searching out pools left by the rain. Then he saw they were the vanguard of a much bigger flock, flying steadily north. In their shadow, blown hither and thither in the rising gale, came a flurry of smaller birds pursued by a gathering swell of dust. There was a sandstorm coming, and it seemed to thunder after them across the plain. His comrades looked at each other anxiously as the sound unfurled - a steady barrage of fire that came from the south and the west.

A red sun issued from the gloom as they slipped and stumbled their way down the ravine. The rising wind smeared ribs of bloody cloud across the sky. Little dust devils whipped along the tops of the dunes and streams of sand snaked along the gulch with a gritty hiss. Within minutes a yellow haze had filled the air and long fingers of dust reached ever higher, as if groping their way to the stars. The sky turned orange and then umber. Kamaran tied his scarf over his nose and mouth and pulled down his hood, leaving just a slit for his eyes. By the time he had finished the howling air was dark brown and filled with sand.

They huddled together in the lee of a boulder at the bottom of the ravine, waiting for the storm to pass. Every now and then the grumble of artillery gusted on the battering wind. It was impossible to tell where it came from, indeed it sounded as if it was all around. Then a new sound scuttled towards them - a gritty patter that hissed over the cliffs, hurling sand and water at their faces.

The rain washed the dirt from the air and they pressed on, their sodden clothes now stiff with sand. After twenty yards Kamaran sat down again. Jamil and Sadiq fumbled with cold fingers at the laces of his boots and worked them from his feet. His socks were soaked with blood. Kamaran peeled the wool from his heels and almost wept with relief as the cold rain spat against his shredded skin. Jamil helped him stand and they trudged on after their comrades, whose distant figures were now shrouded by shifting veils of rain.

As Kamaran hobbled over the pebbles trying to keep pace with his friends, he felt the squelch of mud between his frozen toes. Water had begun to seep up through the silty ground. Within minutes little streams coursed through the grit and carved ferny rills in the sand. He splashed through a puddle, then another. Soon there was nothing but puddles and pools which crept stealthily towards each other. Little waves started to leapfrog towards the bed of the gully, now a swirling, simmering, coffee-coloured lake.

The mud sucked at Kamaran's feet as they floundered towards the dunes at the wadi's edge. Jamil got mired in a patch of boggy silt and slipped over, his arms flailing in the swampy ground. Sadiq stopped to help him up and urged Kamaran to go on. Digging his bare feet into the damp sand, Kamaran clambered sideways up the dune. As he reached the crest a squall of wind whipped into his face and he turned away. Rain spattered against his hood and through it he heard another sound - a steady panting that staggered inexorably towards him.

A tumbling, sepia cloud barrelled along the top of the dune. The pant changed to the roar and putter of an engine and a dark form darted from the murk. For an instant Kamaran stood, transfixed, as he registered the shark's teeth daubed on the helicopter's snout and the stars and stripes of the American flag. Then there was a flash and he felt a blow that smacked him off his feet.

When he came to he was lying at the base of the dune and everything had come to a stop. In the puddle next to him each splash of rain flowered into a perfect crown of droplets and spread slow circles across the milky water. He felt winded and knew he had to breathe. When he tried, pain ripped through his chest as if his ribs had splintered like glass. He heard a scream - his own scream - and then the calls of his comrades, shouting to him through the mist. Jamil appeared at his side and fell to his knees in the mud.

'Kamaran!' he gasped. 'Kamaran! My friend, my brother!'

Like a magician conjuring a string of handkerchiefs, Jamil pulled a black and white *keffiya* from his pocket and tried, with shaking hands, to stem the flow of blood from Kamaran's chest. From the terror in his face Kamaran saw that he was going to die. For a moment he thought the wailing of the wind was his own, last anguished cry. With a final effort he moved his arm and stayed his friend's hand, holding it in his own.

'My life is going, Jamouli,' he said. 'Don't be afraid.'

Jamil's face and the sky beyond faded to a charcoal smudge. Then Kamaran felt himself float upwards, free from pain. From his vantage point above the dunes he could now see everything quite clearly - the simmering water, the humps of wet sand, the trail of footprints leading to a body that Sadiq and Jamil were making frantic efforts to revive. The scene looked oddly familiar and he suspected that he had got things wrong, as usual, and should be saying something heroic to his distraught friends. Jamil dropped his keffiya and let it fall onto the body, where it changed colour from black and white to red. Then, sitting back on his heels, he began to weep.

'Don't give up!' Kamaran wanted to shout. 'I'm not dead after all! I'm not dead!'

But Sadiq was already on his feet and, grasping Jamil by the arm, he dragged him away. Kamaran saw a shimmer around their bodies. Then they began to diminish and fade as he spun higher and higher until he could see, for a brief instant, the entire panorama of the war.

The oil wells of Kuwait, fired in a final act of vandalism by the vanquished Generals, spewed a biblical pall of black smoke across the vast battlefield. The highway to Basrah was choked, mile after mile, with a petrified tangle of buses and trucks and littered with the charred bodies of the retreating troops. In the marshes a regiment of dead soldiers bobbed face down amidst the reeds and across the wide desert below him, thousands of tanks burned like funeral pyres while the tattered survivors and bloodied remnants of the army fled across the stones, or sat slumped beneath white flags, praying for the carnage to end.

Kamaran's heart burst with sorrow for all these fallen men. Then he soared upwards like a flake of fire, until something shifted and he found himself amidst other fragments of his life. A thousand and one moments, some cherished, some long-forgotten, others he had no memory of at all, unfurled around him like the patterns of a kaleidoscope. Rabia was sighing as he explained that the class bully had ripped his shirt, when in fact he had torn it himself climbing a tree. Elsewhere and at the same time Sindbad tottered out of the rushes and his father vanished in a cloud of dust, while Leyla danced before him in all her incarnations. He was kissing her on a train, his hand behind her head, and her curls swept against his skin with the rocking of the carriage. Her fingertips lingered on his face as she brushed a mosquito from his cheek. He watched as she sliced a pomegranate in half and knocked it with the handle of the knife until the red seeds pattered out like rubies. She looked up at him with a shy smile as he put a sprig of jasmine in her hair. Her blue school pinafore flapped in the air as she jumped up and down on his bed. She clambered onto his shoulders to pick a lemon from a tree, and waved wings of palm, her head level with the long grass, as she fluttered along the stream like a bird. Sami, meanwhile, gathered his little grandson in his arms and claimed him for his own. Nasir wept acid, drunken tears. Kamaran poked his fingers into a warm jelly of frogspawn and stood amidst the tombs of Wadi al Salaam, uncertain what he should feel, even as his mother's face - which he had no memory of - shone above him like the moon.

From the smallest gesture to the great dilemmas of his life, each moment had its own note. Strident, jangling, poignant, silvery, pure, they all sounded together like the discordant notes of a tuning orchestra and then resolved, at last, into a coherent tune. He saw that he had loved deeply and quarrelled stubbornly, that the dramas people spin around their lives are trivial and misguided, and that most perverse of all was this war that had just killed him - a conflict which had no more honour than a squabble between spoilt children over a slice of cake. All this danced around him, fragmented into a pattern of light that overwhelmed him with love, blazed like a star - and was gone.

* * *

A week after the ceasefire a British convoy passed through the wadi where Kamaran had been killed. Sadiq, Jamil and the other runaways had perished

290

nearby, unaware of the Allied tanks that had foundered in the quagmire half a mile from the dunes.

The commanding officer called the convoy to a halt. He marked the position on a map and ordered a squadron of soldiers to dig a shallow grave. A second squad searched gingerly in the pockets of the dead. They collected letters, dog tags and identity cards and put them into a black rubbish bag, already nearly full, to send to the Red Cross. One by one the corpses were hauled away. Two soldiers, averting their faces from the smell, rolled Kamaran's body onto a blanket. They checked in the pockets of his uniform and found nothing but a photograph, crusted with blood, which they left to the wind and the rain. Dragging his body across the rough ground, they lowered it into the pit. Their chaplain refused to give a service so the twelve men stood in a moment's silent prayer at the edge of the hole. Then, picking up their shovels, they filled it with sand.

Epilogue

In the spring of 1994 Erin joined a humanitarian group travelling to Baghdad. Engineers, peace activists, nurses and doctors, some from Europe but most of them American, their mission was to assess the impact of the blockade which was still in place, three years after the end of the war. Erin's inclusion in their party, at the invitation of an Irish doctor, had speeded up the process of getting a visa but she felt ill at ease in their company. The whole expedition smacked of charity - which she mistrusted - and she had come under false pretences, having told no-one the real purpose of her trip.

They travelled overland from Amman and arrived in Baghdad in the early hours of a warm April morning. Erin thought it prudent to spend some time with the delegation and for three days she endured a round of meetings and hospital visits, listening to an unending tale of woe: the dinar had no value and everything was scarce. Professionals sold their furniture to buy food and medicine on the black market, while enterprising hustlers, their pockets stuffed with cash, rode in taxis driven by teachers and engineers. The monthly food ration lasted barely three weeks and the flour was full of weevils. Baby

292

milk and penicillin cost more than a poor man's life, and doctors trained to treat heart attacks and strokes, the ailments of the rich, found themselves helpless against famine and dirty water, the forgotten afflictions of the poor.

Erin watched her companions note down the grisly data and take snapshots of dying children as if they were exhibits in a zoo, and her heart rebelled. This litany of hideous facts did such a disservice to the city she remembered she could barely listen. It was as if the body of a famous beauty who had been raped and beaten was being displayed naked for all to see. She recalled her visit to Baghdad four years before - her excitement as she first walked into the market and discovered, in the earthy smells and opulent colours, something longed for and familiar like the tantalizing shadow of a collective dream. She remembered the kindness she had secured with her halting Arabic and how she had been greeted, everywhere she went, with the same few words of English - 'Hello, hello, you are welcome - welcome in Iraq' - and a glass of sugary tea. How she had returned laden with gifts and stories and music, mournful and sedate, wild and free; how she had seen in the faces in the streets the same features that had been chiselled, six thousand years before, on gods and goddesses, princes and queens: that full mouth, the haughty, ungulate nose, those tender, slanting eyes that had inspired a thousand and one poets to compare their lover to a gazelle - eyes she knew so well from the hours she had gazed at Kamaran.

Had she not longed, in visiting the land he loved, to learn something of her friend's heart? To catch, amidst the grandiose ministries and monuments, the dreary high-rises, the flyovers, a glimpse of the city that had him in its thrall? To understand why, when he talked of date palms, his eyes filled with tears? Why he stared out over the ice-bound harbour in Helsinki and thought only of the Tigris in Baghdad? Why that broad stretch of muddy water which slid between scruffy, concrete banks should inspire such rhapsody? Why he would sing, at the drop of a hat, a song that made him cry? Why his face changed when he spoke Arabic, as if its cadence revealed some part of his soul that no other language could express? Why he said that Europe made him sad because the buildings were all straight lines? Why he, who earned so little for work he found so dull, was so compulsively generous and unfailingly produced on the earnings of a skivvy a banquet fit for a queen? So instead of listening, as she should have done, to the facts of the current situation, Erin remembered the city she had seen then. Gripped by nostalgia she pressed her face to the coach window as they drove from ministry to hospital and hospital to ministry, trying to see if it had survived.

At the hotel there was no respite. The gentle, smiling maids and waiters looked wan and thin as ghosts. The only other guests were American

294

weapons inspectors from the United Nations who strutted about, keys jangling from their belts, and took over the bar to trade sneering stories about their hosts. Scrawny schoolboys loitered on the forecourt outside, missing class to shine shoes or hawk bottles of bootleg pepsi, the labels long since bleached by the sun. Desperate, barefoot children dodged through the traffic if they spotted a foreigner, risking death for a few cents. The travel agents in Sa'adun Street were boarded up. Yawning patriarchs kept vigil in the deserted cafés, clacking their worry-beads, their eyes as empty as the tables. Venerable grandfathers and harried mothers queued for their rations, staring at the ground shame-faced, while the once bustling suqs were hushed. The throngs of giggling girls flouncing along the Corniche and the young men pursuing them had gone. Clots of sewage floated on the Tigris and poisoned the water supply, and battered trucks rumbled over the bridges, spewing bilious fumes into the air. The destruction wrought by the bombing had been miraculously patched up but now everything was breaking again and the streets echoed with the death-rattle of failing machines. Like a punch-drunk boxer in a come-back fight, Baghdad staggered up each morning and tried to stay on her feet until the end of the day.

On the third evening of the trip Erin pretended to be ill. The following afternoon she took a small suitcase from her cupboard - a suitcase that belonged to Kamaran. She hurried through the hotel lobby on the look-out for government spies, hailed a taxi and told the driver to take her to the Al Gailani mosque.

It had rained heavily that morning and wide rivers had gathered in the gutters of Sa'adun Street. A couple of children were playing in the puddles and they screamed with laughter as the cab drove by, spraying them with water. At the mosque Erin got out. She crossed the busy road and wound her way into the backstreets, following a burly teenager who was trundling a car wheel over the uneven dirt. He stopped at a cobbler's shop where a boy sat in the window, sewing patches onto a tyre. Erin held open the door as he manoeuvred the wheel inside. In the next street a man in a frayed cap tried to sell her ice-cream from a stall outside a dusty, derelict shop. After that she passed a row of bombed out houses - a low mound of rubble, criss-crossed with paths where people had taken a short-cut between two alleys. A flock of white pigeons clattered over the rooftops as she emerged from the passageway, and she found herself in the square.

She stopped before the entrance and looked up at the lintel to make sure she had the right house. She could just make out the form of two lovebirds in the weathered brick and she recognised the hand-shaped knocker. As she touched its metal fingertips she heard footsteps within. She backed away as the heavy door swung open. A gaunt woman, her haughty face framed in a white hijab, stepped into the alley. She was about to close the door behind her when she noticed Erin and stopped in surprise.

'As-Salaam-Alaikum,' Erin said, taking a step towards her.

'*Wa alaikum as salaam*,' the woman replied with an imperious look. 'Are you lost?'

'I hope not,' Erin said. 'I've been here once before. I'm looking for Kamaran.'

'Kamaran!'

'My name is Erin. I used to know him - when he lived abroad.'

The woman stared at her for a moment. Then, with a swift glance down the alley, she held open the door.

'Please come inside.'

A pleasant smell, humid and dusty, enveloped them as they stepped over the threshold - the smell of Baghdad after rain. Erin followed her guide through the hallway to find the courtyard awash with water.

'Welcome to our lake district,' the woman said, lifting her skirt as she picked her way through the puddles. 'The main drains don't work anymore.'

'Is that so?' Erin said. 'I noticed the streets are all flooded. It's the first time I've been back since the end of the war.'

The woman stopped and turned to face her.

'The war hasn't ended,' she said. 'You people bombed the sewage works and the water plants. Now you prevent us from mending them. Our currency is

297

worthless and we cannot buy medicine or food. Two thousand children die every week. It's very efficient, this biological warfare of yours.'

'I'm Irish,' mumbled Erin. 'The Irish had no part in the war.'

A couple of chairs were propped against a table under the branches of a tree. The woman dragged them forward, letting the legs grate against the tiles.

'Please sit down,' she said, wiping the drops from the seat with her hand. 'I'll go and get Leyla.' Gathering up her skirt again, she forded the puddles and disappeared into a dark stairway.

Erin turned and looked around, hoping to find some clue that Kamaran was home. The green swing-seat she remembered sitting on with Sami had been removed, there was little evidence of family life, and the courtyard looked more like an allotment than the enchanting sanctuary that she recalled. A makeshift scaffold held up one sagging corner of the gallery. Runner beans clambered over the timber like jungle plants, their wet leaves sparkling in the sun. The floor below had been dug up and planted with vegetables, and whispers of steam rose like little wishes from the remaining tiles. Buckets, cans and plastic bottles had been pressed into service as pots, and an okra plant, splashed with creamy flowers, sprouted from the basin of the old fountain. Two brown chickens scratched about this unlikely garden which, surrounded by puddles, appeared to be growing in the sky.

For some time Erin sat alone, listening to the clucking of the hens and watching the glimmering drips of water that splashed from the eaves. She began to wonder if she was right to have come unannounced. Picking up Kamaran's suitcase, she put it on the table. The catches sprung open with a loud click. There was nothing but paper inside - a book's worth of letters, some written on the backs of bills and napkins, others tied together in bundles, all of them covered in the beautiful, swirling handwriting she found impossible to read. Erin smiled at the thought that - for the second time - her excuse for coming was that she had a letter to return. She snapped the suitcase shut again. As she put it back on the ground she heard footsteps and she looked up to see a woman emerge from the stairs.

Her bare, sandaled feet appeared first, then the hem of a black abaya which trailed on the steps behind her like a bridal train. She brushed her hands together as she stepped into the courtyard, sending little puffs of dust into the air. The silky fabric of the gown billowed and rippled around her and she appeared to glide, rather than walk, between the puddles. Her face, framed by the black hijab she had wrapped around her hair, had a stark beauty and Erin had the peculiar sensation, as she looked at her, that the light had changed, or that the air about her quivered like smoke above a fire. She stood up feeling suddenly clumsy and awkward.

'Hello Erin,' the woman said as she stopped before her. 'My grandfather sends his fond regards but he is ill and unable to come downstairs. I am Leyla,' she added, holding out her hand.

They shook hands and Leyla cocked her head to one side, waiting for Erin to speak.

'I've brought some... some things,' she said, 'some things that belong to Kamaran. Things he left in Finland.'

'Where is he now?'

'I hoped I would find him here - or in Baghdad, at least.'

Leyla gave a little shake of the head.

'Have you not seen him?'

Leyla shook her head once more.

'But he left Helsinki as soon as I got back. He told me he was going home.'

'When?' she asked.

'When I got back from my visit here... about a week before the invasion of Kuwait.'

Two lines appeared on Leyla's forehead as if she was working out a very difficult sum. She shook her head again and Erin's eyes brimmed with tears.

'Please!' Leyla averted her face and raised her hand as if to shield herself. She stood still for a moment, her eyes shut, and then she walked away.

Erin watched as she went into an annex off the courtyard. She heard the squeak of a tap. The whole building clanged like a palsied engine as water coughed and spat into the sink. Away across the rooftops a loudspeaker crackled into life and the first, haunting strains of the call to prayer soared like a lament into the air. As they faded Erin heard the hiss of a kettle and the tinkle and clatter that heralded the familiar ritual of tea.

Leyla bent her head as she walked back under the low branches of the tree, carrying a tray. A shower of drops fell onto her shoulders and rolled, like pearls, down the silk of her black gown. She pulled the chairs up to the table with her free hand and they sat down. The little glasses chinked in their saucers as she heaped them with sugar. For a moment the only sound was the chiming of silver on glass as Erin stirred her tea.

'Thank you,' she said.

'You are welcome,' Leyla replied. 'Welcome in Iraq.'

Acknowledgements:

I want to thank everyone I interviewed in Iraq and in the UK and the many other people who have been generous enough to share their stories and insights with me over the last twenty years. They include:
Ali and Haider; Alia, Einam, Hoda, Mohammed, Nada, Zeinab, their parents and Taghred, Moayid, Sarah and Ali; Anwar; Ghazwan, Vian, Jwan, Omar and Ali; Jabbar *aini* and Faris; Leyla; Mohammed; Nasra and Mustafa; Sabah; Sa'ad; Sadiqa; Samir; Tariq; and also Chris Saunders, Dennis Halliday, Hans Von Sponeck and Bob K.

For their help, encouragement and forbearance during the long evolution of this novel I would like to thank Derrick Retieff and Tim F.; my friends Andy, Grant, Deb, Hugh, Lucy and Vivienne; and - above all - my husband Phil and my daughter Adela.

For more information and a bibliography for *Haneen* please visit:

www.miriamday.com

Made in the USA
Charleston, SC
10 June 2013